KATIE'S WAY

KATIE'S WAY

Pleasant Valley
BOOK FIVE

MARTA PERRY

BERKLEY BOOKS, NEW YORK

THE BERKLEY PUBLISHING GROUP
Published by the Penguin Group
Penguin Group (USA) Inc.
375 Hudson Street, New York, New York 10014, USA
Penguin Group (Canada), 90 Eglinton Avenue East, Suite 700, Toronto, Ontario M4P 2Y3, Canada
(a division of Pearson Penguin Canada Inc.)
Penguin Books Ltd., 80 Strand, London WC2R 0RL, England
Penguin Group Ireland, 25 St. Stephen's Green, Dublin 2, Ireland (a division of Penguin Books Ltd.)
Penguin Group (Australia), 250 Camberwell Road, Camberwell, Victoria 3124, Australia
(a division of Pearson Australia Group Pty. Ltd.)
Penguin Books India Pvt. Ltd., 11 Community Centre, Panchsheel Park, New Delhi—110 017, India
Penguin Group (NZ), 67 Apollo Drive, Rosedale, Auckland 0632, New Zealand
(a division of Pearson New Zealand Ltd.)
Penguin Books (South Africa) (Pty.) Ltd., 24 Sturdee Avenue, Rosebank, Johannesburg 2196,
South Africa

Penguin Books Ltd., Registered Offices: 80 Strand, London WC2R 0RL, England

This is an original publication of The Berkley Publishing Group.

PUBLISHER'S NOTE: The recipes contained in this book are to be followed exactly as written. The publisher is not responsible for your specific health or allergy needs that may require medical supervision. The publisher is not responsible for any adverse reactions to the recipes contained in this book.

This is a work of fiction. Names, characters, places, and incidents either are the product of the author's imagination or are used fictitiously, and any resemblance to actual persons, living or dead, business establishments, events, or locales is entirely coincidental. The publisher does not have any control over and does not assume any responsibility for author or third-party websites or their content.

KATIE'S WAY

Copyright © 2011 by Martha Johnson.
Cover art by Shane Rebenschied.
Cover design by Annette Fiore DeFex.
Text design by Tiffany Estreicher.

ISBN: 978-1-61793-382-0

PRINTED IN THE UNITED STATES OF AMERICA

*This story is dedicated
to my children and grandchildren,
with much love.
And, as always, to Brian.*

Acknowledgments

I'd like to express my gratitude to those whose expertise, patience, and generosity helped me in the writing of this book: to Erik Wesner, whose *Amish America* newsletters are enormously helpful in visualizing aspects of daily life; to Donald Kraybill and John Hostetler, whose books are the definitive works on Amish life; to Louise Stoltzfus, Lovina Eicher, and numerous others who've shared what it means to be Amish; to my quilting family and friends; and most of all to my family, for giving me a rich heritage upon which to draw.

CHAPTER ONE

Fast-paced chatter in Pennsylvania Dutch, followed by a ripple of women's laughter, floated through the archway to Caleb Brand's handmade-furniture shop from what used to be a hardware store next door. Caleb forced himself to focus on the rocking chair he was waxing, trying to ignore the sounds of change.

He didn't like change. This building, with its two connected shops, had been a male enclave for years. Now everything was different, because Bishop Mose had decided to rent the other side to Katie Miller for a quilt shop.

Caleb gritted his teeth and rubbed a little harder, trying to concentrate on the grain of the hickory. Rocking chairs were among his best sellers, and this one had turned out to his satisfaction. He'd never let anything go out of his shop that he wouldn't be happy to have in his own home.

Another peal of female laughter. How many women were over

1

there, anyway, helping to set up for the opening tomorrow? It sounded like half the sisters from the church district.

No reason why Katie Miller, newly komm to Pleasant Valley from Columbia County, shouldn't open a quilt shop. He wished her well. Just not next door to him.

The bell on his own front door jingled, and he looked up. Bishop Mose, his white beard fluttering in the mild May breeze that swept down the main street of the village, ducked into the shop.

"Bishop Mose." He half rose, showing the bishop that he was behind the counter at the rear of the showroom.

"Ach, Caleb, I thought you'd be tucked away upstairs in your workshop at this hour." The bishop, his years seeming to sit lightly on him, wound his way through the handmade wooden furniture that filled the room.

"Nobody's here to help out today, so I have to mind the shop." Caleb put the lid on the furniture wax, tapping it down tight. "Can I do something for you?"

"Ach, no." The bishop's blue eyes, wise with a lifetime of service to the Amish of Pleasant Valley, crinkled a little. "Chust thought I should see for myself how you're dealing with your new neighbor."

Caleb glanced down at the rocker to avoid meeting the bishop's gaze. "Fine. Everything's fine, I think."

He didn't understand why Bishop Mose had seen fit to install a quilt shop next to him, but he wouldn't complain. He'd never forget that when it seemed every person in the valley had turned against him, Bishop Mose had accepted his word.

It was eight years since then, and Caleb supposed folks still talked about him and Mattie, though not in his presence. But thanks to Bishop Mose, he still had his place here.

In the brief silence between them, the sound of women's voices came through clearly, talking about how best to display some quilts, it seemed.

"That's gut," Bishop Mose said. "I thought maybe it would be a bother to you, having a quilt shop next door instead of a hardware store."

Absently, Caleb caressed a curved spindle of the rocker, the wood warm and smooth under his hand. Could he drop a hint in the bishop's ear?

"Well, I did think a hardware store was a better fit with my shop." He said the words as cautiously as if he were walking on eggs. "We shared more of the same customers, ain't so?"

"You don't think the folks who buy Katie's quilts will be interested in your fine rocking chairs and chests?" Bishop Mose lifted white eyebrows.

Another burst of laughter scraped at Caleb's nerves. "No. I don't think a bunch of quilting women are likely to want what—"

He stopped—a little too late, it seemed. Katie Miller stood in the archway, and he didn't doubt she'd heard his words. He cleared his throat, trying to think what to say, but she beat him to it.

"Ach, Bishop Mose, I thought I heard your voice." The warm smile she directed toward the bishop probably didn't include Caleb. "Would you like to see what we've done with the shop?"

"We would like nothing better." He reached across the counter to clap Caleb's shoulder. "Komm, Caleb. We'll have a look at your new neighbor's shop, ain't so?"

Caleb hesitated, glancing at Katie. Her blue eyes were guarded, it seemed to him, and her strong jaw set. Katie Miller looked like a determined woman, one bent on doing things her way.

Which was maybe how she'd reached her midtwenties without marrying, an unusual situation for an Amish woman. And at the moment her way most likely didn't include showing him her shop.

But in the next instant her expression had melted into a smile. She smoothed back a strand of light brown hair under the white kapp on the back of her head and nodded. "Komm. I'd like fine to show you what we've done."

With the bishop's hand on his shoulder Caleb couldn't very well pull away. He walked through the archway, feeling as if he were moving into a foreign land.

It looked that way, too. Harvey Schmidt's barrels of nails and coils of wire were long gone, of course. The shop had been stripped down to the bare shelves during Harvey's closing sale. But now—

The walls and shelves had been painted white, as had the counters. Against the white, every color possible glowed in bolts of fabric and spools of thread. It looked like a huge flower garden in full bloom.

And that was saying nothing of the quilts, draped on a four-poster maple bed that had been placed in the center of the space. Another quilt, in shades of blue and yellow and white, sagged between Molly, Katie's cousin and the reason Katie had come to the valley in the first place, and Sarah Mast, Pleasant Valley's midwife. Both stood on chairs, obviously trying to hang the quilt from a rod that Harvey had used to support coils of rope.

"That looks like a dangerous thing to be doing." Bishop Mose was quick to steady the chair on which Molly teetered. "Especially for a new mammi."

Dimples appeared in Molly's cheeks. "Ach, you sound just like my Jacob. Anyone would think I was made of glass to hear him. After all, our little boy is over four months old now."

"Ja, well, komm down anyway," Katie said, going quickly to grasp the quilt from them. "This one I'll put on the bed. I have some quilted table runners that can hang from the rod instead."

Molly and Sarah climbed down, looking a little relieved, Caleb thought.

Sarah took the quilt back from Katie, her normally serious face lighting with a smile. Sarah had been a newcomer to the valley herself not that long ago, when she'd arrived to take over the midwife practice from her elderly aunt. Maybe that explained the connection she seemed to have with Katie.

"We'll put the quilt in place," Sarah said. "You have guests to show around."

Katie nodded. She spread her arms wide in a gesture that took in the whole space.

"Here it is, as you can see. My new quilt shop." A smile blossomed on her face, touching her eyes and bringing a glow to her cheeks.

Happiness. Hope. They radiated from Katie like heat from a stove. Caleb couldn't help but be touched.

But that didn't change anything, he reminded himself. Having the woman's business right next door was going to be a nuisance.

And if she'd heard what folks in Pleasant Valley said about him, it wondered him that she'd want to be near him at all.

. . .

"Are you certain sure I can't stay and help you a bit longer?" Cousin Molly hovered at the door of the shop. "Jacob doesn't mind watching the boppli."

"Get along home." Katie gave her a quick hug. "That little one will be wanting to eat soon, and that's one thing Jacob can't do."

Molly giggled, her face alight with mischief, as if she were a child again herself. "He does get desperate when little Jacob cries. I think it makes him appreciate me more."

"Jacob appreciates you fine, especially after all the months you were apart when he was working out west." Katie gave her cousin a gentle shove. "It is ser kind of you to spend so much time helping me, but now you should get on home to them."

Molly paused again, glancing around the shop. "The place does look wonderful gut, Katie. Who would have thought the old hardware store could change so much?"

"I just hope people like the change." She suspected she already knew of one person who didn't.

Molly gave her a quick, impulsive hug. "I'm so glad you're here. And glad, too, that your parents were willing to part with you." She kissed Katie's cheek and went out, the shop door bell jingling.

Katie had been grateful for all the help today. Still, it was gut to be alone in the place that was everything she had hoped it would be. She touched the end bolt of a row of fabric, feeling the soft cotton slip through her fingers.

Denke, Father. The prayer formed in her thoughts. *Thank you for giving me useful work to do here.*

Molly's parting words echoed in her mind. It wasn't quite true that her parents had been willing to part with her . . . not entirely, anyway.

She'd explained to Mamm and Daad why, after her visit to help when Molly had her baby, she wanted to start a shop here in Pleasant Valley. Her mamm hadn't been convinced. Mamm wanted the same thing for all five of her girls . . . that they get married, have babies, and settle down close to her.

Unfortunately, her eldest daughter was disappointing her on all counts.

Katie crossed her arms, rubbing them, and moved to the display of quilts in the center of the shop. It was lucky that she'd had a number of her own works to put out, since the quilts she expected to sell on consignment from other Amish women had been slow to show up.

It will get better, she assured herself. *Once people see that the shop is open, they'll be more willing.*

As for Mammi . . . well, in the end she'd given way, due in large part to Daadi's persuading. Katie's heart warmed. She owed this venture to him.

She traced the tiny squares of a postage-stamp quilt with her finger. The sign of a patient quilter, that one was, requiring the time to fit together all those small pieces.

She had made that quilt during the long winter after Eli married her best friend. Nearly four years ago now, but she hadn't forgotten. In one brief summer, she had lost both the man she'd expected to spend her life with and her closest friend.

A scrape sounded from the shop next door, reminding her that she was not really alone. Caleb Brand was there, and Caleb was not very pleased with his new neighbor, it seemed. Bishop

Mose hadn't said much about the man when he'd brought her to see the shop he had for rent. Only that Caleb's woodworking business was in the other half of the storefront, and the bishop was sure they'd be good neighbors.

Funny that Molly hadn't said much of anything about Caleb Brand, either. Not that Molly was a blabbermaul, but she'd spent most of her life in Pleasant Valley. She must know him. She knew everybody. If . . .

The thought trailed off as the front door opened. Katie turned, ready to say that the shop wouldn't be open until tomorrow, but the words died on her lips.

"Mammi! What are you doing here?" And not just her mother. Two of her sisters, twenty-one-year-old Louise and sixteen-year-old Rhoda, crowded in behind her.

"We've komm for your opening, ain't so?" Mamm untied her bonnet and took it off, revealing brown hair tinged slightly with gray. "Ach, that's better. That bus bumped us around so much I thought we'd never get here in one piece." Her gaze sharpened on Katie. "Well? Aren't you happy to see us?"

"For certain sure I am." Katie hurried to her mother for a hug and then turned to Louise, her next-younger sister. "I'm just surprised, is all. How could Louise tear herself away from Jonas?"

Something that might have been a snort came from Rhoda, but Louise acted as if she didn't hear it. "Jonas agreed that it was my duty to help Mammi on the trip," she said. "He'd never object to that, even if he doesn't understand why you had to go so far away."

Katie bit back the tart words on her tongue about Louise's intended's opinion. Jonas, the youngest son of a bishop, had a bit too much self-importance for Katie's taste, but that was Louise's concern, not hers.

"I'm sure Katie doesn't care what Jonas—"

Katie interrupted whatever unwise words Rhoda was about to say with a quick, strong hug and a murmured hush in her ear. "It is ser gut to see all of you."

She drew back, waving her hand to encompass the whole of her shop. "What do you think of it?"

Mamm took a few steps around, studying the layout as if comparing it to her own quilt shop back in Columbia County. "It's not as big as I thought it would be."

"There's another room at the back that I can expand into," Katie said. "This is enough for starting off, I think."

"You could be right. The less you have, the easier it will be to . . ." Her mother stopped and then started again. ". . . to take care of."

That wasn't what she'd intended to say, Katie felt sure. *The less there will be to get rid of when you come home again.* That was the thought in her mother's mind, wasn't it?

Katie found she was clutching her arms around herself again and deliberately relaxed.

One year. That was how long she had to prove herself. Daadi had paid Bishop Mose for one year's rent on the shop. At the end of that year, she should be able to sign her own lease.

Or go home in defeat and spend her life next door to Eli and Jessica, watching their growing family.

She cleared her throat. "How long are you . . . will you be able to stay?"

"Ach, chust 'til Friday. Louise is supposed to go to dinner

with Jonas's family on Saturday, so we must get back." Mamm nodded toward the stairway that led up to the second floor. "Will you have room for us in your apartment?"

"We'll make room." Katie thought rapidly. Mamm would have her room, of course, and Louise and Rhoda could share the second bedroom. She'd sleep on the couch. "If you're not comfortable, I'm sure Molly would be glad to have you stay with her."

"No, no, this will be fine." Mamm made shooing motions toward the other two. "Take your bags up now. Get settled. I want to speak to Katie."

Mamm's words sounded serious. If something was wrong at home—

Her sisters vanished up the stairs. Katie studied her mother's face, trying to read the expression. Mammi, for some reason, was avoiding her eyes.

"Is something wrong?" she asked finally, when it seemed her mother wouldn't speak.

"No, no, why would you think that?" Mammi made little sweeping gestures with her hands. "I chust think . . . that is, your daad and I have decided that Rhoda will stay here with you for a time."

"Rhoda?" There was a faint squeak in Katie's voice, and she tried to control it. "But why would you want Rhoda to do that? She has her job at the restaurant, and you'll need her help with Louise getting married in the fall."

And just as important, why would Mammi think Katie should take on the responsibility for a lively sixteen-year-old when she was trying to get a new business started on her own?

Her mother studied a row of spools with concentrated care. "She can be more help to you. As for that restaurant . . ." Mammi's voice seemed to tighten. "We think it better that she not work there anymore."

"I see."

But Katie didn't, not really. It was so unlike Mammi to let one of her chicks leave home without a fight, and Rhoda was only sixteen, just beginning her rumspringa.

Light began to dawn.

"Does this have something to do with Rhoda's rumspringa?" Rhoda, with her quick mind and daring disposition, was probably destined to have a more tumultuous running-around time than either Katie or Louise had had.

Her mother turned toward her, fingers to her lips. "I'm not saying there's anything really wrong. But Rhoda has got herself in some trouble."

"Trouble?" Mamm surely didn't mean—

"No, no, not anything serious." Color stained Mamm's cheekbones. "Staying out later than she should, going off with some of the older girls to an Englisch party."

"That's not so bad," Katie said, going a little weak at the knees at the thought of taking on the supervision of Rhoda.

Mamm pressed her lips together for an instant. "Never did I think a daughter of mine would be so rebellious. You and Louise were nothing like that when you were sixteen. Of course, Louise has always been serious, a perfect fit for Jonas. And you weren't running around a lot because you and . . ."

Mamm let that trail off, but Katie knew the end of that sentence, too. *You and Eli Hershberger were going to marry.* Only it hadn't turned out that way, and she'd had to watch while Eli married Jessica Stoltzfus.

She pushed those thoughts aside hurriedly. Best to concentrate on the current problem. "If Rhoda is misbehaving, wouldn't it be best to have her at home, under your eye?"

Mamm shook her head decisively. "There's Louise to think of. How will it look if Rhoda gets into trouble with her sister marrying the bishop's son? Anyway, your daad and I agree that Rhoda is better off here, and you can use her help. I never thought you should live above the shop on your own, anyway. This way you'll have company."

She certainly would.

"Maybe we should talk about this some more," she began. "If—"

"There's nothing more to be said." Mamm turned away, examining a bolt of fabric. "Anyway, least said, soonest mended. I had to tell you, but no one else needs to know why Rhoda is here."

Katie leaned against a box of quilt batting, trying to settle her mind, and her ears caught a sound through the archway . . . the creak of a rocking chair.

Mammi was wrong. Somebody else already knew, because Caleb Brand was still in the shop next door.

Are you sure you don't want us to help you finish clearing up?" Katie's mother paused at the door after the long opening day of the shop. "We can stay."

But fatigue drew at Mamm's face, and Katie patted her arm. "Ach, no, you and the girls go on to Molly's. She'll like fine to have a longer visit with you, and likely she has supper almost ready. I'll be along soon, for sure. Molly lent me her buggy today."

Mamm nodded, gesturing Louise and Rhoda out to where Jacob, Molly's young husband, waited at the curb with their horse and buggy. Mamm started to follow and then turned back toward Katie.

"This was a gut beginning." She closed the door before Katie could respond.

Katie stood at the window, watching as they moved off down the street, and then locked the door, pulling down the shade. Her opening day was over.

She leaned against the door for a moment, still holding the napkin and paper plate she'd intended to toss in the trash, and felt the tension seep out of her. She hadn't realized how nervous she'd been about this day until now, when she was as boneless as one of the faceless rag dolls she'd displayed along a top shelf.

The opening had been gut, and she imagined Mamm had mixed feelings about saying so. Not that Mamm consciously wanted Katie to fail. She just wanted their lives to go along the way she'd envisioned them.

Maybe that was what Katie had wanted once, too, but that would never be. Only her tiredness let the tears form in her eyes at that thought, and she blinked them away. Eli was as gone from her future as if he'd died. And if she couldn't stop loving him, at least here she wouldn't have to see him and Jessica, happily married and living next door.

A lock snapped in the adjoining shop, and Katie looked through the archway to see Caleb closing up. He hadn't acknowledged her presence except for a polite nod of greeting this morning, but she hadn't forgotten what he might have, must have, heard Mamm say about Rhoda the day before.

He didn't strike her as a man who'd gossip, but she couldn't just leave it, ignoring the possibility. Not giving herself time to think, she walked quickly through the archway.

"I hope all the people coming and going today didn't bother you. I'm sure it won't normally be so busy."

For a moment Caleb didn't speak, the strong planes of his face resembling nothing so much as the wood he worked with. Even his eyes were like the wood—a deep, rich brown—as was his hair. The fact that he was beardless showed the unexpected cleft in his strong chin.

He shrugged, palms open. "It was not a problem. Did you have a gut opening?"

The most words she'd heard from him in a row . . . that might be a hopeful sign. "Not bad. Lots of people came looking. No big sales, but most folks went away with something, if only a quilted pot holder."

He gave a short nod, and turned away. Apparently that was all he had to say to her. But it wasn't all she needed to say to him. If he told other people what Mamm had said about Rhoda, life here could be difficult for her sister before it even started.

"Paula Schatz brought me a whole tray of sweets from her bakery to celebrate the opening." The Mennonite woman's bakery, Katie had learned, was just a few doors down Pleasant Valley's main street. "Can I persuade you to take some home to your family?"

"No. Denke," he added, as if thinking he'd been rude. "My sister-in-law bakes enough for half the county as it is." He glanced at the paper plate in her hand. "I shouldn't think you'd want people eating around your quilts."

"I had the food and drink in the back room. Most people

were sensible enough to keep it there." She shrugged. "It was worthwhile, I think. Serving something brings folks in and makes them feel wilkom. If they stay longer, they buy more, ain't so?"

His brows, a darker brown than his eyes, drew down. "I've no need for such gimmicks. If people want something, they buy it, that's all."

She had to bite her tongue to keep from telling him how wrong he was. "If you have well-made products, buyers will find you. That's true. But there are things you can do to draw people's attention."

His shop was a prime example, and her hands itched to re-arrange things in a way that would highlight their beauty. That rocker, for instance, with the intricately turned spindles—it should be up front where the customer's eye fell on it immediately. The whole space looked cluttered and unwelcoming to her eyes.

He shook his head in a way that dismissed both her and her sales ideas. "Your family . . . have they gone home already, then?"

"Just to my cousin Molly's for supper." Here was an opening to find out what he'd heard about Rhoda, if she could see how best to use it. Did she dare ask such a forbidding personality to keep silent? "They'll be going home tomorrow, except for my sister Rhoda. She's staying to help me for a while."

"I see." Two words only. But he crossed his arms over his broad chest, and glanced down, not meeting her eyes.

She'd dealt with enough customers in her mother's shop to read in his body language what he didn't say. He'd heard, that was certain-sure.

She took a breath, murmuring a silent prayer for guidance. "Caleb, I think that you must have heard what my mother said about why Rhoda is staying here."

His face tightened. "I don't listen to what doesn't concern me."

"Sometimes you can't help but hear something that wasn't meant for your ears." She'd gone this far. She may as well say all that she was thinking. "I just hope you will not repeat it."

She'd thought his face couldn't get any tighter, but apparently it could. There was no mistaking his expression now. Anger. He glared at her for a long moment.

"I'm not a blabbermaul." He spun and walked away from her, shoulders stiff.

She let out her breath in a sigh. She'd have done better, it seemed, to keep her mouth closed.

Chapter Two

Nancy, Caleb's sister-in-law, put a wedge of dried-apple pie in front of him. As he'd told Katie Miller, his sister-in-law always had enough baked goods in the house to feed half the county.

Of course, those five boys she and his brother Andy had produced went through the cakes and pies in a hurry. The old farmhouse was as noisy now as it had been when he and Andy and their brothers were young, even though now Andy did the farming Daad had once done, and Mamm lived in the grossdaadi haus, the four-room house that he'd helped Daad and Andy build onto the side.

After Daad died, they'd decided Caleb should move into the second bedroom in the grossdaadi haus, so Mammi wasn't alone there. That gave Andy's kinder a little more space, too, though sometimes the farmhouse still felt as if it bulged at the seams.

Becky, Caleb's sixteen-year-old niece and the only girl in the family, poured coffee in his mug.

"Denke, Becky. That's plenty."

She gave him her shy smile and moved on to the head of the table to pour a cup for her father. The boys had already been excused, dashing outside to finish their chores and toss a baseball around before the sun disappeared.

"So, the new quilt shop opened up today, I hear." Nancy sat down across from him, her hazel eyes bright with curiosity. "Did a gut lot of folks come?"

"Seemed like plenty of people to me. All women, of course." It felt as if he could still hear them buzzing in his ears. He put his mug down on the pine table, next to the scar he'd put in the smooth edge with his front tooth when he was nine or ten and he and Andy had been wrestling at the table. Daad had punished both of them impartially, as he recalled.

"What is Katie Miller like?" his mother asked, pushing aside the wedge of pie Nancy had put in front of her, causing Nancy and Andy to exchange worried glances. Mammi had eaten like a bird since Daad's death last fall.

"You've seen her at worship," Caleb said, since the question seemed directed at him.

"Ja, I know what she looks like, but I haven't talked to her. It takes some courage to start up a business all on your own, I'd say."

He tried to sort his thoughts. It wasn't Katie's fault that he disliked having her shop right next to his. On the other hand, it *was* her fault that she'd acted as if he were a blabbermaul who couldn't wait to spread gossip about her sister, putting his back up.

To be fair, Katie might not know much about him. Not enough to be aware of all the gossip that swirled around him over Mattie

Weaver's pregnancy, although if she didn't, someone would tell her soon enough.

No, he wasn't likely to inflict the pain of being the object of gossip on someone else.

"Well?" Mamm prompted. "What's she like? And what's the shop like?"

Mamm hadn't shown this much interest in anything in months. That was a gut sign, wasn't it? He'd have to do his best to encourage her, even if it meant talking about Katie Miller.

"She's a nice enough woman. Sort of opinionated, I'd say."

Nancy chuckled. "She'll have to be, to make a success of a new business."

"Ja, maybe." Katie's words still rankled, but Caleb tried to dismiss them and think of something to entertain his mamm. "You'd never know the shop was the same place, with all the quilts and bolts of fabric and rows of thread all over the place. Lot more colorful than the hardware store was. Attracts women, like I said."

Andy frowned. "Is that likely to be a problem for you, having a place like that next door?"

"I'm bound to say I thought the hardware store was a better fit." Caleb shrugged, scooping into the pie. "But the building belongs to Bishop Mose. He can do what he wants with it."

"So she has a lot of quilting fabric," Mamm said. "You know, maybe I should think of starting a new quilt."

"That sounds wonderful gut, Mamm Naomi. Why don't we take a ride into town and see what she has?" Nancy seized on Mamm's flicker of interest with her characteristic energy. They'd all of them been trying to find ways to bring Mamm out of her shell these past few months.

"Maybe," Mamm said.

"Tomorrow," Nancy prompted, never one to let grass grow under her feet. "We can go in tomorrow, and maybe take Becky to—" She stopped suddenly, glancing at Andy.

Something was not being said, it seemed. "Take Becky to what?" Caleb asked. He glanced at his niece, to find her staring down at her hands.

"We were thinking," Nancy said, obviously speaking for his brother, too. "Maybe you could use our Rebecca in the shop a few hours a week. It'd be gut for her to have a job outside the house, and you could stand to have someone clean up the shop for you and wait on customers so you can work. Besides, maybe it'll help her get over being so shy with people."

"There's nothing wrong with being a little quiet," his mother said, reaching out to pat Becky's hand. "I'd rather have our Becky the way she is than as bold as some of the girls are these days."

"She needs to learn not to give in to being shy." Nancy, who didn't have a bit of shyness in her robust nature, was talking about Becky as if she weren't sitting there. And the girl seemed to shrink in the chair, stirring Caleb's heart. Becky might look like Nancy, with her round face and hazel eyes, but she was totally different in personality. And as well-meaning as Nancy was, she didn't understand her only daughter.

He'd like fine to have Becky working for him, if it would help her. It would help him, too, letting him escape to the privacy of his workshop while someone else dealt with the customers.

But, unfortunately, working at the shop would bring Becky into contact with Katie's sister, the one who'd apparently gotten into trouble already for her wildness during rumspringa.

"Maybe Becky doesn't want to work at the shop." If she

didn't, then he wouldn't have to worry about what kind of influence on her the Miller sisters would be.

Becky glanced at him. "I would like that fine, Onkel Caleb," she said. "If you can use me."

He hesitated. Maybe he should say something to Nancy and Andy about the Miller girl. But he'd just told Katie that he wasn't one to go around talking about what he'd heard. How could he go back on that?

He was boxed in. He couldn't go back on his word. And he couldn't disappoint his niece, either.

"That's fine, Becky. You can start as soon as you want."

Her smile radiated pleasure, warming him. But it didn't get rid of the faint resentment he felt toward Katie Miller and her shop. She'd only been open a day, and already she was causing him trouble.

Katie was filled with a mix of relief and apprehension when the bus pulled out the next morning, carrying Mamm and Louise. Relief, because she knew Mamm disapproved of every deviation Katie had made from the way Mamm ran her own shop. And apprehension at the prospect of being solely responsible for her young sister.

"You don't need to worry about me." Rhoda walked beside her down the street, tilting her face to the spring sunshine and seeming to read her thoughts too well. "What kind of trouble can I get into here?" Her gesture dismissed Pleasant Valley and all its people. "I don't know a single person my age."

"I'm not really worried about you. Well, not too much, anyway."

"Why not? Mamm is. And Louise." Rhoda's pretty, heart-shaped face seemed set in lines of discontent, her golden-brown eyes downcast.

Was that bitterness or hurt in Rhoda's voice? Katie wasn't sure.

"You're a smart girl," she said. "Smart enough to know that if you got into trouble again, you'd get a reputation you don't want."

"According to Louise, I already have that," Rhoda muttered.

"Louise listens to Jonas too much." The words were out before Katie thought, and she shook her head. "I shouldn't have said that." But she'd brought a smile to Rhoda's face and a sparkle to her eyes, and she couldn't regret having lessened the strain between them.

"Louise is all right," Rhoda said with the easy volatility of a sixteen-year-old. "Daadi says she'll stop being so preachy once she has some kinder of her own to run after."

"That might be true." Or she might be even worse. Katie spared a sympathetic thought for her prospective nieces and nephews.

They passed Bishop Mose's harness shop . . . open already. She could see Bishop Mose through the window, bending over the counter, his white beard nearly touching the harness he was mending.

Paula Schatz's bakery opened early, too. The scents of cinnamon buns and coffee drifted out as a customer exited the front door. Paula seemed to have quite a clientele, mostly Englisch but also a few Amish, who stopped by for coffee and gossip every morning.

Katie glanced at her sister. Rhoda's face was absorbed, her

attention turned inward. Was she brooding on her fate in being shipped off to Pleasant Valley, maybe?

"This is a nice place," Katie said. "With gut people. And we have family here already, in the Miller cousins. You'll meet some girls your age before long, that's certain-sure."

"If their parents haven't already warned them against me." Rhoda seemed determined to look on the down side.

"No one here knows anything about what happened back home." No one but Caleb Brand. "There's no reason why anyone should."

"Someone will write to a friend or a cousin or a distant relative and blab about it." Rhoda's lower lip jutted out. "You know how that works."

The Amish grapevine, of course. Rhoda might be right, but Katie wasn't going to encourage her gloominess.

"Even if someone from back home does write to somebody here, that doesn't mean they'll think your doings are important enough to relate. Suppose you try to get your mind on something else. Look, there's Molly in front of the shop already, and us not open yet. And she's brought baby Jacob, too. Run and help her with him."

Katie suspected Rhoda's fascination with babies would override her obsession with her own woes. Sure enough, a smile dawned, and Rhoda darted ahead of her. By the time Katie reached the shop, Rhoda was already cuddling little Jacob in her arms.

"We did not expect to see you so early, Molly." Katie bent to kiss the wisp of white-blond hair on top of the boppli's head. "Let me get the door unlocked."

"We can't stay," Molly said, but followed her inside, showing the dimples in her pert face as Rhoda cooed at the baby. "We are on our way grocery shopping, and I must fit it in before this one decides it's time to eat and nap again. But I wanted to drop off a list for you."

"A list?" Katie looked at her blankly.

Molly pressed a folded sheet of tablet paper into her hand. "I know you're fretting about not having enough quilts on consignment in the shop, so I wrote down the names of all the women I could think of who might have some they want to sell."

"That is wonderful kind of you, such trouble as you've gone to for me and the shop." It was kind, and thoughtful, too.

"As if you haven't done as much for me a dozen times over, helping out like you did when the boppli came." Molly gave her a quick hug. "We're cousins. As close as sisters, almost."

Maybe closer than some sisters. Katie had begun to think she didn't know Rhoda nearly as well as she should.

"It's true it has been troubling me, not having as many quilts as I expected. I thought folks would naturally want to sell their quilts on consignment here, like they do in Mamm's shop back home."

"They're just not used to the idea yet, that's all," Molly said. "Mostly if they want to sell, there's a dealer from over toward Mifflinburg who will buy from them. They don't see that they'll make more by selling the quilts through you on consignment. Once they understand, I'm certain-sure you'll have plenty of business."

"I hope so." *Pray so.* She tucked the list under a stapler on the counter. "Denke, Molly."

Footsteps sounded in Caleb's shop, and then women's voices.

Molly looked that way, smiling as the figures came toward the quilt shop. "Naomi. It's ser gut to see you out and about."

Three people walked through the archway—an older woman who was clearly the object of Molly's attention, followed by a younger woman and a girl of about Rhoda's age. Predictably they clustered around the boppli.

"Ach, look at this big boy." The older woman touched his round cheek. "He's thriving, that's plain to see."

"Going to look just like his daadi," Molly responded, a hint of pride in her voice. "But what am I thinking of? Naomi, these are my cousins, Katie and Rhoda Miller. It's Katie who's started the quilt shop here."

"We've been needing a quilt shop since Ruth Stoltzfus retired." Naomi had a sweet smile in a thin face that held lines of strain or maybe pain around her brown eyes. "And I've been hearing all about you from my son."

"Your son?"

"Ja, Caleb Brand, that is my boy. I'm Naomi Brand, and here is Caleb's brother's wife, Nancy, and Nancy's oldest child, Rebecca."

Caleb's mother. What, Katie wondered, had Caleb been telling her? Nothing too bad, apparently, since the woman was smiling.

"Ja, we couldn't wait to see your shop for ourselves," Nancy said, running her fingers along the row of fabric bolts.

"You like to quilt, then." Katie wondered if Nancy's name was on Molly's list.

Nancy shook her head, chuckling a little. "Not me, not with the five boys to sew for besides Rebecca. I don't have the

25

patience for it, anyway. It's Mamm Naomi who is the quilter in the family."

Katie glanced at Molly, who gave a slight nod. Obviously it was Caleb's mother whose name would be on her list.

"Maybe you'd like to see the quilts I brought with me from home," Katie said. "I've noticed some of the patterns there are different from the ones around here."

A spark of interest lit Naomi's faded brown eyes, and she nodded. "Ja, I would. I saw some quilts my husband's cousin in Nebraska made, and they certain-sure were different."

Katie pulled back the sheet she'd spread over the quilts when she'd left the previous night.

"Postage-stamp quilt in a Log Cabin design," Naomi said. "That takes time."

"Ja, it does." Katie's hand rested on it for a moment, remembering. It had taken her all that cold, lonely winter after Eli married. She was tempted to put it away so it wouldn't be a reminder, but maybe the sooner it was sold, the better.

"You made this one yourself," Naomi said quietly.

The woman's perception startled her. "How did you know?"

"The way you touched it." Naomi ran her finger along the binding. "Sometimes I think we stitch our feelings into our quilts, ain't so?"

Katie could only nod, her throat suddenly tight. Caleb's mother was a wise woman, maybe a bit too wise for comfort.

She cleared her throat. "Would you be interested in having me sell any of your quilts for you here in the shop?"

Naomi seemed to consider. "You'd buy them from me to sell?"

"No, I'd take them on consignment." As Molly had said, she'd have to do some explaining. "We would decide together on a price, and then when the quilt sold, I would receive a percentage of the money."

Naomi frowned slightly. "There's a dealer that has shops in Mifflinburg and Harrisburg, I think. Mr. Hargrove, his name is. He sometimes buys quilts. I sold him a Sunshine and Shadows one once. Pulled the bills right out of his pocket and paid me cash."

"Do you mind my asking how much he paid you?"

"A hundred dollars, it was."

Katie flipped the corner of the quilt over so that Naomi could see the price tag. "He probably sold it for at least five hundred. If you put a quilt like this in my shop and I sell it, I take twenty percent commission. That means you'd make four hundred."

"That's if you sold it," Naomi said.

"Ja, that's true. My mamm has a shop back home, though, and most of the ladies who bring their quilts in sell them within a month or two. And small quilted items, like table runners and pot holders, sell even quicker."

Naomi didn't speak for a moment, and Katie held her breath. Getting Naomi's quilts to sell could be just the step she needed.

Finally Naomi gave a small nod. "I will bring in one or two quilts. And we'll see."

Katie let out her breath. "Denke."

"Now maybe you will help me pick out some fabric. I have it in mind to start a new quilt. In a Tumbling Blocks pattern."

"It would be a pleasure." Katie glanced toward the others. "If your daughter-in-law doesn't want to wait—"

"Ach, Nancy is happy enough to chat with Molly. And those two girls seem like they are getting to know each other, don't they?"

Sure enough, Rhoda and Rebecca had drawn a little apart, talking over the boppli's head. A friend . . . that was what Rhoda needed more than anything right now. But Katie was not sure she'd have chosen Caleb Brand's niece as the perfect friend for her sister.

"You're right," she said, trying to focus on Naomi and her quilt. "Now, what colors were you thinking about?"

"Maybe shades of blue, going from dark to light, and—"

"Becky." Caleb's voice was sharp enough to draw Katie's gaze to him. He stood in the archway between the shops, looking at his niece. "Komm, and I'll show you what I want you to do."

"Ach, I nearly forgot one reason we came today," Naomi said. "Our Becky is going to work a few hours each week for Caleb in the shop. He must want her to get started."

Katie watched the girl walk away from Rhoda. Maybe Naomi was right about what Caleb wanted. Or maybe he was intent on keeping his young niece away from her sister.

"Your job will be to keep everything in this part of the shop looking nice." Caleb wiped a cobweb off the spindle of a chair. "Looks like I do need some help in here, ain't so?"

Becky giggled. "I'll keep it spic and span, that's certain-sure."

"I know you will." He patted her shoulder. "You're a gut girl, Becky."

As for Katie's sister . . . well, maybe she was not so good. A bit wild, by the sounds of it.

He'd told himself he would just have to keep Becky away from Rhoda, but Becky had no more than entered the shop when she'd met Rhoda. When he'd looked through the archway and seen those two girls with their heads together, his stomach had tightened up.

It wasn't fair, he supposed, to blame Katie Miller for bringing problems into his life. Still, it was a plain fact that if not for her setting up next door to him, he wouldn't be fretting about Rhoda's influence on Becky.

"What about the workroom upstairs, Onkel Caleb? Do you want me to clean there, as well?" Becky looked poised to fly up the stairs and begin scrubbing. She'd been helping Nancy keep the house clean since she was a small child, and she knew what to do.

"Ja, but that's not so important. Customers don't go up there. The days you're here, you can sweep and dust the workshop, but do that last thing, because I'll dirty it up again pretty quick." He smiled at her eagerness. "Don't count on it staying clean. It won't."

She nodded, as if making careful note of that. "What about customers?" Apprehension entered her eyes. "Will I be waiting on them?"

He considered. Part of the reason Becky was working for him was so she'd become more comfortable being around folks, but he didn't want to pitchfork her into something she wasn't ready for.

He tried to stay away from folks by choice, but it wasn't that way with Becky. If their Becky was shy, it was because God made her that way. He was just grateful that she usually seemed to feel she could talk to him.

"Let's just see how that goes," he said. "You can find out what people are interested in. Then if they seem serious, not just looking, call up to me, and I'll come down and deal with them. All right?"

The worry faded from her face. "All right."

His gaze flickered to the other room. Mamm was picking fabrics out, with Katie's help. Mamm showed more interest than she had in months, and he was glad. He wasn't worried about that. But as for Rhoda . . .

She stood against the far counter, Molly's boppli in her arms, bouncing and crooning to little Jacob. He could bring up the subject, couldn't he, without breaking a confidence?

"You met Katie's sister, Rhoda Miller, I see." He kept his tone casual. "I hear she's staying here with Katie for a while to help out in the shop."

"Ja, that's what she said."

"What did you think of her?"

"She seemed nice." Becky paused, and her cheeks grew a little pink. "Different from me."

"Different?" All his defenses went up. "How is she different?"

"Well, she doesn't know anybody here. Any of the kids our age, I mean. I know them all. I was just thinking how hard it would be not to know anyone."

"That's thoughtful of you." Becky had a kind heart. That was good, but kind hearts were easily bruised.

The pink intensified in her cheeks. "You know the birthday party on Saturday for Thomas Esch?" she asked.

"Ja, I know." Becky had seemed a little hesitant to go off to a birthday celebration with the other teenagers.

"I was thinking maybe I should ask Rhoda to come along

with me. That way she'd already know somebody there. She might like that, don't you think?"

Appealed to, he could only think that seeing Becky go off with Rhoda Miller was the last thing he wanted. Before he could answer, Mamm came in, followed by Katie, who was carrying a bag of fabric, and it was obvious Mamm had heard.

"That sounds like a kind thought, Becky." Mamm beamed at her. "That's certain-sure to make Rhoda feel wilkom." She glanced at him. "Don't you think that's a gut idea, Caleb?"

He hesitated in answering. It was probably only a couple of seconds, but it felt like an hour. They were all looking at him, Katie with an expression that was so intense he knew she feared he was going to tell what he'd heard about Rhoda.

"Ja," he said shortly, turning away from the concern in Katie's eyes.

Mamm patted the counter. "You can put the fabric right here, Katie, and Caleb will load it into the buggy for me when we're ready to go."

Katie obeyed, setting the package on the countertop, not looking at him now.

Mamm held out her hand to Becky. "Komm, and you can ask her now. I chust want to look closer at that one pattern."

Mamm and Becky went out together. Caleb tried to think of something to say to Katie, but his mind was curiously blank. He found he was staring at the slender curve of her neck as she smoothed the fabric pieces in the bag.

She turned and came toward him with a quick step until they stood very close. "Denke, Caleb." Her voice was soft. "That will mean the world to Rhoda." Her fingers touched his hand, and it was as if his skin tingled where their hands met.

His startled gaze went to hers. Something—some awareness that he hadn't expected and didn't welcome—filled the air between them. Her deep blue eyes went wide, and he thought she felt it, too. She probably didn't know what to do with the feeling, either.

He stepped back, pulse thudding. "I could not stop her. Becky has a sympathetic heart."

"Ja. She does."

That almost sounded as if she thought he didn't. He stiffened, knowing he had to give fair warning. "If there is any trouble for Becky because of her kindness to Rhoda, I will have to tell what I know."

Katie's lips pressed together, her eyes narrowing. "There won't be," she said sharply, and turned away.

CHAPTER THREE

*K*atie couldn't shake off the warning in Caleb's words. All through supper, even as she and Rhoda washed and dried the dishes, she fretted over it, wondering whether she should say anything to her sister.

The pan Rhoda was drying clattered to the countertop. "You don't want me here." The words burst out as if Rhoda couldn't hold them back. "It's not as if I had a choice, either."

"Rhoda, what are you talking about?" Katie dried her hands on the dish towel and reached toward her little sister.

Rhoda jerked back as if she'd been stung, brown eyes snapping with anger. "You might as well admit it. Daad and Mamm wanted to be rid of me, so they pushed me off on you. And you don't want me, either."

"That's not true. Mamm and Daadi . . ." Katie hesitated, not sure what to say. "Well, maybe they thought you'd do better here."

"You mean Mamm was afraid I'd embarrass Louise and her precious Jonas."

Since that was just about what Mamm had said, Katie could hardly deny it. She tried to smile. "Ach, you know how excited Mamm is about getting one of her daughters married off, after being disappointed by me. We just have to be patient with her."

Rhoda's lips trembled, and she pressed them together, scowling. "Everything's always about Louise. I'm sick of hearing about her, and the bishop's son, and all the plans for the wedding."

Rhoda sounded fierce, but Katie could read the hurt behind her anger.

"I know." She reached out tentatively to touch her sister's arm. It was stiff and rigid, but at least Rhoda didn't pull away again. "I know it's hard. That's probably how Rachel and Kathy Ann feel about you."

"Them?" Rhoda dismissed the mention of their two youngest sisters with a sniff.

"Don't you think they envy you, starting your rumspringa?"

Rhoda considered. "Maybe. But nobody's telling them they have to be good, and be careful, and don't draw attention, and don't do anything to embarrass Louise."

A wave of sympathy rippled through Katie. Mamm loved all five of her daughters, but she had trouble showing that love when they weren't doing what she wanted. Katie had felt the same way Rhoda did only too often herself.

"Komm, now." She put an arm around Rhoda's shoulders. "That's only Mamm worrying. You know that."

"Maybe." Rhoda's voice wavered a bit. "But she said I'd have to stay with you, and now you don't want me, either."

Careful. She was responsible for her little sister, and she didn't want to make a mistake. "Why would you say that?"

"You hardly said a word to me all through supper," Rhoda pointed out. "And you looked like you were a million miles away."

Not a million miles. Just down in Caleb's shop, feeling that astonishing warmth between them. Warmth that had turned too quickly to ice when he'd said what he did about her sister.

"Ach, you mustn't mind me." Katie tried to make her tone light. "Since I moved into the apartment I've been so busy getting the shop ready to open, I haven't thought about anything else. I guess I've gotten into the habit of being quiet. It's not that I don't want you here, that's certain-sure."

Rhoda looked at her as if measuring the truth of what she said. She must have been convincing, because Rhoda's heart-shaped face relaxed a little. "You're sure?"

"Ja, I am."

"It seems like a fine place to be." Rhoda's gesture seemed to take in the four-room apartment. "I'd love to live like this, having my own place right above the street where you can look out and see what's happening if you want. Or be quiet if you want. With Rachel and Kathy Ann around, I don't get enough peace to think for a minute."

Katie decided to ignore the comment about their little sisters, who were a bit noisy, come to think of it. "The apartment is nice." She couldn't deny that she enjoyed having a place of her own, even if it was only rented from Bishop Mose. "I can concentrate on the shop for now. But you know, I found it was getting a little lonely, too. Now that you're here, I don't have to worry about that."

"Are you sure?" Some of Rhoda's natural liveliness came back into her face.

"I'm sure." She gave her little sister a hug. "It's early yet. Komm, let's walk down to the corner and get an ice cream for our dessert. To celebrate our first day in the shop together and having you here with me." She needed to know what Rhoda had done that had so upset Mamm, but tonight wasn't the time to ask. Tonight she'd just try to cement their relationship.

"You mean it?" Rhoda loved ice cream, but it was a rare treat at home, unless Daad got out the old ice-cream maker when the berries were ripe.

"I'll tell you a secret," Katie said, gathering her keys and money. "Having an ice-cream cone might be the best thing about living in town."

Rhoda giggled. "I'll take ice cream over another talk about Louise's dower chest anytime. I guess Mamm has to be excited about it, being the first wedding that really—" She stopped, looking stricken. "I mean—"

"It's all right." Katie managed a smile and hoped it was convincing. "Really. That's in the past."

"You're not still sad about Eli?"

"Not a bit."

Sad wasn't exactly the right word. She was still mourning the life they should have had together.

The truth was that she still loved Eli. The fact that he'd decided he didn't love her couldn't alter her feelings.

She followed Rhoda down the stairs, unable to prevent herself from glancing into the dim interior of Caleb's shop. Those moments when she'd touched him, when she'd thought she felt something—well, that was a mistake. She couldn't feel anything for anyone else because her heart belonged to Eli, and it always would.

After a week, she and Rhoda had fallen into a comfortable pattern, Katie decided. She glanced toward the back room, where Becky was helping Rhoda clean. The two girls had formed a rather surprising friendship in such a short time, and when her work in Caleb's shop was finished, Becky tended to show up in the quilt shop, lending a hand with whatever Rhoda was doing.

"Hanging out," Rhoda called it, a term that no doubt came from those Englisch friends Mamm had deplored so much. Fortunately, there had been none of those problems here. The birthday party Becky had invited Rhoda to had gone smoothly, with no ruffles to annoy Caleb.

Katie felt her own little spurt of annoyance. Becky was such a shy, quiet little thing—certainly not a description anyone would apply to Rhoda. In Rhoda's lively, talkative company, Becky seemed to come out of her shell a bit. Caleb ought to be happy about that, but Katie didn't suppose he was.

She paused in rearranging fabric bolts to glance into Caleb's shop. No one was in sight. Apparently he was upstairs in the second-floor workroom. Becky's handiwork was evident, though. The floor was spotless, the front window shone, and every piece of furniture on display seemed to glow. Did Caleb appreciate all that his niece was doing? Manlike, he might not even notice.

Katie's hand lingered on a length of flannelette she'd gotten in for folks making baby clothes and children's nightgowns. The Amish wouldn't buy quilts, since they either made them or received them as gifts. But they might start coming to her for their other fabric and sewing needs, instead of making the trip to Lewisburg or Mifflinburg to a fabric store.

The sale of quilts and quilted items depended on Englisch customers, and so far, her store traffic hadn't been nearly what she'd hoped.

It had only been just over a week, she reminded herself. Things would pick up. She'd put an ad in a weekly shopping paper that other local Amish shops advertised in. That should help.

But the ad had cost more than she'd expected. Everything did, and when she'd sat down to reckon up her expenses on Saturday evening, she'd been appalled at how quickly her savings were melting away.

The sound of footsteps crossing the other shop pulled her away from that depressing line of thought. Caleb. She'd already learned to recognize his firm stride.

He came through the archway carrying a large, paper-wrapped bundle in his arms.

"Katie." He put the package carefully on the countertop. "There are three quilts here from my mamm to put up for sale in your shop."

Relief made her smile warmer than it might otherwise have been. She'd heard nothing more from Naomi and begun to fear that she'd changed her mind.

"Denke, Caleb. That is wonderful gut. I hoped she'd bring some in. I understand from Molly that she is an accomplished quilter."

One of the best in the valley, Molly had implied, but Amish humility didn't allow you to claim to be better than your neighbors. You did things to the best of your ability and for the good of the community, as was pleasing to God.

Caleb's firm expression actually relaxed into a half smile for a moment before it tightened again. Did he regret the absence of a married-man's beard to help hide his emotions and that appealing cleft in his chin? He certainly didn't want to show his feelings, at least not to her.

"I think Mamm's only regret in her children was the lack of daughters," he said. "She wanted someone to pass her gift to."

"Your sister-in-law doesn't quilt, I understand."

"No, Nancy claims she doesn't have the patience for it. Becky seems to take an interest, but I'm not sure she has the love for it that Mamm does." He glanced toward the door into the back room as he spoke.

"Those girls are talking as fast as they work," Katie said, interpreting his look. "That's certain-sure. If you need Becky . . ."

"No, no, let her stay, as long as she's being useful and not a hindrance."

"That she is." Katie began unwrapping the quilts. "Those two are cleaning out the back room for me at the moment."

The paper fell away, and Katie's breath caught. Here was artistry for sure—a Sunshine and Shadows quilt done in such a combination of colors slipping from dark to light that the pattern actually seemed to move when you looked at it. Named for the alternating patterns of sunlight and shadows across the land, the design seemed also to reflect the happy and sad times in life.

"This is lovely. There aren't many quilters with such an eye for the effects of color." She smoothed her palm over the quilt and glanced up at him. "Are you all right with my having your mamm's quilts to sell?"

Caleb looked honestly taken aback. "Why wouldn't I be?"

"When I opened, you didn't seem exactly happy to have a quilting shop next door to you."

That might actually be embarrassment in his deep brown eyes as he glanced away from her. "Maybe I thought a quilt shop wasn't a gut mix with my shop." He shrugged. "But it's not so bad."

She smiled at the grudging admission. "Ach, you were afraid the place would be full of chattering women, ain't so?"

His gaze met hers again, and his face relaxed into the first real smile she'd seen from him, crinkling his eyes and making him look years younger all at once. Her heart seemed to give a few extra beats. She'd think a smile like that would have women lining up to relieve Caleb of his single state.

"Looks like I didn't do such a gut job of hiding my feelings."

"Not very." She ought to wipe the silly grin from her face, but she couldn't seem to manage it. "I could use a few chattering women in here. It's been quieter than I expected."

"For me, as well." He leaned against the counter, crossing his arms across his broad chest. "It seems like most folks are a bit more cautious with their money these days, Englisch and Amish."

She nodded. The Amish tried to live as independently as possible, but everyone was affected by the economy, especially those in business.

"Maybe this wasn't the best of times for starting a new business," she admitted. "But the opportunity opened up, and I was ready for a new challenge."

He was studying her face with an intentness that made her nervous, as if he was trying to see through to her motives. "You like a challenge, do you, Katie?"

"I do." She lifted her chin. "I'd rather start my own place and fail than spend my life wondering what would have happened if I'd not tried."

He tilted his head a little, as if weighing her words. "Weren't you in business with your mamm before?"

"I worked in her shop. But it was hers, not mine." Could he possibly understand the difference?

He nodded slowly. "Ja. You wanted to see how your ideas would work."

"Exactly." She found herself more in charity with Caleb than she had since the day they'd met. "But if I don't get some more Englisch coming in here, I'm afraid all the ideas in the world won't help me."

"Englisch?" He looked startled for a moment, but then he nodded. "Ja, I see. Amish aren't likely to buy a quilt from a shop."

"They're the sellers. Like your mamm." She lifted the top quilt off, revealing a baby quilt done in the softest of pinks, blues, and yellows. "Ach, this baby quilt would sell for sure, if only we get some tourists coming through this summer."

She carried the first quilt toward the bed on which she displayed quilts, and was a little surprised when Caleb moved to help her.

"Can't say I'm eager to see any tourists," he said, taking one end of the quilt and helping her spread it across the bed. "Peeking into windows and wanting to take your picture."

It was on the tip of her tongue to point out the money tourists brought to the area, but maybe it would be best to back away from the subject. She didn't want to destroy this new amity between them by arguing.

Seen spread out to its full width, the Sunshine and Shadows

quilt was even more inspiring. "Wonderful," she breathed. "Did your mamm make this recently?"

"Last year, I think. Mamm hasn't done any quilting since the fall."

"No? Winter is usually a fine time for quilting, once the other work is done."

He hesitated, staring down at the quilt, and she had a sense he was wondering how much to say to her. She studied the strong, averted face with its broad cheekbones and square, hard jaw. A little muscle twitched under the skin near his mouth, a testament to his indecision, and she found she wanted him to speak.

"Daad passed in the fall," he said finally. "Since then, Mamm has been . . ." He hesitated, plainly searching for the word. "A little lost, and not feeling well herself. She hadn't taken an interest in much of anything until she heard about your shop."

"I am sorry for your loss," Katie said quietly, trying not to imagine what her life would be like without her daad's steady presence. "You must be worried about your mamm."

"Ja." He paused again, still not looking at her. "I like it fine that she's excited about quilting again. I just don't want her to try to do too much."

Was that comment aimed at her? Katie wasn't sure. "I wouldn't urge her to overdo," she said cautiously. "But if she wants to quilt again, that's a gut thing, for sure."

She felt an urge to touch him, to reassure him, but she pressed her hands against her sides, remembering all too clearly what had happened the last time they'd touched.

"Ja," he said finally. "I hope so." He met her eyes then, his gaze probing and serious. He jerked his head toward the back room at a peal of laughter from the girls. "Your coming here has changed things, Katie Miller. I just hope all the changes are gut ones."

Caleb took a step away from Katie, wondering at himself. Now, why had he said that? He was trying to stay away from the woman, not confide in her.

And telling her all his concerns about Mamm—well, how ferhoodled could he be? Katie was just a little too easy to talk to, with that quick interest that sprang to life in her dark blue eyes and the warm sympathy that filled her face.

Maybe having her shop next door to his hadn't presented some of the problems he'd expected, but it seemed Katie was creating new ones.

Katie cleared her throat, and he had the sense that she was looking for something less personal to talk about.

"Ach, I just remembered a question I wanted to ask you. I was wondering if you have any quilt racks in stock just now. Becky mentioned that you made one for her."

He nodded. Quilt racks was a safer subject of conversation. "Ja, I have a couple of them."

"Maybe you'd be interested in putting one of yours in the archway between the shops, and I could display a quilt on it." The enthusiasm was back in her face again, and when her face lit that way, it was nearly beautiful. "It might draw the customers' attention to both your wares and mine."

Maybe she hadn't believed him when he'd said he didn't depend on gimmicks to sell his pieces. "I don't think that I—" He stopped when the bell over her shop door jangled.

"We'll talk about it later," she said, all her attention focused on the man who came in. With his plaid shirt and tan pants, a ball cap pushed back on his bald head, he looked like an Englisch tourist ready to buy something.

Caleb knew better. He'd seen this particular Englischer before—Bennett Hargrove, his name was. He owned a couple of shops in bigger towns, and he came through Pleasant Valley a few times a year, looking to buy Amish-made goods to resell.

Katie approached the man, greeting him pleasantly in Englisch, asking if she could help him find something.

Caleb frowned. Seemed like Katie should know she was talking to a dealer, not just a casual shopper.

It wasn't up to him to interfere. He kept it to himself. It was none of his business.

But he couldn't quite manage to walk away, either. Hargrove was a shrewd bargainer, always intent on getting Amish-made goods as cheaply as possible. And Katie, for all her talk of the shop she'd helped her mother run, might find herself in difficulty dealing with him.

Hargrove wandered along the counter, looking dismissively at the various pieces Katie had displayed. He stopped when he reached the baby quilt Caleb's mother had made.

"Now, this might be something I'd be interested in." He lifted the quilt, shaking it out to its full length. "For a gift, you know."

Katie nodded, catching the quilt before its edge could touch the floor. "It is a lovely piece for a nursery. Made by a gifted local quilter. The design . . ."

Hargrove chuckled. "Don't know much about quilts, or need to. But like I say, I might give it as a gift. If the price is right, that is." He flipped over the edge as if looking for a tag.

"This piece just came into the store today," Katie said. "It is not marked yet, but it is priced at two hundred dollars."

"Two hundred dollars? What's it made of, gold?" Hargrove let go of the quilt. "I can't spend that much on a gift."

"Think of the hours of work that went into it." Katie folded the crib quilt, her hands gentle. She held it for a moment against the blue dress she wore, as if it were wrapped around a boppli. "Look at the fine stitching, all done by hand. It's not just a baby quilt. It's an heirloom, something a mother will pass on to a daughter."

"Very nice." Hargrove stepped back, brushing his hands together as if to say he was finished. "My niece would be happy to have it, with the new baby coming and all, but I can't afford that price. Now, if you said seventy-five dollars . . ."

Katie didn't look at Caleb, but he seemed to know what she was thinking. She hadn't made much money in her first week, judging by what he'd seen, and maybe any sale was better than no sale.

"It may be for his niece." He surprised himself with his own words, spoken quickly in Pennsylvania Dutch so that Hargrove wouldn't understand. "But he is a dealer with a couple of shops of his own. Buys cheap and sells dear, so people say."

Katie's face warmed with gratitude. "Ja, denke, Caleb."

"Something wrong?" Hargrove looked from one to the other, his eyes narrowing.

"No, not at all." Katie had switched back to Englisch, her voice firm. "The price is two hundred. Now, if you're interested in taking some pieces on commission for your shop . . ." She let that trail off.

Hargrove's lips tightened to a thin line, and he shot an

annoyed glare at Caleb. "I don't deal in commissions. Never have, never will. And if you want to make a success of this place, you won't, either."

"It is a way that is fair to the quilter," she said mildly.

"It's a good way to go broke," he snapped. He turned, stomping toward the door. "Suit yourself. Your place will go belly-up before the year's out, anyway. Not enough traffic through this out-of-the-way place."

He grabbed the door and yanked it open, the bell jangling furiously. "Let me know when you have your going-out-of-business sale. Maybe I'll buy something." He punctuated the words with a slam of the door.

For a moment silence filled the shop.

"Well." Katie let out a long breath. "I hope I don't have many visitors like that."

Her tone was light, but Caleb saw her fingers press against the countertop until they were white.

"You don't want to listen to somebody like Hargrove." He wasn't very good at finding comforting words to say. "You'll do fine."

"I hope so." But the confidence was lost from her voice.

None of his business, Caleb reminded himself. Still, he had to do something.

"I'll go and get that quilt rack," he said. "Which quilt do you want to hang on it?"

Her gaze met his, and the sparkle came back into her eyes. "Ach, your mamm's baby quilt, of course. What else?"

CHAPTER FOUR

This feels familiar, ain't so?" Molly tilted her head toward the grounds around the township fire hall, her dimples showing when she smiled. "You had Mud Sales at home, I'm sure."

"Ja, you're right." Katie glanced across the grassy area, already turning muddy from all the people who crowded around stalls selling everything from plants to funnel cakes to the latest kitchen gadgets. "Except there I knew everyone."

She wished the words back immediately, reminding herself that "everyone" included Eli and Jessica.

Molly squeezed her arm. "You'll soon get to know folks here."

"For sure." She pinned on a smile.

Aaron, Molly's oldest brother, caught up with them. "What are you looking to buy today, Cousin Katie? A pan of sticky buns or a vegetable chopper or a new harrow? Whatever it is, someone has it."

Her smile broadened. Aaron's happiness was contagious as he looked forward to his fall wedding to Sarah Mast, the midwife. "I don't think I need anything, but you are the one to shop today," she said. "You'll be setting up housekeeping with Sarah at the birthing center before long. There must be some things you both need."

Aaron's face gentled, as it always did at the mention of his intended. "Sarah's aunt has lived in the house for so long that it's well-furnished. Still, Aunt Emma will be moving furniture into the grossdaadi haus once it's finished, and we might need a few things."

Aaron, a carpenter, was building an addition to the old house for Sarah's aunt, a semi-retired midwife who still helped out with the births.

"Go along with you." Molly flapped her hand at her brother. "You know you want to check out what they have at the auction. And if you see Jacob, tell him I'll take the boppli whenever he wants."

Nodding, Aaron moved off through the crowd.

"I think everybody in the township is here today," Molly said, nodding to an older couple who passed them. "You should have just closed the shop and let Rhoda komm, too."

"Rhoda will have her chance this afternoon. I'll go back and take over for her."

That arrangement had not been to Rhoda's liking, since she'd wanted to spend the whole day at the sale with her new friends. But Katie hadn't been able to get the words of that Englisch dealer out of her mind, try as she might. He was convinced she would fail, and her dwindling bank account only reinforced that idea. Even if she made only one sale today, she had to stay open.

"Look, there is Rachel Zook's stand. Komm, we must say hello."

Katie let herself be tugged along by her cousin. She knew full well what Molly was doing. She was determined that Katie should meet everyone, make friends, and be happy here.

Rachel had a welcoming grin as they approached her stand, which was laden with flats of flower and herb seedlings. "Molly, Katie. It's gut to see you. Katie, this is your first Mud Sale here, ja?"

Katie nodded. She'd talked with Rachel several times after church, of course, but Rachel had always seemed busy with her young family. "You have so many plants. They look wonderful gut."

"Rachel was born with a green thumb," Molly teased. "And now that she has her greenhouse, her business is thriving."

"It does all right." Rachel flushed slightly at Molly's words. "I never thought I'd be running a business, that's certain-sure, but it has worked out just fine for me."

Katie nodded. This wasn't the life she'd envisioned for herself, either. But Rachel had a loving husband and young children, in addition to her business, so she had the best of both, it seemed.

"This is a gut place for you to make sales?" she asked.

"Ja, I go to all the spring sales, and also to the farmers' market. It's worthwhile, I think. Even if folks don't buy from me on the day of the sale, they might remember my name and seek me out afterward."

Katie nodded, considering Rachel's words. "That didn't occur to me. Maybe I should be following your example. I could take some things from the shop out to sales."

"Gut idea," Molly said, her face lighting up with her typical enthusiasm. "I'd think you could sell a lot of the smaller items at a sale like this, and once folks saw what you have, they'd want to visit the shop. Why, you could hit a sale every weekend, this time of year, if you didn't mind hiring a driver, and—"

"Ach, Molly, don't overwhelm her." Rachel seemed to read Katie's reaction. She reached across the counter to pat her hand. "Not every sale, for sure. That would tire you out. But I am planning to go to the one in Fisherdale in two weeks. If you're interested, you could go with me and share my stand."

The unexpected offer, coming when she had been feeling increasingly worried, nearly brought tears to Katie's eyes. "That is ser gut of you. But I don't want to impose."

"It's not imposing. I would be glad of the company." Rachel squeezed her hand. "Other people helped me when I was getting started. We businesswomen need to stick together, ja?"

"Ja. Denke, Rachel." Rachel's words seemed to sweep away some of Katie's doubts. "I would like to do that, if you're sure."

Rachel nodded briskly. "I'll stop by the shop this week, and we can make plans."

An Englisch woman approached the stand. "Rachel, I see you have the best plants as always." She included Molly and Katie in her smile.

Katie found it difficult, sometimes, to judge the age of an Englisch person, but the woman's gray hair, worn short and windblown, seemed to say she was middle-aged, at least. Smile lines crinkled around green eyes that seemed to match the shirt she wore with jeans and a corduroy jacket.

"Molly, it's so nice to see you. How is the baby?"

"Ach, he is thriving." Molly beamed at the mention of little Jacob. "I don't think you have met my cousin, Katie Miller. She has the new quilt shop in town. Katie, this is Mrs. Macklin. Her gift shop is just down the street from your shop."

"Lisa, please." The woman's warm smile included Katie. "In Pleasant Valley we're all just down the street from each other, aren't we? I'm sorry I haven't been in to welcome you yet."

Katie wasn't sure whether to respond to the introduction or to the woman's comment. "It is nice to meet you, Mrs. . . . . Lisa," she amended. "Are you interested in quilting?"

"Interested, but not very good. Still, I'd like to learn more about the lovely quilts the Amish make. I'll stop by sometime next week, okay? Main Street merchants have to support each other."

It was a variation on what Rachel had said, and it warmed Katie still more, making her feel that she was not alone.

"I'll look forward to seeing you soon, then."

Lisa Macklin nodded. "You know, you might be interested in a project I'm working on. I've been thinking that if all of the merchants got together, we might find ways of drawing more tourists into town. That would be good for everyone."

Certainly good for her, Katie knew, but she couldn't jump into anything without considering it carefully, especially if it would cost money.

"I would like to hear about it," she said politely. "But now I must go. I told my sister I would be back to take over the shop so that she can come and enjoy the sale."

"We'll talk about it when I stop by your shop, then." Lisa nodded, turning to Rachel's plants.

Katie moved away, her spirits a bit lighter. She hadn't come to the sale today with any particular hopes, but in a short time she'd gained a friend or two and lost some of the apprehension that had been dogging her. She'd been praying for guidance, and perhaps those two very different women were God's answer.

Molly caught up with her. "I'll walk along with you as far as the auction tent. The boppli might be getting hungry."

"You just can't bear to be away from him, that's all," Katie teased.

Molly glanced toward the tent, maybe looking for Jacob. "There is Naomi Brand with her family. I'm glad to see her out and about."

Katie looked in the direction Molly indicated. Naomi seemed to be surrounded by her entire family, except for one person.

"Caleb isn't there," she pointed out. "He must be keeping his shop open today, too. So I'm not the only one who didn't close."

"Caleb doesn't go out to events like this very often." Molly closed her lips, as if she'd said something she shouldn't.

"Why is that?"

"Why what?" Molly tried unsuccessfully to look as if she didn't know what Katie was talking about.

Katie gave her arm a little shake. "You said Caleb doesn't go out to events like this. What did you mean?"

"Nothing. I—nothing."

Katie tightened her grip on her cousin's elbow. If Molly held the key to unraveling the puzzle that was Caleb Brand, she wanted to know it.

"Molly," she said warningly.

"Oh, all right." Molly took a quick look around, as if to ensure that no other Amish were within earshot. "You must have noticed already how Caleb would rather stay away from people."

Katie considered. He did seem to keep to himself, but she'd thought maybe that was just with her. It was unusual among the Amish, to whom family and community meant so much.

Molly took a deep breath and blew it out. "He's a bit older than me, so I don't know as much as some might. Maybe you should talk to Aaron."

Katie recognized an evasion when she saw it. "I'm talking to you."

"Ja. Well, when he was younger Caleb and Mattie Weaver were going to make a match of it. Everyone said so, and they were together all the time. The wedding date was set, even. And then one day Mattie was just gone."

"Gone?" Startled into immobility, Katie let a group of Englisch flow around her. "What do you mean?"

Tears sparkled in Molly's eyes. She wasn't enjoying telling the story. "She ran away, without a word to anyone."

"That . . . That's terrible." For Caleb, and for Mattie's family.

"But that wasn't all." Having started, Molly seemed intent on getting the whole story out. "A few months later, the community learned that she was living in Harrisburg. And she was pregnant."

Katie tried to absorb that. "But if she was going to have his baby, why didn't she come back?"

"That's what nobody knows. You can imagine the fuss it caused. Caleb went before the bishop and the ministers. He said he still wanted to marry Mattie, but she wouldn't have him. Bishop Mose even went to Harrisburg and talked to her, and she said the same. No explanation, but she wouldn't come back."

It was a painfully unfinished story. "That's all?"

Molly shrugged. "What could anyone do, when she had left and wouldn't return?"

Katie grappled with it. "But Caleb stayed here."

"Ja. He stayed. I think he might have been under the bann for a short time, but then . . . well, it should have wiped the slate clean."

"But it didn't," Katie said, knowing that must be the case. "People didn't understand, and so they remember."

"Ja. Folks don't forget. If Caleb had married, gone on with his life, maybe they would have. But he didn't, and he just stays away from people when he has a choice."

Maybe Caleb couldn't go on with his life. And maybe Katie understood just a little of what he felt.

"What about Mattie's family? Did they leave, too?"

Molly shook her head. "They're still here . . . in fact, they're here today—the older couple we passed when we were going to Rachel's stand." Molly let out a sigh. "I always feel so sorry for Ruth. I'm sure she would forgive what her daughter did, but her husband, Ephraim, is so strict. He'll never have their daughter spoken of, even though she hadn't been baptized yet when she left."

"That is so sad. Families can be torn apart over things like that." It was heartbreaking for everyone concerned. Did Caleb still love Mattie, despite what she'd done?

Small wonder that people still talked. What could have been so bad that the woman refused to marry the father of her baby?

Katie couldn't seem to let go of the revelation about Caleb. She walked back toward the shop along the village's main street, her thoughts churning as she passed under trees leafing out in their pale green colors.

Certainly it wasn't unheard of for a young couple to become pregnant before the wedding. Nobody wanted that to happen, but young people could be heedless, swept up in the emotion of the moment.

Normally, the couple made a confession to the bishop and ministers, and a hurried-up wedding would be arranged. A source of embarrassment to the parents, maybe, but beyond that it would be quickly forgiven and forgotten. A situation like this one Katie had never heard before.

She passed Paula's bakery, then the tiny shop that sold everything from paper clips to drain cleaner. Like many of the stores, including hers, it was located in what had once been someone's home. The only new building in town was the bank, and even that had been built of a faded brick so that it didn't stand out for its newness.

Was it possible that Caleb's love—Mattie, her name was—had wanted to leave while Caleb wanted to stay?

Maybe so. But Katie thought they could have come to a compromise when a baby's future was at stake.

She stopped at the corner. Pleasant Valley boasted one traffic light, where the state route crossed Main Street. She waited obediently at the curb, even though no traffic appeared in either direction. Molly had been right—everyone was at the fire hall for the Mud Sale on this fine, sunny Saturday.

But not Caleb. As she approached, she could see that his door stood open. Another few steps, and she glimpsed him bending over the counter in his shop.

Averting her gaze, she hurried past toward her own shop. How could she face him with this knowledge so fresh in her mind?

She couldn't. She'd just have to avoid him until she could talk to him without her knowing being written all over her face for him to see.

Katie scurried to her door, reaching out to open it, and stopped, staring. CLOSED. The sign on the window had been flipped to read CLOSED.

Surely not. Maybe she'd forgotten to switch it when she opened up this morning. She grasped the knob and twisted. It didn't turn. The shop was dark and locked. And Rhoda was supposed to be here.

Panic grabbed her, shook her. She was responsible for her little sister, and something had happened to her.

Common sense asserted itself. That was foolishness. Nothing could happen to Rhoda in broad daylight on a quiet street. Not with Caleb barely twenty feet away in his shop.

Katie yanked out her key and unlocked the door, sweeping inside to the jangle of the bell. "Rhoda?"

Her voice echoed through the silent shop. The back room? She hurried across the floor. Nothing. It was empty.

Rhoda must have gone up to the apartment—maybe to the bathroom or to get something to eat. In that case she'd probably close the shop. It was silly to imagine anything else.

Katie trotted up the stairs, calling her sister's name. It took no time at all to check out the four rooms. Rhoda was nowhere to be found . . . her bed made, her closet door closed, everything as neat as a pin.

Beating back the worry that ate at her, Katie returned to the shop. No note lay on the counter. The cash register was locked.

She stood for a moment, staring at the counter, biting her lip. There was no helping it. Evading Caleb was now out of the question. She had to ask if he knew where Rhoda was.

Walking to the archway, she paused for a second before continuing into the shop. Caleb was working on a small chest, running a polishing cloth along its surface. When he saw Katie he stood up, watching without a word as she approached.

"Caleb." She forced herself to meet his eyes. "I just got back from the Mud Sale." *Where I learned something shocking about you.* "I thought Rhoda was here. Did you see her leave?"

An expression of distaste appeared in Caleb's face and was as quickly gone. Who did he disapprove of? Her? Rhoda? Both of them?

"Ja, I saw her." His face was as wooden as the chest. "She closed up and went out about half an hour ago."

"Did she say where she was going?" Katie hated to pursue it in the teeth of his obvious reluctance, but she had to.

"Not to me." He ran a cloth over the chest, as if to suggest that he was busy.

Katie's jaw tightened. If he thought . . .

Her shop door opened, and she spun around. Rhoda stood there, holding a foam mug in her hand, a wisp of steam rising from it, partially obscuring the guilty look on her face.

"Katie. I didn't think you'd be back so soon."

Stalking back into her own shop, Katie seemed to feel Caleb's disapproving gaze on her back. "That is obvious, I think."

"I don't know what you mean." Rhoda's gaze evaded hers. "Just because I went for a coffee . . ."

"When you were supposed to be keeping the shop open." The worry she'd felt for Rhoda was rapidly being replaced by annoyance. "You could have waited until I got back. Or gone up to the kitchen for coffee."

"Nobody came in here all morning." Rhoda flared up in an instant. "You can't expect me to hang around for no reason at all."

Katie tried to hold on to her temper. "We had an agreement. You'd watch the shop while I went to the sale, and then I'd take over so you could go."

"It's no big deal."

Sulkiness turned Rhoda into a grown-up replica of her six-year-old self, pouting because Louise was allowed to go to a quilting and she wasn't. That was Rhoda, as quick to anger as she was to laughter or to tears or trying something none of her sisters had done, just for the fun of it.

"Don't let's argue." Katie put her hand on Rhoda's arm. The girl was only sixteen, after all. Katie couldn't really expect grown-up behavior from her. "I was worried, that's all, when I came back and there was no sign of you."

"Ja, well, I'd have left a note if I thought you'd be here before I returned. I just ran down to the corner to get a coffee to go and came straight back."

But Caleb had said she'd been gone for half an hour. It didn't take half an hour to do that.

Confront Rhoda? Katie was tempted, but that would mean letting Rhoda know that Caleb had told her. She'd be resentful, and maybe rightfully so.

Katie closed her eyes for a moment. Taking responsibility for her little sister was proving considerably more challenging than she'd expected.

"Katie?" Rhoda's voice had gone soft, and she clasped Katie's hand. "You're not mad at me, are you?"

That was the little sister she remembered—her soft heart leading her to regret a moment after she'd done something foolhardy.

"No, I'm not mad." She squeezed Rhoda's hand. "But next time—"

"I won't do it again, I promise. I won't let you down again."

"All right, then. We'll forget it." She turned toward the counter, careful not to let her gaze stray toward Caleb. He probably thought she was being too easy on the girl, but it wasn't his business, and she didn't care what he thought. "Go on to the sale, now. Don't spend all your money in one place, ja?"

Rhoda's smile was like the sun breaking through the clouds. "Denke, Katie. I won't." She scurried out the door as if she were afraid Katie would change her mind if she lingered.

Maybe she should have insisted Rhoda stay at the shop. That's what Mamm would have done.

Katie rubbed her forehead. They still hadn't had a talk about whatever it was that had led Mamm to bring Rhoda here. She felt hamstrung, knowing too much but not enough. Still, she wasn't Rhoda's mother. All she could do was try to be the best sister she could.

Flipping the sign to OPEN, she walked back to the counter. She probably wouldn't have a customer all day, but she'd said she'd stay open, and she would.

Like Caleb, and his shop. Except that Caleb's reason was apparently far different from hers.

The three-hour worship service moved toward its conclusion. Caleb tried to keep his attention focused on the bishop's words. Or on Gideon and Rachel's barn, with its rafters rising above their heads and its floors swept and scrubbed, where the service was being held this Sunday. He'd best think of anything, in fact, but Katie, who sat a few rows ahead of him on the women's side.

Or, for that matter, from focusing on the teenagers, who sat in a row toward the front with a solemnity that didn't disguise their interest in each other.

He glimpsed the back of Becky's kapp, the soft brown hair fastened securely under it. Next to her sat Rhoda Miller, head turned slightly to the side so that he could see the resemblance between her profile and Katie's. Rhoda's kapp tilted, and he thought she whispered something to Becky.

He frowned. He was trying to be fair to the Miller girl, but he couldn't help feeling she wasn't the best friend for their Becky.

And now he was looking at Katie, unable to escape the feeling that she'd handled the girl incorrectly yesterday. She'd let Rhoda get away with her irresponsibility.

As for that story of the girl's, he knew full well Rhoda had been gone far longer than it would take to get a cup of coffee. Probably flirting with one of the boys along the way.

Katie, slim and erect on the backless bench, seemed oddly vulnerable when he was looking at the curve of her nape instead of at the stubborn jaw and snapping eyes she so often showed him. Katie was too young, in his opinion, to have charge of a high-spirited teenager like Rhoda. Her parents should have kept the girl at home and dealt with her themselves.

He tried to imagine Mamm and Daadi shipping one of them off to live with someone else. He couldn't. Mamm and Daadi had handled any mischief or disobedience themselves, with love and kindness, but firmly.

Well, folks were different, and he had to hope Katie's parents knew what they were doing. As for Katie . . .

He suspected he was past the point of staying detached from Katie Miller's concerns.

His brother Andy, sitting next to him, dug his elbow into Caleb's ribs, just as he'd done when they were kids and he'd thought Caleb wasn't paying attention. Caleb grinned at him, reminding himself that he lived with his older brother, just as Rhoda now lived with her older sister.

But that was different. He wasn't a difficult teenager. His smile disappeared. He focused his gaze on Bishop Mose as he began the final prayer, but he found his mind forming a prayer of his own.

Show me what is right, Lord, and I will do it.

In a few minutes the service had ended. The barn doors swung open, letting in a path of May sunshine. The usual after-service bustle began. Women collected young ones and herded them outside, while others, along with a flock of teenage girls, headed for the kitchen to bring out food.

Caleb joined Andy and the other men in converting the backless benches into tables for their meal.

"Thought you were dozing off there toward the end of the service," Andy said, flipping the bench up with the ease of long practice.

"Caleb wouldn't do that." Gideon, their host, joined them, adding some extra muscle to the task. "He's the serious one of the family, ain't so?"

"So folks say, but I've known him too long to buy that," Andy retorted.

"Don't listen to him," Caleb said, relieved at the interruption. He certainly didn't want to talk about the reason for his distraction during worship. "At least I've never dozed off during the sermon."

Andy grinned. "I'd been up all night helping that stubborn mare give birth, and you know it."

"So you tell us." He was in a mood to be glad of the careless teasing that went on among them. He'd known Gideon near as long as his own brother, and Gid had been one of the few who hadn't ever doubted him.

"Looks like your Becky has made a new friend." Gideon straightened, nodding to where Becky and Rhoda, heads together, were walking toward the house.

"Ja, that's so," Andy said. He leaned against the table they'd just erected. "Becky is doing some work for Caleb at the shop now, and she's gotten thick with Rhoda Miller. A gut thing, I think." He gave a short nod. "Becky is so quiet and shy, we figure it helps her to have a friend who's as lively and outgoing as Rhoda."

Andy wouldn't say that, Caleb guessed, if he'd heard what

Caleb had the day before. Caleb was caught like a fly in a spider web, not knowing whether to speak or not. If he said something, if Andy and Nancy discouraged the friendship between the girls, Katie wouldn't have any doubt about who to blame. Not that that would prevent him, if he was sure he was right.

But he wasn't sure, and he didn't like the feeling. He wanted to know what was right and do it, no matter how that might look to anyone else. Or what it might cost him.

"Maybe that gives Becky a little more confidence," Gideon said, seeming to agree. "I hear we'll see her at the singing tonight."

Gideon and Rachel, having hosted worship that morning, had said they might as well have a singing for the young folks tonight, since the barn was all cleaned up. Getting ready for when their own young ones launched into their rumspringa, Caleb supposed.

"Ja, Becky and Rhoda are coming together." Andy put out a hand to slow down his youngest boy as he went spurting past. "You and Rachel will keep an eye on things, ja?"

"That's certain-sure." Gideon grinned. "But I guess we might have to let a few kisses go unnoticed, with the older ones."

"Ach, stealing a kiss is all part of growing up," Andy said, his own smile reminiscent.

Say something? Or not? If Caleb did, word would get around. People would start talking about Rhoda, and he didn't like the idea of causing that.

Gideon clapped his shoulder. "We could use a few more adults tonight, Caleb. How about if you join us, ja?"

"I don't think—"

"Ja, that's a gut idea. Becky would hate it if her mamm and I came, but she wouldn't mind seeing her onkel there." Andy sounded a little too jovial, knowing as he did the trouble that had emerged during Caleb's rumspringa. "You go, Caleb."

Caleb couldn't help how stiff he got at the words. "I'm not such a gut example for the young people." He tried to turn away, but his brother's hand on his shoulder stopped him.

"That's foolishness," Andy said, his voice firm. "Nobody thinks about that old story anymore. It's forgiven and gone. You can't act like a hermit because of that."

It was so unlike his normally taciturn brother that Caleb could only stare at him.

Andy reddened a little. "You know it's true, what I say. You never look at a woman, never go to anything you can get out of. It's not the way you should be living, I'm certain-sure of that."

"I don't—"

"Then prove it," Gideon said. "Komm tonight. You know Becky would like that."

He didn't like this surprise attack, but Gideon was right about one thing. Becky would be happy to see him there tonight. And if he was at the singing, he could observe Rhoda's behavior for himself.

"Ja, all right," he said finally, knowing when it was best to stop arguing. "I'll be here."

"Gut," Gideon said, slapping his back. "I'll tell Rachel. She'll be glad we have some extra help. And since you're coming, you could do something else for me."

"What is it? Do you need soda? Snacks?" He might have known they'd have more for him to do.

"You can swing by and pick up Rhoda and Katie," Gideon said. "Katie's coming to help out, too."

Gideon walked away before Caleb could object.

And anyway, what would he say? To refuse would be unkind to a sister, and he couldn't do that.

But he was being thrown together with Katie and her sister, as if he didn't already see enough of them, and he didn't have to like it.

CHAPTER FIVE

*K*atie wasn't sure what was more awkward on the ride to the singing that evening—the endless giggles of the girls in the backseat or the utter silence that stretched between her and Caleb in the front. Amish men typically didn't chatter, but she'd think he could say something as the horse clopped along. She'd assumed at first that he was concentrating on the traffic, but once they turned onto a winding gravel road, that wasn't an issue.

The road wound between pastures and through dense stands of hemlock and hickory trees. Slanting sunlight touched the fresh green growth, so much lighter and brighter than it would be later in the summer. She looked toward the distant ridge, where the setting sun had begun to turn the clouds to purple. Still . . . everything was so still, save for the girls' soft voices and the clop of the horse's hooves.

She slanted a glance toward Caleb, but his strong-featured face gave nothing away. Probably it would be better if she could clear the air between them over Rhoda's behavior the previous day, but she could hardly do that with Rhoda sitting behind her.

Katie could be imagining the heavy disapproval that came from Caleb, but she didn't think so. It was only too obvious that he didn't care for the friendship that had grown between his niece and her sister.

Well, if he wouldn't speak, she would. "It was kind of you to pick us up tonight for the singing, Caleb."

"It's nothing." His gaze was fixed at a spot between the horse's ears. "Gideon suggested it."

Did that mean that Caleb wouldn't have made the offer if Gideon hadn't thought of it? Probably. She tamped her annoyance down.

"I am used to having a horse and buggy of my own," she said, "but it wasn't practical to try and bring them this far. My cousin Aaron has a buggy I can use, so I'll probably buy a horse."

That got Caleb's attention, and he swung toward her, brown eyes seeming to frown. "Where will you keep them?"

She stared blandly back at him. "Bishop Mose said that I can share the stable behind the building with you. After all, you only use it during the day."

A muscle twitched in his jaw. "I'm sure your cousins would be happy to take you anywhere you need."

"Ja, they would, but I'm used to getting myself where I want to go." She hadn't particularly looked for such independence, but it had found her.

"If you were my cousin, I would not want you to have to do things like that." His voice grated on the words.

"Then it is a gut thing you are not my cousin, ain't so?"

He didn't bother answering, just turned in at the farm lane behind several other buggies, all headed for the barn where they'd worshipped that morning. A small white sign announced the presence of RACHEL'S GARDEN, NO SUNDAY SALES.

Katie clamped her lips shut. She'd said too much, no doubt about it.

If Rhoda were to be happy here, she needed friends like Becky. For Rhoda's sake, Katie should make an effort to get along with Becky's uncle. Too bad he had the ability to bring out all the worst aspects of her nature with just a look.

Caleb drew into the row of buggies parked along the lane, and a couple of boys ran to help. Rhoda and Becky slid out in a hurry, obviously eager to get to the fun, and Katie followed more slowly.

"We want to join the volleyball game. All right?" Rhoda said, nodding to where a net had been set up on the lawn near the barn, a safe distance from the greenhouse where Rachel obviously grew the plants she sold. A fair-sized group of boys and girls, maybe thirty or more of them, milled around the net, probably more interested in each other than in the game.

"Of course." Katie bit back the impulse to remind Rhoda to behave properly. Rhoda wouldn't appreciate it, and no wonder. Katie certainly wouldn't have at that age. "I'll go and see if Rachel needs any help in the kitchen."

The two girls darted off. As Katie turned toward the house, Caleb clasped her hand to stop her.

"Katie..."

Whatever he was about to say seemed to vanish from his lips. His fingers warmed against her skin, and that warmth began to spread up her arm. She stared at him for a brief, disorienting moment, seeing his eyes darken, feeling the ground seem to shift under her feet.

He surely could feel her pulse pounding against his hand. She should . . .

Caleb dropped her wrist as if he'd touched a hot stove. He took a step back, bumping into the buggy. He shook his head, maybe denying that anything had happened between them.

"I'll keep an eye on Becky," he said abruptly. "I hope you'll do the same for your sister."

For an instant Katie felt like bursting into tears, but a flare of anger came to her rescue. "My sister is fine. She doesn't need anyone to keep an eye on her."

The fact that Katie had come for just that purpose was none of Caleb's business.

His jaw clenched. "Yesterday—"

She'd known he'd bring that up sometime. "What happened yesterday was a misunderstanding. It was between me and my sister. No one else."

"You mean it's none of my business," he said, clearly not agreeing.

"It's not." She gave him back look for look. He could make of that what he wanted.

Finally he turned away, making a small gesture with his hand that seemed to dismiss her and her sister entirely.

Clearly he didn't approve of the way she'd handled Rhoda yesterday. But then, there didn't seem to be anything about her that didn't draw that same reaction from him, did there?

That moment when they had touched was different, a small voice in the back of her mind said. Very different.

. . .

"So some of Becky's friends are going to get together to go shopping on Saturday, and they invited me." Rhoda's tongue had been running faster than her hands as she and Katie got ready to open on Monday. "I can go, can't I?"

The efforts Becky had made to introduce Rhoda into Pleasant Valley's teenage society were obviously working, but that left Katie with one challenge after another.

"That is ser gut of them, but I'll need to know a bit more about it. Who is going, and how are you getting there, and—"

"And, and, and," Rhoda interrupted her. "You sound like Mammi. Can't you trust me?"

Katie reminded herself that she'd been just as impatient to grow up at sixteen. "Mamm and Daadi left you in my care. I have to do things the way they would. I didn't say no, just that I must have more information. That's not too much to ask, ain't so?"

"If I find out all that, will you say yes?" Rhoda was nothing if not persistent.

"If it sounds appropriate," she said cautiously.

"Ach, you'll see. They are all nice girls, Becky's friends." Her good humor restored, Rhoda seized the end of the sheet Katie had put over the quilts on the display bed and began folding. She paused, sheet in her arms. "Should we put a different quilt on top?"

Katie touched the Tumbling Blocks quilt Caleb's mother had made. "Let's leave this one on top a bit longer. There hasn't been much traffic in the shop since I put it out."

And there was the crux of her problem. How long could she

keep going if sales didn't pick up? Of course, Saturday had been the Mud Sale, so people hadn't been out shopping in town. And she couldn't expect to have fantastic sales the first week. Things would get better.

She kept telling herself those same reassuring words. They were beginning to sound a little hollow.

"Thomas Esch is awfully nice-looking, don't you think?" Rhoda asked the question with such studied casualness that it was obviously important.

"Thomas?" Katie mentally scanned the faces of the young folks she'd met at the singing. "Tall? Kind of gawky?" Of course that described at least half the boys there.

"He's not gawky," Rhoda said, her tone indignant. "I think he's handsome, with those brown eyes and light hair."

"Ach, ja. I was thinking of the wrong boy." Katie tried to make amends. "Thomas is good-looking, for sure." Rhoda thought so, and that was the important thing. "Did you talk to him?"

Rhoda shrugged. "A little. He's in the same gang as Becky, and they said I could be, too."

"I'm glad."

The word *gang* probably had a different meaning in the outside world. To Amish teens, it was a loose group of friends who did things together. For sure it was important to a newcomer like Rhoda to belong to a gang, and Katie could be confident that Becky's group would be an appropriate one.

She felt a surge of gratitude toward Becky. Despite Caleb's attitude, Becky had gone out of her way to welcome Rhoda.

Not that Caleb was always so judgmental. Katie uncovered the quilt rack, letting her hand rest on the smooth curved wood for a moment, and glanced into his shop. No one was there, but from the second floor came the rasp of a saw. Caleb was obviously getting in some work time before he opened up.

Rhoda, humming something Katie suspected was a popular song, began sweeping the floor. Despite Caleb's unbending attitude toward her sister, there had been moments when she'd almost thought they might be friends.

When Caleb had helped her out with that Englisch dealer, for instance. She might very easily have given in to his ridiculously low offer for the crib quilt, just for the sake of selling something, if not for Caleb's timely warning.

She touched the fine feather stitches of the quilting. The piece was worth every penny of the price she'd put on it, and she'd be foolish to take less.

Thanks to Caleb she hadn't. And when he'd brought the quilt rack in to display, she'd thought surely they were done with disagreeing.

Not so. Caleb's disapproval of how she'd handled Rhoda set her back up. Unfortunately, it made her question her judgment, as well. What did a maidal like her know about raising a teenager?

Still, Caleb was no more a parent than she—

Katie cut that thought short. Caleb *was* a parent, if Molly's story was true. Somewhere out there in the Englisch world, he presumably had a child. It was inexplicable.

"Katie, someone's here." Rhoda, picking up the broom and dust pan, scuttled behind the counter.

She was right. Lisa Macklin approached the door, and in a moment she'd entered, a smile crinkling the fine lines around her eyes, her short gray hair ruffled from the spring breeze.

"Good morning, Katie. I said I'd stop by, and here I am."

"Wilkom, Mrs. Macklin." She handed the sheet she held to Rhoda, brushing a thread off her skirt. "You are out early."

"I don't open my shop until ten on Mondays, so I thought I'd stop by. And you're going to call me Lisa, remember?" She approached the counter, turning her smile on Rhoda. "And who's this?"

"This is my sister, Rhoda, komm from home to help me with the new shop. Rhoda, this lady is Mrs. Macklin. She has the gift shop down the street—the one with all the candles in the window."

Rhoda nodded politely, still clutching the broom. "I have seen your shop." She glanced at Katie. "Shall I sweep in the back room, then?"

"Ja, do that." Had Lisa come to buy, perhaps? Katie fervently hoped so.

Rhoda and the broom disappeared into the back room, and Katie returned to her visitor. "Can I help you find something?"

"I'll just look around a little," Lisa said. Katie's heart sank. People who said that were seldom serious about buying.

She tried to think of something to say that wouldn't sound as if she were pushing Lisa to buy. "Have you had your shop for a long time?"

Lisa shook her head, a tinge of sorrow in her eyes. "No, only about two years. It was a retirement dream of my husband's—to run a little gift shop in a small town like this. Mark was so enthusiastic about it. He had so many ideas for the place. But he passed away after we'd only been open a few months."

"I'm so sorry." Katie's heart went out to the woman, whose dreams had been shattered so quickly. "Yet you still run the shop?"

Lisa tilted her head to the side, as if she were considering the question. "It does seem strange, in a way. The shop was Mark's dream, not mine. At first I suppose I found the routine comforting, and the idea of selling the place was overwhelming when all I could do was get through one day after another. Then one day I woke up and realized that I was enthusiastic about it, too."

"So your husband's dream became yours."

"I guess so. Mark would laugh about that." She smiled, though a hint of sorrow touched her eyes. "Running the shop suits me, and I want to make it a success."

Success was not a word an Amish person would use readily in that regard. A business should pay its way and provide a living for its owner and a means of supporting the community.

The trouble was, Katie had begun to worry that her place would not even do that. "Tell me," she said impulsively, "do you make enough sales here in Pleasant Valley to . . . well, to be worth it?"

"Not as much as I'd like," Lisa said. Her gaze sharpened on Katie's face, as if she'd said something insightful. "It's not easy to make a go of a shop in a small farming community unless you're selling something lots of people need. Like Bishop Mose and the harness shop, for instance."

Katie nodded. What the woman said was true enough, and folks here didn't need quilts.

"That's why I've been trying to organize the shop owners to try and increase the number of visitors to town," Lisa said, her eyes sparkling with enthusiasm. "We need people coming to Pleasant Valley who will want the unique things we have to offer, like your quilts and Caleb Brand's furniture."

"Ja, I see. But how would you get more people to come?"

"That's not as hard as you might think. We need to reach the people who would stop by if only they knew about us. For instance, a website on the Internet would draw people's attention." She gave Katie a questioning look, and Katie nodded.

"Ja, I understand about that."

"Good. And I thought if we ran some special promotions it would help. For instance, say we all had sales at the same time. Or we could have an outdoor sidewalk sale on a particular Saturday. Or place an ad in the tourist booklets they put out in Lewisburg. Or — "

Lisa cut herself short, laughing a little. "Sorry. I do run on, but for someone who wasn't that enthusiastic about running a shop, I suddenly find I have too many ideas. I can't go into anyone else's shop without thinking what I'd do if it were mine."

"Ja?" Lisa's enthusiasm was infectious. Katie found she was smiling back. "So if this shop were yours, what would you do?"

Lisa glanced around. "Well, the decor is just right . . . so cozy and colorful. What you need is something to bring more people into the store. For instance, what if you had a quilting class, or if you started a quilting group that met here? I'll bet you'd find lots of people who were interested in that. And once they came, they'd want to support you."

"You mean, Englisch people?" Katie turned the idea over in her mind.

"Sure thing. It would be a big attraction to learn quilting from an Amish person. Or, even if a person were an experienced quilter, it would be nice just to be in a group that met and quilted together. People enjoy the comradeship, and there isn't a quilting group here in town."

The dozens of quilting parties Katie had attended helped her visualize that clearly. What Lisa said was true—the joy of a quilting party wasn't just the finished product. It was the pleasure of working together, with tongues flying as fast as the sewing needles.

"You really think people would come to something like that?"

"I really do." Lisa's eyes sparkled. "Tell you what—let me make up a flyer for you. I'll give them out in my shop, you can give them out in yours, and maybe Paula Schatz would do that at the bakery. I bet you'd have a group in no time."

Lisa was going almost too fast for Katie, but she found her mind racing. She couldn't just sit around and hope she got more customers. She had to make it happen.

"If I'm rushing you . . ." Lisa began.

"No, you're not. You're waking me up." A wave of energy swept through her. "Let's do it."

"You're on," Lisa said. "I'll be the first one to sign up. And what about the other idea? Will you join me in trying to promote Pleasant Valley's shops?"

Caution put a hand on Katie's enthusiasm. "Let me speak to Bishop Mose about it, ja? If he doesn't object, then I will help you if I can."

"It's a deal," Lisa said promptly. "Now, let's go ahead and pick the day and time for the first quilting meeting, and I'll run off some flyers."

Katie pulled a calendar from under the counter, feeling all the excitement she'd had that first day bubble within her. She had friends and allies here now, and with their help, in a year's time she would be signing the shop lease on her own.

. . .

He hadn't been acting unreasonably. Caleb had been telling himself that since the awkward encounter with Katie at the singing Sunday night. The problem was that after three days of saying so, he still didn't quite believe it. He'd interfered in his neighbor's business. Maybe his motives had been good, but that didn't excuse him.

He wiped down the rocking chair with a soft cloth. Another coat of wax, and the chair would be ready to put on display. He glanced around the front room of the shop, vaguely dissatisfied. In comparison to the quilt shop next door, his own place looked kind of bare, especially on a day like today, when rain dripped down from a gray sky. The only spot of color or softness was his mother's baby quilt, hung over his rack in the archway between the shops.

He tossed the cloth on the counter. Not only was Katie causing him worry over his niece—now she had him questioning his running of the shop.

That was foolish, for sure. He had plenty more experience in business than Katie Miller did. He didn't need to learn a thing from her.

His shop door creaked in a welcome distraction, and he had a quick smile for his cousin William Brand.

"William. I hoped you were a customer on such a wet day, but it's gut to see you anyway."

William snatched off his hat, showing his thick thatch of light hair, damp at the neck where the hat didn't protect it from the rain.

"S-s-sorry." William's face creased in a grin. His stammer kept him from talking easily to others, girls in particular, but around family he didn't let it bother him. "Was ist letz, Caleb? Isn't business gut these days?"

Caleb shrugged. "You know how it is. Folks seem to be watching their money tighter anymore. But I'm doing all right. What brings you into town?"

"I s-s-stopped at the house, b-but you'd left." He laid his hat on the counter and leaned across it to get a better look at the rocker. "Th-th-that's turned out fine, it has."

"Ja." Caleb ran his hand along the curved back, feeling the grain like a living thing under his palm. Pride was a sin, but he couldn't help knowing when a piece turned out even better than he'd expected. "The grain came up wonderful gut on this one."

William came around the counter to bend over the chair for a closer look. Even though he spent most of his time working his brother's farm, William had a bent for carpentry. It was a shame he had so little chance to put that gift to use.

William ran his fingers along the arm of the chair much as Caleb had done, his touch gentle. Then he straightened. "Ach, I am near f-forgetting why I came. You w-wanted some help carrying a piece down from upstairs, ain't so?"

"Ja, denke." Caleb had nearly forgotten mentioning that after worship. "I guess with the rain, Isaac didn't need to keep you close today, ja?"

William's oldest brother, Isaac, was a worthy man, but he had a tight rein on anybody who depended on him. Too tight, Caleb sometimes thought.

"Right." William started toward the stairs, and Caleb followed. "S-s-seems like there's not as much for me to do anyway, what with Isaac's boys getting b-big enough to be a real help.

And now that Rachel and Gideon are married, she d-doesn't need me so much."

That sounded a little . . . well, lonely maybe. Caleb felt sure William didn't begrudge Rachel her happiness in marrying Gideon more than a year after his brother had died, but William no doubt still thought her a member of his family, since she'd been his sister-in-law for so long, and he was onkel to her three kinder.

They reached the top of the stairs, which led into the large, loftlike area where Caleb had his workshop. The space that had been turned into a small apartment on Katie's side of the building had been left open here, and it suited him perfectly, with plenty of room for two workbenches, storage, shelves, and racks for his tools. On a sunny day the light poured through windows at the front and side, but today it seemed a bit gloomy.

"This cabinet is what I want to take down." He indicated the large piece that an Englisch owner would probably use to hold a television. Well, it wasn't his business what someone bought it for.

"Nice." As always, William had an appreciation for the quality of the piece. He glanced around. "You've g-got some quilt r-racks to finish, ja?"

"Ja, I started a few of them. They sell pretty well, and they don't take long to make."

"W-w-with the quilt s-shop next door, you'll maybe sell more." William jerked his head toward the adjoining wall. "Getting along all right?"

That depended on who you asked, Caleb supposed, but all he could do was nod.

"Rachel l-likes K-K-Katie Miller," William volunteered, putting his hands on one end of the cabinet. "I saw the s-sister with your Becky at church."

"Ja." That was too short a response. Caleb didn't want William thinking there was a problem. "The two girls have got to be friends." He picked up the other end of the cabinet. "I'll go backward."

William lifted, and they edged together toward the stairs. The cabinet was a big piece, too much for one man to move, especially since Caleb didn't want to go knocking it against the wall on the way down.

He stepped back carefully, his chest against the side of the piece. "Take it slow."

"I w-won't make you t-tumble." William started down. In a couple of minutes, with William's muscle added to his, they got the piece down without a nick.

Caleb set it down at the foot of the stairs, catching his breath for a moment.

"Wh-where t-to?" William said.

Caleb nodded to the space between the windows on the outside wall, and they picked it up again, edging it across the floor to set it carefully in place. "Gut." He patted the cabinet. "Denke, William."

"Glad to. Anything else I c-can help with?" William looked . . . well, hopeful. Maybe he was feeling at loose ends, not quite so needed anymore.

If so, Isaac ought to be setting the boy up in some job or other, not keep him hanging around to help out. And William wasn't really a boy anymore—he was only a couple years younger than Caleb.

"Would you want to work on those quilt racks I started?"

Caleb asked the question with a bit of hesitation, not sure how William would react. Or Isaac, for that matter.

But William's grin was answer enough. "Ja, I w-would like that."

"Gut, gut." Caleb clapped his shoulder. "Let's go, then."

They'd headed for the stairs when William stopped. "Ach, I near f-forgot. Your mamm says to r-r-remember her f-fabric."

For an instant Caleb's mind was blank, and then he realized that he was supposed to pick up from Katie something Mamm needed for her quilt. "Right. She told me last night, and I was forgetting already. Go ahead up, and I'll be along in a couple of minutes."

If it had been anyone else who needed something, he might have made some excuse to avoid talking to Katie. But he couldn't do that to Mamm. She'd see through it anyway, and he'd have to explain.

So he'd poke his head into Katie's shop and get this errand over with quick. No need for more than business between them.

As soon as he stepped through the archway, he realized Katie was taking care of a customer . . . an Englisch woman he didn't know. He would retreat, but Katie had seen him, so he pottered along the shelves as she finished.

Katie had a nice, easy way with the Englisch customer. He'd noticed that before . . . envied it a little, if truth be known. He got near as tongue-tied as William when a strange Englisch woman ventured into his shop.

Not that he was all that talkative with the Amish, either. Maybe that was why he liked having William around when he needed help. No need to chatter with William or pretend interest he didn't feel.

Not that Katie was putting on anything. Her manner to the woman was as open and friendly as it was with everyone else. That warmth of hers just seemed to be something she was born with, as far as he could tell.

The woman left, finally, calling good-bye over her shoulder as if to an old friend. Katie turned to him, and he wasn't imagining how her face changed, how it became wary. Obviously it wasn't quite everyone who got her warm side.

"Can I help you with something, Caleb?" Her tone was brisk.

He pulled the square of fabric Mamm had given him from his pocket. "My mother wants another three yards of this." He handed the fabric over, trying to avoid his fingers brushing hers. "Something about changing the pattern a bit. She said you'd understand."

Katie's expression eased as she stroked the material. "Ja, I do. She's decided to make this color more dominant. I like the idea. Your mamm has a wonderful gut eye for design."

She walked quickly down a row of fabric bolts, pulled one out, and carried it to the counter. She began unrolling the material, measuring it with deft hands against a yardstick fastened to the countertop.

"She makes beautiful quilts, that's for sure," he said. "And it's wonderful gut to see her take an interest in it again."

"I'm glad." Katie's tone went warm on the words. "How is she doing?"

He shrugged, not sure how he'd gotten into talking to Katie about Mamm. "We're always trying to get her out of the house and visiting with people, but she still says no more often than ja."

Katie frowned, apparently in concentration, as she cut the

piece. She folded it, hands smoothing the fabric as she did. "I wonder . . ."

He lifted his eyebrows. "What?"

As if making a decision, she pulled a sheet of paper from under the counter and showed it to him. He frowned, reading the piece. It was a flyer advertising a quilting group.

"I'm starting a group to meet here at the shop once a week to quilt together," Katie said. "Everyone from beginners to experienced quilters is most wilkom. I wonder if maybe your mamm would like that. We would love to have such an accomplished quilter join us. Do you think she might?"

He doubted it, but he hated to say so to Katie, who was being kinder than he probably deserved. "I'll show it to her. Denke, Katie. That is ser gut of you."

She smiled, putting the paper in a bag with the material. "Your mamm would be doing me a favor if she came."

"I will tell her that." He hesitated. He could, maybe should, walk away now, his errand complete. But there was something else that needed to be said. "Katie, about your sister . . ."

Her blue eyes turned to ice. "My sister is not your concern."

"I know. You were right to be upset with me at the singing. I shouldn't have spoken about it. And I have to admit everything went fine."

She didn't thaw, at least not that he could see. "You have to admit? That sounds as if you think you have a right to judge how my sister behaves during her rumspringa. Of all people, you—"

Katie stopped midsentence, her cheeks turning scarlet.

So, she knew. Someone had told her about him. He tried to ignore the faint, bitter taste of it.

"Considering what I got up to in my rumspringa, ja?" His jaw felt as if it would break if he said anything more, but he forced words out. "Someone has been telling you about me."

She looked as if she would speak, but he shook his head.

"It's all right. Everyone in Pleasant Valley knows about me." He couldn't help it—the bitterness seeped into his voice. "I am not a gut pattern for any young person to follow, ain't so?"

It was useless. He couldn't talk about this. He turned away.

Katie grabbed his wrist. He was so startled at the feel of her slim, strong fingers against his skin that he couldn't move.

"I am sorry for your pain." Warmth colored her words, seeming to ease through him.

He turned slowly to look at her, seeing the sympathy in her face. And not just sympathy. Something more. Something that seemed to say she understood how much love can hurt.

"Denke, Katie." His throat closed. But he didn't have anything else to say anyway.

"The past should be forgiven," she said earnestly, gazing into his eyes as if she had to be sure she impressed him. "It should be forgiven and forgotten, Caleb. Can't you do that for yourself?"

He shook his head, the black anger he sometimes felt threatening to overwhelm him. "It's not so easy as that. Do you think you could forgive and forget when you've been hurt badly by someone you love?"

Her face changed, the bright color fading, as if she'd come up against something that frightened her. "I . . . I don't know." She stumbled on the words, then put her hand to her lips, looking stricken. "I don't know."

What had he done? He wanted to erase that expression

from her face, but he didn't know how. If he could find the words . . .

But she moved away, shutting him out. She fumbled with something on the counter, her rigid back saying she was fighting for control. And that anything he had to say would be unwelcome.

CHAPTER SIX

Katie picked up the large black umbrella that lived in a milk can next to the door. The milk can was a silent invitation to anyone who came in with a wet umbrella that here was the spot for it—not dripping on the floor.

She hadn't had much use for umbrellas since she'd opened. Until yesterday, May had been fairly dry, which meant that everyone would welcome today's steady, gentle rainfall.

She glanced at Rhoda, who leaned on the counter, staring gloomily out at the rain.

"I'm going to bring flyers around to some of the stores. Take care of things until I get back, ja? Then you can have a lunch break."

Rhoda's lower lip came out. "Why do you bother to stay open on such a rainy day? No one will be out shopping anyway."

"You have someplace very important to go, do you?" Katie raised her eyebrows.

"No place to go and nothing to do here, for sure. If I was home—"

"If you were home, you'd be helping Mammi with the ironing today. Would you rather do that?"

Katie couldn't help the slight exasperation in her voice. Had she been this annoying when she was a teenager? Dealing with Rhoda was sometimes like coping with a tired two-year-old.

Rhoda didn't dignify that question with an answer. Well, there wasn't anything she could say that would make Katie change her mind anyway. As long as Rhoda was here, she had to pull her weight in the shop.

"Keep the store open. And be pleasant if anyone comes in."

"No one will," Rhoda muttered, determined to get in the last word as Katie went out the door.

The patter of the rain on her umbrella was better than the discontent in Rhoda's voice. Becky had not come in to work at Caleb's today, which was probably the main issue, but Rhoda could hardly expect to have a friend in every day.

At least she shouldn't expect to have that. Maybe Rhoda was missing her pesky little sisters more than she wanted to admit. Katie felt that way at times, that was certain-sure.

Mamm's most recent letter had been full of chatter about the things she and Louise were making for Louise's marriage. About the plans they had started already, even though the wedding was not until November. The letter had not said a word about Rhoda coming home.

Katie pressed her lips together. She should be ashamed of herself, thinking of that. Rhoda was her little sister, and she was always welcome.

She reached the corner and stepped back to avoid being splashed by a car that took the turn too fast, sending up a spray of water. Rhoda actually had a point about customers. No one seemed to be out on Main Street today.

Funny, that people would let the weather keep them inside, because the day wasn't really all that unpleasant. The air was warm, and the rain had settled down to a gentle drizzle. The tulips in pots along the sidewalk seemed to lift their heads in welcome.

Katie knew what she was doing. She was using Rhoda, the rain, and anything else she could come up with to avoid thinking about Caleb's words. And more important, about her reaction to them.

She'd seen the pain in his face when he'd talked about his past, and she'd longed to comfort him. The words about forgiving and forgetting had just seemed to say themselves.

And then he'd turned her own words back on her, and it was as if Caleb had shone a bright light onto her very soul, showing the dark things that dwelt there.

Caleb didn't know about Eli and Jessica. How could he?

Anyway, she had forgiven them. She'd prayed about it and she'd forgiven.

As for forgetting . . . well, maybe she of all people should have known better than to suggest that Caleb could forget. Caleb couldn't forget the pain of that betrayal any more than she could.

Katie had reached the bookstore that was her destination and paused in the doorway, shaking out the umbrella and ordering her thoughts carefully before entering. She stepped inside, glancing around at the shelves of books . . . brightly colored paperbacks and hardbacks of all types. There was even a rack of used books on sale for only fifty cents each.

She felt herself drawn toward those books and pulled back firmly. She didn't have money to spare right now, and as much as she loved to read, the shop seemed to take all her time and energy. To say nothing of Rhoda taking any energy that might be left over after the shop. And Rhoda's idea of fun wasn't sitting in a comfortable chair losing herself in a book.

"Morning. Can I help you with anything?"

The white-haired man who emerged from behind the counter sounded as if he hoped not. He had his finger marking a place in a book, and with his hair ruffled and wire-rimmed glasses sliding down his nose, he looked as if he had been enjoying a rainy day by immersing himself in his own stock.

"Good morning. I'm Katie Miller. I just opened the quilt shop down the street."

"Oh, yes, I think I heard something about that." The vagueness of his expression said he hadn't paid much attention. "I'm Cliff Wainwright. Owner of Cliff's Books, obviously."

He started to hold out his hand, realized it held a book, and stopped, putting it down and dusting his fingers on a white handkerchief he pulled from his pocket. "What can I do for you, Ms. Miller?"

"I have some flyers here." She caught a negative expression on his face and hurried on. "For a quilting group I'm starting at my shop. I hoped you would be willing to give them to any of your customers who might be interested."

He stared at the papers she held out, and then he nodded toward the counter. "There's room right by the register, where people will see them when they check out. You can leave them there if you want, so people can pick one up if they're interested."

"Denke. Thank you," she corrected herself. "I appreciate it."

She wasn't sure what room he referred to. The counter was nearly covered with books and magazines, to say nothing of a fine layer of dust. Books, she supposed, would generate dust, just as fabric generated lint. Since there wasn't an empty space, she put the flyers on top of an existing pile.

"Thank you," she said again. "I am sorry if I interrupted your reading."

He stared at her for a moment, and then he chuckled, the sound catching her by surprise. "You caught me. To tell the truth, I enjoy the days when nobody comes in. Then I can read to my heart's content."

"But a shop needs customers."

Mr. Wainwright shook his head. "Only if you're in business to make money." He chuckled again. "Owning a bookshop in a small town always seemed to me the perfect life, so when I retired I opened this place. I love everything about it . . . the books, the quiet, the atmosphere."

"I can see why." The comfortable clutter of books appealed to her, too.

"I like everything except the customers, always coming in and asking for the latest bestsellers as if they have to read what everybody else does. Yep, running a bookstore would be perfect if not for the customers."

He shook his head and glanced toward the leather chair behind the counter, a reading light strategically placed.

"That's an interesting idea." But not a very practical one, she'd think. "Thank you again for your help."

When she reached the door and bent to pick up her umbrella, she looked back. He was already ensconced in his chair and engrossed in his book.

She had to smile. If Lisa Macklin wanted help in her campaign to bring tourists to Pleasant Valley, she'd probably best not come to Cliff Wainwright.

Katie passed two empty storefronts and then Paula Schatz's bakery. Paula had already taken a stack of flyers, and one of them was displayed prominently in the front window. Katie would have stopped to say hello, but she could see through the window that Paula was clearly busy with her lunch crowd, even on a day like this.

The hardware store was next. Katie hesitated a moment, but women did go into hardware stores, didn't they? Maybe even women who liked to quilt.

The cash register was located in the middle of the store, and Katie walked past plumbing supplies on one side and paint cans on the other. The paint color chart was huge, displaying so many different shades that it was dizzying. How did people make a choice when they had that many options?

The young woman standing behind the counter had curly brown hair pulled back into a ponytail and fastened with a bright red clip that matched her shirt. She had a quick, friendly smile for Katie.

"Hi. Can I help you with something?"

"I hope so. I am Katie Miller, owner of the quilt shop down the street."

"You are?" The young woman, Melanie according to her name badge, thrust out her hand. "I'm glad to meet you. I was just looking in your shop window on Saturday. You have some beautiful things."

"You should come in. No need to buy, if you don't want to. Just come in and look around."

"I'd like that." The girl wrinkled her nose. "This job doesn't give me much extra cash for things I don't really need. I have to account for every penny."

Probably not a good customer, then, Katie thought, but she liked the way Melanie's lively features changed quickly with her mood. Katie handed her a flyer. "I hoped you might be willing to give these out. They're about a quilting group that will meet at my store."

Melanie's expression clouded. "I don't know." She glanced uneasily toward the back of the store. "The boss doesn't believe in putting up signs and things for other businesses. Doesn't want to distract the customer, he says."

"I see. Well, thanks for your time." Katie started to turn away, but Melanie reached across the counter and snagged her sleeve.

"Wait a sec. How about if I stick one in the bag of anyone I think might be interested? That's the best I can do."

"That would be wonderful, Melanie. Denke."

"It looks like a neat idea." Melanie put her finger on the printed sheet. "Do you mean this, about beginners being welcome?"

"Ja, sure. Are you interested in quilting?"

"I like to sew. And crochet. My grandma taught me. I've always wanted to try quilting."

"Come and join us then," Katie said quickly. "You could start with something small, just to see if you like it."

"I'm not sure . . ." Melanie let that trail off, stuffing a stack of the flyers under the counter. "I'll think about it. Maybe I'll see you there."

"I hope so. Thanks." So far she only seemed to be recruiting Englisch members, but maybe that was natural. Most Amish women had too much to do this time of year with gardens to put in and spring cleaning to do. Quilting tended to be a wintertime activity for them.

Still, that wasn't a bad thing. If she turned a few Englisch women into quilters, or at least introduced an appreciation of quilting, they might turn into good customers.

She went out onto the street to find that the rain had nearly stopped and the sun was trying to peek through the clouds. She glanced at the clock above the bank. She had time for one more stop, and Bishop Mose's harness shop was just a step away.

The bell over the door jingled, and Bishop Mose looked up with such a pleased smile that he might have been waiting all day just to see her.

"Katie. This is nice, for sure. Are you staying dry this wet day?"

"Ja, and I think the rain is over already."

"We had enough to perk the gardens up, anyway." Bishop Mose put aside the piece of leather harness he'd been working on. "How are things going at the shop?"

"Not bad." She leaned against the counter. "Not great, either."

"Ach, it's early days yet." His gnarled hands, stained from the leather he worked with, lay relaxed on the counter, as if he had all the time in the world for her. "Business will pick up."

"I hope so." She produced the flyers. "This is one thing I'm trying to bring more people into the shop. I'm hoping that if women join a quilting group, they will tell others."

He studied the flyer. "It's a gut idea, that. Selling quilts is not like mending harness, ja?" His blue eyes twinkled. "Folks always have leather to mend, even if they aren't ready to buy new. Buying a quilt is something folks will study on for a while, ain't so?"

She nodded. "That's why it's important to get them into the shop, even for some other reason. Then, when they're ready to buy, I hope they come to me."

"I'm sure they will. What can I do to help?"

"I thought maybe if you had any customers who might be interested, you could give them a flyer?" She ended up putting it as a question, a little surprised at herself for asking the bishop, of all people, such a thing. Maybe she shouldn't—

But at once he smiled and nodded. "I will. And I will put one in the window, as well. That way folks will see it when they pass. Everyone looks in here when they walk by."

It was easy to see why. Bishop Mose made people feel good just to look at him.

"Denke, Bishop Mose. It is ser kind of you."

He shook his head. "A little thing."

She felt a bit bolder, thanks to his quick response. "I have been talking with Lisa Macklin, who owns the gift shop."

"Ja, I know Lisa. A nice woman, and a hard worker, I think, running the shop all alone since her husband passed."

"She has the idea that we can bring new customers to town if we all work together on it. She asked if I would help her." She paused, not sure how to frame the question.

"And you told her you would talk to the bishop, ja?"

"Well, I can't forget that I am new here. I don't want to offend anyone, but if I don't get more customers . . ." She let that trail off, knowing that the alternative would be obvious to him.

"I see no problem in working with Lisa, if that is what you are asking. I'm sure you have a gut sense of what to do and what not to do."

"Denke. I would ask for advice if I questioned any of her plans." It was nice to think that someone as wise as Bishop Mose had confidence in her judgment.

"Gut. Now, tell me. How is everything going for you yourself? I know you are close with your cousins, but still, it can't be easy settling in a new place. And taking on responsibility for a young sister, as well."

Was there a question in that? She wasn't sure, but she found herself answering as if there had been.

"Mamm and Daadi were uncomfortable at my living alone above the shop, and they thought Rhoda would be company for me." She'd stop there, but those wise old eyes seemed to probe deeper, to see more.

"My sister Louise is going to marry the son of the bishop back home this fall. Mamm is all excited about the wedding, and she felt that Rhoda . . . well, that having a teenager just starting to run around . . ."

"Ach, you don't need to say more than you want." He reached across the counter to pat her hand. "Sometimes folks think the bishop's kin should be perfect, and we're none of us that."

She nodded, relieved that he seemed to understand what she didn't say. "Rhoda is not wild, you know. Just young and high-spirited. And Louise and Jonas are both so serious that I some-times wonder—" She stopped, not wanting to sound critical.

"It takes all sorts to make a family. Or a church. Maybe the Lord puts us together with others who are different from us just so that we can learn how to forgive."

Her heart winced at his use of the word. But she'd heard enough of Bishop Mose's sermons to know that humility and forgiveness were two of his favorite themes.

"Forgiving isn't so easy." She thought of the pain and bitter-ness she'd seen in Caleb's face, heard in his voice.

"'Forgive if you would be forgiven,'" he quoted from the Lord's Prayer. "God doesn't offer us forgiveness on any easier terms, does He?"

Her throat tightened. "If someone has wronged you, you must forgive. I know. But folks say that you should forgive and forget, and that . . ." She stopped, not able to follow through to the conclusion.

"Scripture tells us that God wipes the slate clean when He forgives, but we are not God. Maybe for us, it's more important to remember and be thankful."

"Thankful?" The word almost choked her. "How can you be thankful when someone has hurt you? Especially someone you love?"

His smile was very gentle. "When we've lived for a while, we look back at our lives. And sometimes we see that the trouble that was very hard at the time brought us gut results in the end. We can't see the whole pattern of our lives. But God can, and He knows that today's pain may be a step on the path He has for us, if we just trust."

She nodded, her throat tight. If she could be sure of that, perhaps her heart would not be so troubled. "Denke," she whispered. "Thank you, Bishop Mose."

Katie hurried back to the shop, aware that she'd been longer with Bishop Mose than she'd intended—and told him more, far more, too. How much he'd guessed beyond that she didn't know.

Time to think—that was what she needed, and that would be difficult with Rhoda as fratched as she was today. Maybe her disposition would improve now that it wasn't quite so gloomy out.

Katie's own spirits lightened when she opened the door and heard the familiar little jingle of the bell. The color and texture of everything in the shop seemed to reach out and draw her in. Did others feel that, too? She hoped so.

The shop was empty. For an instant she thought Rhoda had left again, and then she heard a giggle as Rhoda and Becky emerged from the back room.

"Becky, how nice. I didn't think you were coming in today."

"Her onkel didn't need her today, but her mamm had things to do in town, so she is here." Rhoda's bad mood was clearly a thing of the past, and Becky gave her a shy smile.

Katie set her umbrella in the milk can. "It's always nice to see you, Becky. And, Rhoda, you might let Becky speak for herself."

"She doesn't mind," Rhoda said. "You haven't heard the best part." She practically danced across the floor. "Becky's mamm invited me to spend the night tonight. I can, can't I, Katie? I said I was sure it would be all right."

"And I said we must talk with your sister." Becky's mother appeared in the archway. Caleb was a step behind Nancy, and Katie's stomach seemed to lurch at the sight of him.

"Nancy, how are you? It's gut to see you. Is Naomi here as well?"

"Ach, I could not get her to stir from the grossdaadi haus this morning." A shadow crossed Nancy's broad face. "But she joins me in saying we hope that you and Rhoda will komm to us for supper tonight."

Katie's mind scrambled for an excuse. If she went, Caleb would be there, and how could she sit across from him with his still-raw pain so fresh in her mind?

"That is ser kind of you," she said. "But Rhoda said . . ."

"The girls are putting things backward, ja? First is our invitation to supper. Next, we thought your Rhoda might stay the night. If she can stand all the noise and commotion from Becky's brothers, that is." Nancy chuckled at her own joke.

They were all looking at Katie expectantly, and she had to answer. "Rhoda will love to spend the time with Becky, for sure. But it is too much trouble to have to bring me back as well."

Besides, she had a pretty good idea who would be asked to take her home.

"It makes no trouble." Caleb's voice might be a little deeper than usual, but no one else seemed to notice. "You and Rhoda will go home with me, and I will bring you back after supper. I know my mamm looks forward to showing you her quilt pattern."

A message seemed to pass between them without the need for words. She could be a means of bringing Naomi out of her shell. She nodded, managing a smile. "Denke. We will like that."

The two girls hugged each other. It was such a small thing to make them happy. She should be ashamed of herself for hesitating, but there was more involved here than anyone else could guess.

The afternoon seemed to go slowly, and that was both positive and negative. It put off the moment at which she'd get into the buggy with Caleb, but it gave her too much time to ponder her feelings. She began cutting the pieces for a Lancaster Rose quilt, thinking she'd make it during the quiet times in the shop, and since it was a pattern she'd never made before, it should keep her mind occupied.

Bishop Mose's words kept echoing in her thoughts. Forgiveness was such a given in their lives that she had never questioned it in relation to Eli and Jessica. She'd forgiven them for hiding their feelings from her. She'd wished them happiness. She just didn't want to stay around and witness that happiness. Surely that wasn't wrong.

Her fingers moved among the pieces she'd chosen for the quilt, trying one combination and then another. She had forgiven. That was all God expected of her, wasn't it? But Bishop Mose's words seemed to say that as long as she dwelt on it, it wasn't forgiven.

By the time they climbed into Caleb's buggy in late afternoon, Katie's mind had spun itself into numbness. She wouldn't think about it anymore. She wouldn't.

The two girls scrambled into the back, of course, leaving the seat next to Caleb for Katie. She climbed up quickly, not giving him a chance to offer to help her. Things were difficult enough between them without the risk of feeling . . . what? She didn't want to put a name to that shimmer of sensation each time they touched.

The silence in the front of the buggy contrasted with the rapid chatter behind them. It had reached the stage of awkwardness when Caleb finally cleared his throat and jerked a nod toward the backseat.

"I just have brothers, and Becky is the only girl. Are girls always like that?"

Katie smiled, glad enough to talk about something so neutral. "Ja, pretty much. With five girls in our family, when we were younger Daadi always said it was only quiet when we were all asleep."

Caleb glanced at her as if measuring what she'd been like when she was younger. "You don't seem like a chatterbox to me."

"Ach, that's because you haven't seen me with folks I've known all my life. I've been on my best behavior here."

One eyebrow lifted, and there was actually a hint of humor in his face. "This has been your best?"

"Ja, it has." So they could joke with each other. That was gut, wasn't it?

The two girls collapsed on the seat in a spasm of laughter. Caleb's firm lips curved. "It's nice to hear Becky having so much fun."

"Ja," Katie said softly. "Rhoda, too. She needed a friend in Pleasant Valley."

With Caleb's strong hands relaxed on the reins, the horse seemed to find its way home without guidance. They were headed west, and the sunset painted the clouds along the hillside in shades of orange and yellow, fading off to a soft pink at the edges.

"It's hard to imagine you and your sister behaving like those two," he said.

"Louise, you mean? Well, I have to admit that Louise is seldom silly. Sometimes I think she was born serious."

The corner of his mouth twitched. "But not you?"

"No, not me."

He was actually teasing her as if they were friends. Maybe clearing the air between them had been a gut thing.

"Who did you giggle with, then?"

She'd walked right into that question, and she had to answer. "Jessica Stoltzfus. She lived next door, and she was just my age." Her voice didn't give anything away, did it?

"You and Jessica are still close?" He put the question casually, but she sensed that he had heard what she didn't say.

"No. I mean, well, she married. And I moved here, and . . ." Her voice petered out, because he was looking at her. And he was hearing the emotion that lay under the words.

She sucked in a breath. She didn't have to tell him. She didn't have to tell anyone. But . . .

"Eli Hershberger and I planned to marry. But he married Jessica instead." There must be something light she could say, something to show that it was over, that she didn't care anymore.

But there wasn't. She'd shown him that she knew too much about his past, and now he knew too much about hers. If she tried to pass it off with a lie now . . .

Somehow she didn't think he would believe it.

"I thought there was something." His voice was a low rumble. His hand moved from the reins to touch hers where it clasped the seat between them. "I'm sorry."

For the second time that day she was brought to the verge of tears by someone's unexpected understanding. It was painful, having her secret exposed. But it also seemed to form a bond between them, and that . . . that felt good.

CHAPTER SEVEN

Caleb drew up at the rear of the store a few mornings later. Blackie, accustomed to the routine, stopped in his usual place and then whickered, his ears coming forward. An answering whicker came from the small stable.

So. Apparently Katie had done as she'd said—she'd found a horse for herself. Caleb slid down and began unharnessing Blackie. Katie was an independent woman, for sure. She hadn't even mentioned the new occupant of the stable to him.

Well, the stable belonged to Bishop Mose. Maybe she figured that it was not Caleb's business. Still, he felt that they were growing to be more like friends since the evening he'd taken her to Andy and Nancy's house for supper. She might have mentioned it.

The stable door opened. Katie stepped out into the yard, the sunlight picking up glints of gold in her brown hair. "Caleb, komm and see what my cousin Aaron surprised me with."

"I can hear it already." It had been a surprise, then. Somehow that eased the prickle of irritation he'd felt.

"Her. Aaron found the sweetest little mare when he was on a job over toward Fisherdale. He took her on a trial basis, just to see if she suits me."

Caleb followed her into the stable. "From the way you sound, the answer must be yes, ain't so?"

"I sound like a new mammi, I'm afraid." Katie reached up to pet the neck of the bay mare, and the mare rubbed against her sleeve. "Her name is Daisy."

"She doesn't look much like a daisy." He patted the animal's shoulder, running his palm along her back. She seemed like a nice, sturdy animal. Aaron had a good eye for horseflesh, he knew. "But if she makes you smile, that's probably as gut a name as any."

"It was already her name, so it's not as if I had a choice. But I think it suits her."

"Like I said," he responded. "It makes you smile. Isn't that what you do when you spot the first daisies along the road? So, how does she drive?"

"I haven't had time to take her out yet. It was after supper when Aaron turned up with her, and I wouldn't try her for the first time at dusk." She pulled her gaze away from the animal to look at him. "You don't mind that I'm using part of the stable?"

"How could I mind? You look like a little girl who's gotten a wonderful-gut gift for her birthday."

Katie's smile lit her eyes. "That's how I feel, I think. I can't wait to take her out."

Maybe it wasn't so smart to stand here watching that smile. Caleb moved back to Blackie and started taking the harness off.

"Why don't you go for a drive?" he said. "Can't Rhoda watch the shop for a bit?"

"She can, but not today. I have the quilting group coming for the first time."

"I'd nearly forgotten." He coiled up the lines and hung the harness from its peg. "Mamm said to tell you she'll be here for sure."

"Gut. I'm excited. And a little nervous, too, to be honest."

"I don't see why." And here he was, looking into Katie's eyes again. "They are just people who share your love for quilting."

"Ja. I'm being foolish, maybe, but I want so much to have this work well."

He thought it might be the first time she'd shown that she questioned herself, and he wanted to wipe the apprehension from her face. His hand moved, as if to touch her, and he pressed it flat against his leg.

"It will turn out for the best." He stepped back outside. "You know, maybe we should keep the two horses separated for a bit, so that they don't get into a fight over who's the boss."

Katie moved away quickly, as if maybe she'd been expecting . . . something, he wasn't sure what.

"Ja, that's fine. I can leave Daisy in the stall for now, if you want to turn Blackie out into the yard."

"Right, sure." He grasped Blackie's halter and led him through the gate into the small fenced paddock that took up most of the backyard. "We can switch them at lunchtime, if you want."

"Ja. Sounds gut." Katie spoke naturally, and whatever moment of strain he'd imagined was gone.

Imagined, that was the word. He and Katie were easy with each other now, maybe because they each knew the other's pain.

Katie hadn't said anything more about losing the man she'd expected to marry, but he understood. He didn't talk easily about private things, either.

He suspected that Katie no longer considered marriage a possibility, based on the way she'd looked when she'd spoken of the man she'd loved. Maybe still loved, for that matter.

So, if he couldn't have another man sharing the shop space, at least Katie wasn't a danger to his heart.

He gave Blackie a final pat. Katie still stood by his buggy, looking into the stable at the mare.

"If it doesn't rain this afternoon, maybe I'll take her out on the road."

He glanced toward the sky. Yesterday's clouds seemed to be clearing off. "I think we're done with the rain for a few days, at least. Gut thing. The creek is running pretty high." He jerked his head toward the stream behind the stable.

"Ja, we could hear it from inside when we went to bed last night." Katie fell into step with him as they walked toward the shop. "I hope it's not going to rain on Saturday. I'm supposed to go to the Mud Sale over at Fisherdale with Rachel Zook."

"Sunny and mild, that's what I heard." He glanced at her face. "So you will try to sell some quilts over at Fisherdale?"

"I'm not sure whether I'll take any quilts or just some smaller things." Katie's forehead wrinkled. "I don't know yet how much space I'll have, sharing a booth with Rachel and her plants."

"Is your sister going with you?" They'd reached the porch, and he held open the door to her side of the shop.

Katie shook her head. "She'll watch the shop in the morning. Then in the afternoon I told her she could close and go to the mall with Becky and her friends."

His fingers tightened on the doorframe. "I didn't know about the trip to the mall."

"No?" Her eyebrows lifted, and her tone asked why he would expect to.

"No." He would not apologize for caring about his niece. "I am surprised that Andy and Nancy are allowing Becky to go. I wouldn't."

Katie stared at him for a moment, her chin very firm. "Then perhaps it is lucky for Becky that you are not her father." She closed the door between them.

"Let's put the quilting frame against the wall. We don't need it for the group today, but I'd like to have it out, especially so the new quilters can see it." Katie held one end of the folding quilt frame and Rhoda held the other.

Rhoda slid her end against the wall of the shop's back room. "How's that? Gut?"

"Ja, I think that does it."

Her little sister smiled at the quilting frame. "It reminds me of gross-mammi. She was such a gut quilter. And so patient."

Touched, Katie put her arm around Rhoda's waist. "It wonders me that you remember her so well. You were only about five when she passed."

Rhoda considered. "About that. I wasn't in school yet. But I guess you don't forget somebody who loved you that much."

Katie hadn't looked for such a mature thought from Rhoda. "Ja." She dropped a kiss on her sister's cheek. "I don't think I was so wise at sixteen."

Rhoda flushed, obviously pleased, but then moved out of

Katie's embrace with the quick change of mood of a teenager. "I suppose I have to watch the shop while you're busy with the quilting group."

"You suppose right." She frowned at the chairs. "I wish I had more seats for people. What if more turn up than I expect?"

"You're nervous," Rhoda said, wonderment in her voice. "I don't believe it."

Katie made a face at her. "Don't you dare tell anyone. But ja, I am. Why is that so surprising? This is important to the success of the shop."

Rhoda shrugged her slim shoulders. "I just thought . . . well, you always seem so sure of what you're doing. Really, you shouldn't worry. It will work out fine, I know. For sure Molly will be here, and Naomi Brand." She touched Katie's shoulder lightly. "It'll be all right. Honest."

Despite her smile, Katie had to blink back a tear. Her little sister was comforting her. That was a change in their roles she hadn't expected.

"Denke, Rhoda." Her voice was husky.

"I'll get the extra scissors you wanted to put out." Rhoda whirled. "And the pattern books."

Katie looked after her, a little bemused at seeing such enthusiasm from Rhoda. She was settling down here, finding friends and useful work. Surely Mammi and Daadi would be pleased.

As for Caleb . . . well, every time she thought Caleb had gotten over his suspicions of her sister, he said or did something that proved her wrong. They'd been having a nice talk about the horses, and she'd felt that they were actually cementing their friendship. Hadn't she trusted him enough to tell him about Eli?

And then Caleb had gone and spoiled it with his disapproval over the girls going to the mall.

Well, she couldn't stand here thinking about Caleb Brand. She had things to do. She started putting supplies out on the long table.

Some of the women, like Naomi, would bring quilts they were already making the patches for. Others might be starting from scratch. Katie could only pray that her idea to mix beginners and experienced quilters in the same group didn't backfire on her.

Footsteps sounded in the shop, and then Caleb was standing in the doorway carrying a small, armless rocker in each arm. Startled, she could only stare at him.

"I thought maybe you could use these for your group," he said. "Mamm always likes to sit in a rocker when she's hand-sewing."

"But these are two of your new ones." After their tart exchange on the back porch, Katie hadn't expected to hear a word from Caleb for the rest of the day.

"It's fine." He carried the chairs in and set them down in the corner. They rocked gently from the movement and then stilled. Like everything in Caleb's shop, they were skillfully made and lovingly hand-polished to a high sheen.

Maybe this was in the nature of a peace offering. And maybe she was the one who'd overreacted. After all, his objection had been to his niece going to the mall, and that hadn't been Rhoda's idea.

"Denke, Caleb. It is kind of you."

He shrugged. "It's nothing." He looked at her for a moment

longer, and Katie thought he was going to say something more, but then the bell on the door jingled. "I'd best let you get back to work."

She stood unmoving for a moment after he'd left, trying to still the butterflies in her stomach. This group was what she wanted, remember?

She walked into the shop to the sound of voices. Naomi Brand was here already, carrying a bag that undoubtedly held her new project, and with her was Emma Stoltzfus, aunt of Sarah Mast, the midwife. Katie had already heard that she was a very skilled quilter. Rachel Zook came in behind them, pushing a carriage holding her youngest, a little boy not quite three months old.

Rachel hurried into speech. "Ach, Katie, I hope you don't mind that I brought little Josiah. The older ones are in school, and my mamm is watching Mary, but I thought it might be better to have him with me. Gideon loves to watch him, but he's doing some work on my greenhouse today."

"Of course it's fine." Katie went to peek at the sleeping baby. "Goodness, look at those fat cheeks. Naomi, Emma, have you seen this bu lately?"

Naomi put her bonnet on the counter, and they came to bend over the carriage, both smiling at the sight. Sarah said that her aunt Emma had aged since she'd had a mini-stroke back in the winter, but she seemed lively enough at the moment, looking at one of the babies her niece had delivered.

"Ach, what a lamb he is, for sure," Emma said. "And sleeping so peacefully." She patted him with a gentle hand.

"It won't be long before he's running all over the place with the older ones," Naomi pointed out.

"Don't remind me," Rachel said. "I'm going to enjoy the

baby stage while it lasts. Now, he stays in one spot while I'm working with the plants. Soon he'll probably be pulling them up by the roots." She pushed the carriage into the corner. "Maybe he'll sleep through some of the time, at least."

"He'll be fine," Katie said. "And Rhoda loves babies, so she'd be glad to help out. We're going to use the back room." She led the way, but then turned back at the sound of the bell. "You go ahead and get settled."

Lisa Macklin hurried in, smoothing her hair down where its sleekness had been disturbed by the breeze. She looked as casually elegant as she had at the Mud Sale, with turquoise earrings dangling from her ears and a matching bracelet just visible beneath the sleeve of her soft jacket.

Katie wasn't tempted by Englisch clothing. She never had been. But the fabric . . . she longed to touch it just to see if it was as soft as it looked.

"I hope I'm not late. The girl who helps me in the shop didn't get in as early as I'd expected."

"Not at all. People are just now coming," Katie assured her. Aside from her large leather shoulder bag, Lisa was empty-handed. "Do you have a project you're working on?"

"Afraid not. You'll be starting from square one with me when it comes to quilting, but at least I know how to sew." Lisa's eyes shone with enthusiasm. "I can't wait to pick out material for my first project."

"Gut, gut."

Katie was a little wary of that enthusiasm. From what she knew of Lisa, she was a busy woman with lots of irons in the fire. Katie wouldn't want to encourage her to start on a big project that might take more time and patience than the woman had.

"Why don't you go on to the back room and introduce yourself? There are some pattern books on the table you might want to look at."

In the next few minutes two more women arrived . . . Myra Beiler, a shy young mother Katie had gotten to know at church, had brought along her baby as well. The other person was an Englisch woman Katie was sure she hadn't seen before.

Myra, with a quick look at the other woman, vanished into the back room carting the baby and a large bag, which had to hold a quilt in progress. Katie wasn't concerned about Myra fitting in, since she would know Naomi and Rachel and Emma, of course.

The Englisch woman was another story. Katie smiled at her. "Are you here for the quilting group?"

"That's right." The woman's answering smile warmed a strong-boned face. "I'm Donna Evans. I hope it's not a problem that I didn't let you know I was coming."

"No, of course not. You are welcome, Mrs. Evans. I'm Katie Miller."

"Please, call me Donna." The woman looked around the shop with frank curiosity. "This is certainly a far cry from the hardware store that used to be here."

Katie nodded. Mrs. Evans . . . Donna . . . was probably about the same age as Lisa, but there the resemblance ended. Her brown hair was pulled back carelessly and fastened with a clip at the base of her neck. She wore little makeup, just a touch of lipstick, and her plain white shirt was tucked into the waist of a denim skirt.

"Have you quilted before, Donna?" It would be helpful to know what she was dealing with.

"A little," she said. "I took a class once and made a table runner, but I never felt comfortable enough to try anything larger. Your group seemed the perfect place to get going on a project."

"That's fine." Katie hoped her relief didn't show in her voice. It would be difficult to deal with two beginners. "Komm. We're meeting in the back room."

They walked back together. The woman's appearance and manner eased any apprehension Katie felt about her fitting into the group.

Lisa and Rachel were already deep in conversation, while Myra looked on and nodded sometimes. Myra's little girl sat at her feet, contentedly playing with cloth blocks. She looked up, smiling with the instant love that Down's syndrome babies seemed to show the world, and Katie smiled back, her heart melting.

Naomi was showing the patches for her new quilt to Emma. They all looked up when Katie and Donna entered.

"This is Donna Evans. Donna, I'm not sure if you know anyone here . . ."

"Of course I do." Donna went immediately to where Naomi and Emma sat. "We are old friends."

"Gut, gut." Katie took a deep breath, her butterflies returning. "I hope we'll enjoy our time together, helping each other with our quilts."

Smiles and nods greeted her comment.

"Maybe we can start by showing what we're working on, those of us who've already started something, and . . ."

A step sounded behind Katie, and she turned to see the young woman from the hardware store, Melanie, peering in uncertainly.

"Is it okay if I join you?"

"Ja, of course." Katie waved her in. "This is Melanie, every-one. Or maybe you know her?"

No one seemed to, but they smiled in welcome, and Rachel, who was comfortable with the Englisch, probably because of her greenhouse business, beckoned her to a seat.

"I haven't been in town very long, and I haven't gotten to know anyone yet. Except Mike, who manages the hardware store. He's my fiancé." Melanie looked around, her eyes wide with interest.

"So you came here to Pleasant Valley to be close to him," Lisa said.

"Yes, well, he really wanted me to settle here." Melanie fixed her gaze on Katie. "I just hope I can keep up with the group. I don't know a thing about quilting, but I want to learn."

Lisa reached across to pat her hand. "That makes two of us, then. Don't worry. I know all these ladies are going to help us."

That seemed to set a good tone on which to begin. Katie led them through introductions, and those who were already work-ing on projects showed them. Donna had everyone laughing at her story of her first experience with learning to quilt.

Soon everyone was occupied. Donna, it turned out, had al-ready chosen a simple one-patch design and brought her material, so Rachel helped her lay it out and start the cutting. Emma, who seemed to have a natural authority after having been the valley's midwife for so many years, took on helping Melanie choose an easy pattern for a wall hanging.

Mindful of her plan not to let Lisa take on too much, Katie guided her to a table runner as a suitable first piece. She quickly realized that Lisa, as she might have expected, had an excellent sense of color.

After an hour, as they had planned, Rhoda brought in coffee and coffee cakes. Then, as if irresistibly drawn, she settled on the floor next to Myra's baby, helping her to stack blocks.

Katie listened to the chatter among the women as they helped themselves to food, her heart warming at the sound. It was just as she had hoped. Amish and Englisch were finding common ground. The roomful of women might look like a crazy quilt of colors and styles, but even a crazy quilt was united by a single purpose.

Eventually their time was up, and they began gathering their belongings. Lisa came to clasp Katie's hand.

"This was lovely," she said. "I can't tell you how much I enjoyed myself."

"Me, too." Melanie's smile lit her face. "I can't wait until next week. It's so nice to finally know some people in town."

"You'll find Pleasant Valley a gut place to live," Katie assured the young woman. It had certainly proved to be that for her.

"We just need to let more people know how lovely our town is," Lisa said. "Once we get more tourists coming through—"

"Tourists?" Donna shook her head, putting a wealth of scorn into the word. "What would we want with tourists? The last thing we need is to turn Pleasant Valley into another Lancaster County, with its miles of tourist traps and everybody cashing in on the Amish name."

Fortunately that comment hadn't been aimed at Katie, because she wouldn't have known how to answer. Lisa just shrugged, brushing off the remark with a smile.

"Not hordes of tour buses," she said. "Just a few travelers with money to spend at local businesses. That benefits everyone."

Donna didn't look convinced. "Once you start something like that, you can't control it. Mark my words, we're better off as we are."

Emma nodded, apparently agreeing, while even Naomi looked troubled.

Katie's heart sank. She'd thought Lisa's plan to bring more visitors to Pleasant Valley was a gut one. But it certainly wouldn't be gut to divide the community, would it?

Chapter Eight

*R*achel goes to Mud Sales several times in the spring, and she says that most of them are just as gut as this one was."
Katie had been telling Rhoda about the sale all through supper. She just couldn't help bubbling about it. This might have been the best sales day she'd had since she'd opened the shop.

"So you could go to more of them, ja?" Rhoda was making an effort to sound interested, at least. She helped herself to another spoonful of the tuna noodle casserole she'd had ready when Katie got home.

Katie had been surprised, and a little touched. She hadn't thought of asking her sister to fix supper, not being sure what time she and Rachel would return.

"I think I might. And maybe I'll take more things to sell next time, since I sold out of everything I brought today."

"It's gut advertising for the shop, ain't so?" Rhoda said. "You could give out cards with the shop address, or even make flyers."

"I hadn't thought of that." Katie studied Rhoda's face, the pointed chin tipped up, the broad forehead furrowed in thought, liking the signs of interest. "Do you think you could design something?"

"You mean it?" Rhoda's golden-brown eyes lit up. "Ja, I could do that. Maybe something with quilt designs on it. I could use the computer at the library."

"You know how to do that?" Katie wasn't really surprised. Many Amish used computers in their businesses these days, or had Englisch workers to handle the computer side of the work.

"Ja, for sure I can. I'll start working on some ideas right away."

Rhoda's enthusiasm touched Katie's heart. Maybe all her sister wanted was what she herself did . . . to be needed and of value.

"That will be great." Katie smiled, shaking her head ruefully. "I've been talking so much I didn't even ask how your day went."

"Okay, I guess." Rhoda made a face. "I thought I was going to sell a quilt this morning, but the woman just looked at every quilt twice and two of them four or five times, and then she walked out without buying so much as a pot holder."

Rhoda sounded so disgusted that Katie had to smile.

"But that's all part of a sale," she said. "After all, a quilt is a major purchase. Naturally people are going to look around for a while before they decide. Did she say how she heard of us?"

"She said Lisa Macklin told her about us. Oh, and Mrs. Macklin came in to buy some thread. Do you really think that other woman will buy?"

"If we have the right quilt for her," Katie said, cautious. "And if she does, it will be because you sold her on it."

"Ja?" Rhoda's face lit up. "You mean I did it?"

"If she buys, it's your sale," Katie assured her. She had promised Rhoda a small commission on anything she sold, and obviously Rhoda wanted to collect. "Now, tell me about going to the mall. Did you have fun?"

"It was okay." The brightness seemed to fade from Rhoda's expression. "We looked at lots of stuff. Becky bought a little locket on a chain. She said her mamm said she could get it as long as she wears it under her dress where no one will see."

"Did you buy anything?"

"Just some lip gloss. Not for color," she added quickly. "Just to keep my lips from getting dry."

Katie nodded. She remembered making the same statement to Mamm at that age. Mamm hadn't been impressed, but she wasn't going to make an issue of it.

Rhoda fell silent, seeming distracted, all her earlier enthusiasm gone. Katie sought for a subject to bring it back.

"Did you get something to eat at the mall?"

Rhoda nodded. "We went to the food court for a snack. Some of the boys happened to be there, so they met us."

There was probably no "happened" about it. Some things didn't change. What was the name of the boy Rhoda had thought was cute?

"Was the Esch boy there?"

"Tommy?" Rhoda met her gaze for a moment, and then her eyes slid away. "Ja, he was there."

This wasn't the response Katie had expected. "Did you talk to him?"

Rhoda pushed her chair back and picked up her plate, heading for the sink. "No."

"But I thought . . ." Katie let that trail away when she saw how stiff Rhoda's back was as she stood at the counter.

Rhoda swung around, the plate clattering into the sink. "Becky likes him, okay? The other girls were teasing her about him."

"Becky is your friend. You can't—"

"I know that." Rhoda flared up in an instant. "That's why I didn't talk to him. But it's not like he's her komm-calling friend or anything."

"You still can't—"

"You think I don't know that? Just because your best friend did that to you, you don't need to think I would." Rhoda tossed a dishcloth on the counter. "There's a letter for you from Mamm that came today. Probably to ask if I'm behaving."

She rushed across the kitchen and headed toward her room. The door didn't quite slam, but close enough.

Katie took a shaky breath, not quite sure where all that emotion had come from. She probably hadn't handled the situation very well, but . . .

She fetched the letter from the hall table and sat down with it. She could understand Rhoda being upset because the first boy she'd found interesting here wasn't available. But her accusation about Katie's situation was ridiculous. Just because she didn't want to be seeing Eli and Jessica every day, that didn't mean . . . well, anything.

She ripped the envelope open and began to scan Mamm's round, clear writing. Family news first, of course. Everyone was well. Louise had started a new quilt for her wedding, and some of her friends were making another one for her. The strawberries were starting to ripen, and Mamm had made some rhubarb jam.

As Rhoda had predicted, Mamm asked if she was behaving. *We know you will keep her from getting into any trouble.*

Katie skipped on to the next paragraph. *Some happy news in the neighborhood. Eli and Jessica are expecting their first boppli in the fall. You will want to send her your good wishes.*

The paper crumpled in Katie's hand. Her stomach clenched so hard that she nearly doubled over.

She took a deep breath, forcing her fist to relax, and put the letter on the table, smoothing it out with fingers that weren't quite steady.

Eli and Jessica would have a baby. That was a natural thing. She'd expected it, hadn't she? So why did she feel as if she'd just missed a step in the dark?

The off Sunday, when they didn't have worship, was usually a quiet day, Caleb reminded himself. A day for visiting with extended family members.

But there was nothing quiet about today. Andy and Nancy had invited the Brand cousins for supper, and since it was raining again, the children were all inside.

It wasn't that Caleb didn't enjoy his nephews and nieces and young cousins, but the din had reached such astonishing levels that Andy and the other men finally slipped off to Andy's shop for a little quiet conversation until supper was ready.

"What a day. More rain than we need, for sure." Isaac, the eldest of the cousins and William's older brother, shook the water from his hat. His florid face creased with concern. "If the ground doesn't dry out soon, we'll have trouble with the first hay cutting in the south field."

"Ja, it's a bog in there." Isaac's oldest, another Caleb, was generally called Cal to avoid confusion. He was married now, but he still helped his father work the home farm.

Andy joined in with a comment about planting, and for a few minutes the conversation centered on the growing season. Caleb found himself in his usual position of watching and listening, a little apart from the group even when it was family.

Not that he wasn't interested in farming . . . he helped Andy as needed, of course. But Isaac tended to dominate any conversation he was in. A good man, in his way, but a bit bossy.

Someone else was a quiet onlooker, as well. William sat on the work bench, hands linked closely in his lap. He seemed to be studying the kitchen chair that lay on the bench, its leg a victim of some roughhousing by the ten-year-old twins. Caleb moved next to him. "Andy told Nancy he'd have that fixed by today. I should have just gone ahead and done it."

William's solemn face relaxed in a smile. "Ja, I know wh-what you mean. Anything g-g-gets broken at Isaac's place, it's for me. Isaac knows the horses and the d-dairy cows, not woodworking."

". . . wish I could convince Rachel to sell her place to me, so I'd have it for one of my boys." Isaac was talking about Rachel Zook, his former sister-in-law. It always rankled with Isaac that his brother had died and left the property to Rachel.

"S-she wants it f-f-for—" William began.

"Everyone knows she says she's hanging on to it for her boy," Isaac snapped, cutting William off as he always seemed to. "Even so, she might give some thought to us. My brother would have been pleased to have one of his nephews own the farm."

Since it was impossible to know the truth of that, no one could argue.

"Or he might have wanted William to farm it," Caleb said, more because Isaac's treatment of William annoyed him than because of anything else.

"William!" Isaac puffed out his cheeks. "That's nonsense."

It made as much sense as anything to Caleb, but there was little point in starting an argument. "Ja, well, I suppose you couldn't get along without William at your place."

"William's a gut helper," Isaac said. "Course, with my boys getting old enough to be more help . . ." He stopped short.

Still, it was enough. William had said something of the kind the day he'd helped Caleb move the chest. Caleb glanced at the boy. No, not a boy. William was a man grown, even though his beardless face and the shy manner that went with his stammer made him seem younger than he was.

Caleb's gaze caught Andy's for a moment, and he knew Andy was thinking what he was—that Isaac wasn't doing right by his youngest brother. Too bad William didn't have the kind of relationship with Isaac that he had with Andy.

Caleb cleared his throat, interrupting Isaac's monologue on the correct time to plant corn. "That being the case, I wonder if William might be free to work a few days a week for me. I could use the extra help."

That wasn't as true as he'd like it to be. Still, he couldn't deny that it would be helpful to have someone else turning out things like the quilt racks and smaller items so he could concentrate on bigger projects.

Isaac looked startled, and not very pleased with him. But then, Isaac didn't like any idea he hadn't come up with himself.

"That's for William to say," Andy said before Isaac could speak. "But it surely would be a help to Caleb. What do you say, William?" Andy put the decision in William's hands, bypassing Isaac neatly, and Caleb felt a surge of gratitude for his brother.

William's color came up at being deferred to, but the look he turned on Caleb was lit with enthusiasm. "Ja, I would like that fine. If Isaac can spare me."

Isaac shrugged. He could hardly back down now, since he'd already implied that he didn't need William's help. "It's nothing to do with me. Do it if you want."

"Gut." Caleb clapped William on the shoulder. "We won't talk business on the Sabbath, but komm over on Monday, if you want."

The dinner bell clamored on the back porch, no doubt rung by one of the boys with more energy than skill. It cut off the thanks William was trying to stammer out, and they all moved, shoulders hunching as they stepped into the rain again.

Caleb pulled his coat higher, trying to keep the rain from dripping down the back of his neck. First Becky, and now William. What had possessed him? He'd always valued the solitude of the shop, and now here he was, giving that away.

But it wasn't Becky or William who'd broken through first. It was Katie. And that hadn't turned out so bad, had it? No sooner had he thought that than a sense of shock went through him. Was he really saying that he liked having Katie Miller as part of his life?

The noise that accompanied a big family meal effectively prevented him from thinking too much for the next hour. Once they'd eaten their way through roast chicken and ham, along with mashed potatoes, dried corn, and the dozen side dishes Nancy considered sufficient for company, everyone was too full to think of anything but sitting down. But Nancy had decided they would have homemade ice cream for dessert, and there was no getting out of it.

Ordinarily they'd do the ice cream on the porch, so the kinder could run around and play, taking an occasional turn with the crank. In view of the rain, Caleb and Andy had set the ice-cream maker up in the laundry room Daadi had built onto the back of the house years ago. That was the easiest place to clean after a messy job. Nancy mixed up the batch, using the last of the peaches she'd canned in the fall.

At first, the young ones clamored to help, but soon they tired of it. Finally Caleb was alone, sitting on a stool next to the barrel holding the ice, feeling the crank turn harder and harder as the ice cream thickened. It was nice, sitting here by himself for a bit. The rain on the tin roof was loud enough to mask the noise from the house, and he took pleasure in the rhythmic turns of the handle.

The door opened, and Becky slipped in, closing it behind her.

"Not quite ready yet," he said.

"I know." She slid a stool next to his. "I just wanted to keep you company, Onkel Caleb."

"That's as gut a treat as ice cream," he said.

The barrel rocked a bit with his effort, and Becky grabbed the sides to steady it. "That was a nice thing you did for William."

"He's a gut man with wood, and he'll be better with some practice."

"Ja, I know." She stared at the ice-cream cylinder. "A lot of folks don't understand what it's like if you don't talk easily."

He glanced at her. It sounded as if Becky was speaking about herself, not William.

"Ja, maybe that's so," he said cautiously. If Becky wanted to talk, he would listen, whether he could help or not.

"That's what is so nice about having Rhoda for my friend. It seems like she understands me better than girls I've known all my life. They just think, oh, she's shy, and don't bother to try and find out what I think, but Rhoda's different." Becky looked at him, eyes shining. "That's why I know how William must feel about you being his friend."

Caleb put his arm around her shoulders, and she tilted her head against him in a gesture of trust.

He dropped a light kiss on her head, touched by her confiding in him. "Denke, Becky. And now I think this ice cream is about ready. Will you ask your daad to help me get it out?"

She nodded, going quickly to the door, her step light. His heart wrenched a bit when she looked back at him and smiled.

He'd like fine to have a daughter like Becky, but that couldn't be. He'd decided a long time ago that it was better to be alone than to share his days with someone you couldn't trust completely.

He was satisfied with his life. He didn't want any changes. But somehow, changes were being pushed on him, whether he wanted them or not.

The rain still poured down when Katie and Rhoda reached home after spending Sunday afternoon with Molly and Jacob and their family, so Katie drove straight to the stable.

"You can go on inside if you want." Katie slid down and hurried to unhitch the mare. "No sense both of us getting wet."

"I'm already wet," Rhoda said, grasping the harness on the other side. "But not so wet as Daisy. You're a gut girl, aren't you?" She patted the animal, and Daisy turned her head and whickered.

"There, see, she knows what you're saying," Katie said. She and Rhoda agreed that the little mare had to be one of the smartest horses they knew. "Ach, let's get her in."

With two of them working, it took less than no time to finish the job. They rubbed the mare down, one on either side, working companionably.

This was gut, being together. Rhoda had had her ups and downs, and probably still would. That was in the nature of being sixteen. But she was settling down, and seemed happy here. This morning she'd been as cheerful as could be, as if she'd totally forgotten her upset last night.

"You know, I'm ser glad you're here." Katie turned the mare into her stall while Rhoda poured a scoop of oats into the feed bucket.

Rhoda's lips quirked. "You didn't think that at first, ain't so?"

"Maybe not." Katie smiled. "But I have to admit, it's really nice having you around."

Rhoda gave the mare a final pat. "I like it, too."

They reached the stable door and stood for a moment, watching the downpour while Katie opened the large black umbrella.

"Look how high the creek is." Rhoda took a step closer to Katie, nodding toward the stream behind the barn, and Katie put her arm around her sister's waist.

"Ja, I know. But I think I'm more worried about how the water is pooling next to the back of the house." That spreading pool hadn't been there when they'd left this morning, had it? Surely she'd have noticed.

"Is that bad?"

Katie's first instinct was to deny it, but she quickly realized how silly that was. Rhoda was a part of the business now, and old enough to help face any problem.

"It could be. Let's get inside. We'd best check the basement."

Together they ran for the house. The umbrella helped, but the cold rain still blew at them, and water splashed up at every step.

They were inside in a moment, and Katie tried to shake off the chill. She grabbed a flashlight. Jerking open the cellar door, she directed the beam downward.

A pond of water spread there, too, dangerously close to a carton of felt squares she hadn't unpacked yet. Dismayed, she hurried down the steps.

Not another setback, please, Lord, just when things were looking brighter.

She reached the carton, and tried to pick it up while holding the flashlight on it. Water lapped at her shoes.

"I've found the battery lantern." Rhoda scurried down the stairs, bringing light with her. "Ach, what should we do first?"

"Take this upstairs." Katie thrust the box into her hands. "We'll have to try and get everything off the floor."

"What about Caleb's things?"

Katie swung her flashlight beam toward the other side of the cellar. Caleb had wood and some unfinished pieces on the floor where the water might reach them, but most of his supplies were stored on shelves he'd probably built himself.

"His, too, but we must get the fabric first. It will be ruined faster by the water."

Katie lifted a carton, not even sure what it contained. She should have finished unpacking these boxes and had shelves put up. She hadn't, and now she would pay for that.

Two more loads up, but the water was moving faster than they were. Katie paused to take a breath, her mind working feverishly.

"Ach, this is not doing it. We have to find a way to slow the water down. Run and get the mops and that box of cleaning cloths."

Rhoda, her face intent, nodded and raced back up the stairs.

Water coming from the other end of the back wall crept closer to a quilt stand. Katie hurried over, grabbed it, and hoisted it onto Caleb's shelves, standing on tiptoe to try to push it in. But the legs kept catching on something.

The door at the top of the stairs creaked open again.

"Rhoda, hurry and help me with this."

"It's not Rhoda. It's me." Caleb thudded down the stairs. He reached over her head to shove the quilt rack into place. "Denke, Katie. You should not be worrying about my things."

He seemed to tower over her as he stood close to reach up. She could feel his nearness, and his size and his warmth took her breath away. She stepped back.

"What are you doing here? Did you see Rhoda?"

"Ja, I sent her to Bishop Mose's place. He'll get some help and be here in a couple of minutes, I'm sure."

Katie hadn't even thought of that, but of course Bishop Mose would be concerned. It was his building.

"But how did you know something was wrong?" She seized

one end of a board that was about to be drenched, and Caleb took the other. Together they lifted it to the shelves.

"I got worried. We haven't had a steady rain like this in a long spell, and with the ground already saturated from the other day, it seemed like we might have problems."

Without asking, Caleb crossed to her side and began picking up boxes, carrying them over to his shelves.

"Has this happened before?" If so, someone might have told her. She picked up a shopping bag and the bottom promptly fell out of it, scattering spools of thread on the wet floor.

"Not in many years." Caleb stooped next to her, collecting spools and dropping them into the box he'd just picked up. He looked up and smiled, his face tilted a bit. "You're thinking I should have warned you."

"Well . . ." She let that trail off, unable to resist returning the smile.

"And so I should, but I just didn't think of it. Too much else going on, I guess. I really didn't start getting concerned until I heard my brother talking today about how wet the fields are already."

She picked up a sopping wet spool. "I'll lay some of these out to dry up, but they're probably a total loss."

"I'm sorry."

He looked so concerned that she shook her head. "It's not a problem. They were just some extra spools from my mamm's shop that she sent along. The colors weren't that popular anyway."

Caleb took the box she'd lifted, his fingers brushing hers. She stood with her feet wet and the bottom of her skirt dripping, but the warmth of his touch flowed through her, chasing the chill away.

He cleared his throat, seeming to have trouble focusing. "So . . . um . . . different colors are popular in quilts, are they?"

"Ja." Her own voice sounded a little funny. "With the Englisch, mostly. They want quilts that match whatever colors are popular in home furnishings, so I try to keep up with that."

"Sounds more complicated than wood furniture." He set the box with the wet spools on the stairs. She'd carry it up when she went.

"Well, I guess it is. But I'll bet some kinds of wood sell better than others."

He seemed to consider that as he lifted the last box of hers. "Maybe so. But it's more about how the grain lends itself to certain pieces." His face intent, he nodded toward the wood stacked against the far wall. "A fine, sturdy oak desk, now . . . you can't do better than that, to my mind."

"If that's so, maybe we'd best get those pieces moved before they're watermarked."

"Ja, for sure." Caleb went quickly to the wood, his shoes sloshing through the water.

"Listen." She stopped, standing halfway across the cellar, realizing what she'd just noticed. The rain wasn't beating against the narrow cellar window any longer. "I think it's slacking off."

He angled his head, listening. "You're right. Course it might start up again, but maybe we can get ahead of it before then."

"Ja." Recalled to the job at hand, Katie hurried to help him with the last of the lumber. "You were wise to put these shelves up. I should have thought of that. And I should have unpacked those boxes long since, for that matter."

"You've had plenty to do," Caleb said. He took the piece she held and lifted it to a top shelf. "As for the shelves, my cousin William is going to help me with the furniture-making for a bit. He and I can knock together a wall of shelves for you in no time. I have plenty of odd pieces we can use, so it won't cost you."

"That wouldn't be fair. I'd be grateful if you'd take on the job, but only if you let me pay you what anyone else would."

He raised his eyebrows. "Then how much do I owe you for the clutter of mine you cleaned up before I got here?"

"Don't be foolish," she said tartly. "The two things aren't the same at all."

"I don't know about that." He shook his head in mock sorrow, amusement glinting in his eyes. "It seems to me you ought to be getting a fair wage for all this work. That piece you're lifting now—I'll bet that would cost me a pretty penny to pay you for moving."

She tried to keep her lips from curving. "If you don't stop this foolishness, I might have to drop it on your toes."

"Can't let you do that." He grabbed the board, she tugged back, and laughter bubbled up in her.

"Caleb—" Her protest died as her foot slipped on the wet floor. She lurched, dropping the board, and would have fallen, but he caught her in an instant, holding her up.

"You'd best be careful or you'll be sitting in a puddle." His arms were strong around her, his brown eyes creased with laughter.

She clasped his arms to steady herself, feeling hard, strong muscle under the fabric of his shirt. He held her firmly, protectively, and it felt like the most natural thing in the world.

And then his eyes darkened, moving over her face with such intensity that it seemed he touched her skin. The dank cellar faded away, as if all she could see was Caleb.

He bent his head slowly. And then his lips found hers.

She should pull away. But instead she leaned into the kiss, feeling his arms draw her closer, his breath on her skin warming her, changing her.

Heavy footsteps sounded above their heads. Caleb drew back slowly, maybe reluctantly, looking at her with something almost questioning in his expression.

The door creaked open, and by the time Bishop Mose appeared, Caleb and Katie were several paces away from each other. Katie bent to brush off the hem of her skirt, certain she didn't want anyone seeing her face right then.

"Did you think you had to do this all alone, Katie?" Bishop Mose stepped down onto the wet floor. "The fire company is on its way with their pump. We'll have this cleaned out in no time at all."

"Denke." She managed to straighten, to smile at him. "In that case, I'd better go put some coffee on for everyone."

She hurried up the steps as if someone were chasing her, knowing full well that the only thing pursuing her was her own sense of panic over what had just happened.

CHAPTER NINE

*W*e'll stop by and check on you later, but I think we got it solved." The volunteer fire chief gave Katie a beaming smile that suggested bailing out her flooded basement was the most fun he'd had lately. "Don't you worry about it, now."

"I won't. You have been so kind. Thank you."

"My thanks also, Ronnie." Bishop Mose clapped the man's shoulder. "Though I know full well that you enjoy nothing more."

"Flooding is a challenge all right. You can put a fire out, but rising water . . . well, you can't fight that. Just try to control it." He chuckled. "Remember what it was like in '72 with the Agnes flood? We were cut off from outside help, and we didn't get more than an hour's sleep in four days 'til the water finally went down."

"Ach, I remember fine. It seemed like half the state was under water then. I was young enough to do something useful in those days."

It appeared the bishop and the fire chief were old friends, and that didn't surprise Katie. Bishop Mose knew everyone, Amish and Englisch, in the valley.

"Were you a member of the fire company then, Bishop Mose?" she asked.

"First Amish volunteer firefighter," the chief said promptly. "We couldn't run the company now without our Amish firefighters."

"Our houses and barns are just as likely to catch fire as anybody's, ain't so?" Bishop Mose started up the steps from the cellar. "I am sorry for this mess, Katie. And you, also, Caleb. I will be over first thing tomorrow to see about improving the drainage, ja?"

"Denke." Katie followed him upstairs, her shoes squishing with water. It would be a relief to get into some dry clothes.

Unfortunately, it would take more than dry clothes to ease the tumult in her heart. That kiss . . . how could she have let that happen?

It was no sense telling herself she'd been taken by surprise. She'd known it was coming. She'd sensed it in time to have stepped back.

Caleb probably thought . . . Her cheeks grew warm. She didn't feel anything for him. She couldn't.

She loved Eli. Even though he didn't return her love, even if he'd made a happy life with someone else, she wasn't a person who could turn off her feelings. The only thought that comforted her was the knowledge that she was faithful.

She emerged into the hallway that led to the back door. Rhoda stood there, holding a tray with the used coffee cups. She wasn't alone. One of the Englisch volunteer firefighters was with her—a boy probably about her age. He held the coffeepot, but he didn't seem to be doing anything useful with it. He leaned toward Rhoda, intent on her face as he talked.

Rhoda sparkled—there was no other word for it. Her golden-brown eyes laughed at whatever foolishness he was saying.

Obviously they hadn't heard Katie.

"Rhoda." Maybe her tone was a bit sharper than it should have been. Both young faces swung sharply toward her.

"We're just talking," Rhoda answered her in Pennsylvania Dutch.

Did the boy understand? Maybe, because his freckled face reddened. "I guess we're all finished here, so we'll be going." He looked around awkwardly for a place to put the coffeepot and ended up handing it to Katie.

"Denke. Thank you very much for your help." She tried to sound cordial. After all, the boy probably wasn't at fault. Rhoda was a pretty girl, and no doubt she'd attract boys wherever she went. But now wasn't the time, and he certainly wasn't the boy. Small wonder the parents of teenagers spent so much time on their knees in prayer.

Rhoda's lower lip pouted. She'd undoubtedly have let her displeasure spurt out, but the rest of the firefighters were coming through, rolling up hoses and depositing still more dirt on Katie's once-clean floor.

She thanked each one, trying to concentrate on them and ignore the fact that Caleb was at the end of the line. And then she couldn't ignore it any longer, because he was in front of her.

She focused her gaze on the front of his shirt, which didn't really help. It just made her notice the breadth of his chest. "Denke, Caleb. I appreciate your help."

"And I yours," he said, his voice as calm and natural as if that kiss had never happened. "We'll help with the rest of the cleanup tomorrow. Good night." He nodded to Rhoda and was gone.

The door closed behind him. Now Katie had to deal with Rhoda, and it was the last thing in the world she wanted to do right then.

Rhoda didn't wait to speak her mind. "You didn't need to act as if I was doing anything—"

"I know," Katie said quickly. "I'm sorry."

Rhoda blinked. "You are?"

"I am, believe it or not." Katie managed a smile, praying she was steering the right course with her sister. "I was just startled, that's all, to see one of the firefighters looking at you as if you were an apple dumpling."

Rhoda's anger dissolved into a giggle. "He didn't, did he?"

"With whipped cream on top," Katie assured her. She hesitated, but there was more she needed to say, and she'd best get it out now. "I know you're feeling disappointed about Tommy. I'm sorry for your hurt."

She wanted to say there'd be other boys, but that wouldn't help right now. Besides, how did she know that was true? She'd been about Becky's age when she fell in love with Eli.

Rhoda nodded, her eyes filling with tears. She blinked them back. "Ja. But being friends with Becky is more important."

"Komm. We'll put the cups in the kitchen and deal with them tomorrow. Just now we need to get out of these wet clothes."

"Ja." Rhoda peered down at her running shoes. "These will never be the same."

They trudged up the stairs. Katie wasn't sure when she'd ever been so tired. Not just physically tired. She set the coffeepot in the sink. Heart-tired, confused, probably in need of some time in prayer.

Rhoda put down the tray. She turned as if to go to her room, and then stopped, touching Katie's shoulder.

"I'm sorry. About what I said last night. I mean, about Eli and Jessica. I shouldn't have."

Katie's throat tightened. "It's all right. Maybe it's true."

"You . . . You still think about him?"

She hated to admit it. But Rhoda deserved the truth, even though she wasn't sure what that was anymore.

"Ja. I forgive them. But I . . . I still can't forget. Sometimes I do for a long while, but then something reminds me."

Something like learning that Jessica was having Eli's baby. How much did that affect what had happened between her and Caleb? Had she been longing for a kiss just to assure herself that she was still attractive? If so, that didn't say anything very good about her.

"I'm sorry." Rhoda gave her a quick, impulsive hug. "Thank you for telling me. For acting like I'm grown-up enough to understand."

"You're getting more mature every day." Katie patted her sister's cheek. It seemed such a little time since Rhoda was toddling around after her, and now she was practically a woman grown. "As for understanding—well, I'm not sure I understand myself."

Caleb's face intruded in her mind, and she tried to push it away. She would not let that be anything important. She couldn't. Too much stood between them. The promises she'd made to Eli, the woman who had left pregnant with Caleb's child . . . Those were impossible barriers to feeling anything at all for Caleb.

By the time she'd bathed and changed into her nightgown and warm robe, Katie had begun to regain her balance. What had happened with Caleb would be quickly forgotten—he was probably as eager to do that as she was. And the flooded cellar hadn't caused near as much damage as it might have.

"Denke, Lord," she murmured.

A tap came at her door. "Katie? I brought you some hot cocoa. Can I bring it in?"

"For sure." She quickly finished the center braid she put her hair in at night.

Rhoda came in, carrying two mugs of steaming cocoa.

"This is so thoughtful of you." Katie took a mug and sat down on the bed, leaning against the headboard. "Komm, join me."

Rhoda, looking like the little girl she'd been so recently with her hair in a braid, nodded, curling up against the footboard. "I thought cocoa would warm us up."

"Gut idea."

But Katie suspected Rhoda had more on her mind than cocoa. For a moment she was tempted to shirk her responsibility, tell Rhoda she was tired and wanted to go to sleep. That would be true, but it would also be irresponsible.

She patted Rhoda's knee. "You were such a help today. Denke."

Rhoda nodded, but it was as if she hadn't really heard Katie's words. She frowned down at the quilt, tracing the scallop edging with one finger.

"You never asked me what I did that made Mammi and Daadi send me here." Rhoda thrust the words out, as if wanting to get them away from her.

"No, I didn't." Katie paused. Should she have asked? "It's not that I don't care. But I thought you should tell me when you wanted to."

Rhoda pressed her lips together, and then sniffed a little, as if tears were not far away. "I want to tell you now. Like you told me about Eli and Jessica."

That truth had been painful to share, but maybe it would have a benefit she hadn't expected. "I would like to hear, Rhoda."

"I . . . I went to a party with some older kids. There were Englisch kids there, too, and I knew they would have beer and that I shouldn't go."

"So why did you?" Katie kept her voice neutral. Sometimes knowing what was right didn't keep you from doing something foolish.

Rhoda made a face. "It was dumb. But one of the kids dared me to go, and Louise had been lecturing me all afternoon about how I had to behave now that she's going to marry the bishop's son, and I just—well, I just went."

"I see." Katie did see. She wasn't sure she wouldn't have done the same, if Louise had been lecturing her. Which was a sad comment on her maturity.

"So, anyway, I didn't enjoy it that much. They were all drinking and acting stupid."

To Katie's relief, it sounded as if her little sister had had the right reaction. "I think maybe drinking and acting stupid go together sometimes."

"Ja. Well, anyway, I wanted to go home, but I didn't have a ride, and I couldn't make the kids I came with take me." Her fingers clenched the quilt. "There was an Englisch boy . . . he seemed really nice. He had his car there, and he said he'd take me home."

Katie thought she knew where this was headed, and her heart ached for her little sister. "What happened?"

"Just what you're thinking," Rhoda said. She tried to smile, but tears glistened in her eyes. "He didn't take me home. He kept driving, and then he wanted to park up by the lake, and he wouldn't listen when I said I wanted to go home."

Katie took her hand. "You must have been scared."

"I was, but I was mad, too. He kept trying to kiss me, so I gave him a shove and got out of the car. And he said if I felt that way about it, I could just find my own way home. And he drove off."

A completely non-Amish desire for vengeance swept over Katie. "I'd like to—" She stopped, took a deep breath. "That was a terrible thing, leaving you out there all alone."

"Ja, but it was better than being in the car with him. So I started walking, but I didn't know how I was ever going to get home, and I knew how Daadi and Mamm would be worrying." Rhoda wiped away a tear that had spilled over. "I had plenty of time to think about that while I walked, that's certain-sure."

"But you were all right? Nobody else tried to bother you?"

Rhoda wiped away another tear. "A car stopped, and I was scared, but it was two of the Englisch girls from the party. They said the boy came back and bragged about leaving me up there, so they told him off and came after me." She sniffled. "They were really nice, and they tried to make me feel better. But all I could think was how disappointed Daadi would be."

"I know," Katie said softly. Somehow that had always been the case with her, too. The fear of seeing disapproval instead of love in Daadi's eyes had kept her from doing some foolish things, too.

"But it was the middle of the night when I got home, even so. And Mamm cried and said how I'd embarrassed the family, and Daadi was disappointed, and Louise kept lecturing me . . ." Rhoda's voice trailed off, and she put both hands over her face, surrendering to tears.

Katie pulled Rhoda into her arms, her own tears spilling over. Poor, foolish Rhoda. Of course she'd done wrong, but surely she didn't deserve being made to feel like an outcast.

"It's over now," she said, holding her close. "Over and done with, and it will soon be forgotten. We all do foolish things, ja? Even Mamm, even Louise, even me."

Rhoda looked up at her through swollen eyes. "Not Louise."

"Ja, Louise," Katie said firmly. "She's just being a different kind of foolish. Now, you dry your eyes and finish your cocoa. You made a mistake, but you learned from it. That's all any of us can do, ain't so?"

Rhoda blew her nose and nodded.

"Gut." She patted her sister's cheek. "Now let's forget it, as if it never happened."

Forget. That was good advice for herself, too, if only she could take it.

Katie spent much of the next day trying to avoid Caleb. At the moment he was in the cellar, mopping the floor, so she had sent Rhoda down to help him, saying she'd watch both shops.

Not that he had made things difficult for her. His attitude toward her seemed the same as ever. No one watching him could guess that just yesterday they had been smooching in a wet basement.

Fine. That was how she wanted it. If they could both forget it had happened, she'd be happy. The trouble was that she couldn't forget.

Annoyed with herself, she set one of the boxes from the basement onto the counter and pulled off the packing tape that sealed it. There was a perfectly logical reason why she'd been . . . well, maybe *vulnerable* was the best word. Yes, she'd been vulnerable to Caleb's kiss because she still felt adrift after learning of Eli and Jessica's expected baby.

That wasn't a very admirable way to feel, but it was better than thinking she'd begun to care for Caleb. She couldn't.

She jerked her thoughts away from that particular treadmill, knowing she'd just go round and round on it. Much better to focus on the work at hand. Mamm had packed this box, judging by her printing on the outside, and Katie couldn't think what it contained.

The bell on Caleb's shop door jangled, and she stepped away from the counter to see who it was. Not a customer who needed attention—it was Becky and Naomi. Seeing her, they walked through the archway to her side.

"Naomi, how nice to see you. And Becky."

"Not such a nice weekend for you, ain't so?" Naomi came to clasp her hands. "What a thing to happen so soon after you moved in. Did you lose much?"

"Not as bad as it would have been if Rhoda and I hadn't gotten home when we did. A box of thread got soaked, and some fabric will have to be washed to see it if can be saved. Mostly it was just the mess."

"And Caleb tells us that you and Rhoda were already moving his materials out of danger when he got here. That was ser gut of you."

"It was nothing," she said quickly. "He did the same. We helped each other." She could only hope she wasn't blushing.

"Is Rhoda here?" Becky asked, looking around hopefully.

"Down in the basement, helping your onkel Caleb with the last of the cleanup."

"I will go and help, too."

Naomi watched her granddaughter head for the stairs, lips curving in an indulgent smile. "She means she and Rhoda will visit together until their chatter drives Caleb out of there, I think."

"Probably." Katie returned to her box. "It is nice of you to stop and see how we're doing."

"Not chust that." Naomi took off her bonnet, smoothing her graying hair back. "I will help, too. Are these things to be unpacked?"

"Ja, but . . ." Katie wasn't sure spending time with Caleb's mother was the best way to forget about that kiss. "You don't need to help. I think half the town has been in at some time today to see if we needed anything. Some of the other shops had a little water, I hear, but none as bad as we did."

"Ja, I saw Bishop Mose out in the backyard with Sam Troyer's crew. They will make sure the cellar doesn't flood again. But I want to help you." Naomi pressed her hands against the counter, looking down at them for a moment. "It has been too long since I have done for others. Too long since I realized that God still has work for me here, even though my George has gone ahead of me."

It felt as if she had squeezed Katie's heart with her words. "You have been grieving. Lonely. Everyone understands that."

"Others are grieving, too. Others miss him." Naomi shook her head. "I cannot use that to excuse myself. George would be ashamed of me."

Katie put her hand over Naomi's. "I never knew him, but I am sure he loved you too much ever to be ashamed of you."

Naomi's eyes shone with tears, and she squeezed Katie's hand. "Denke, Katie, for understanding." She shook her head, as if to shake off her sorrow. "Now, let us get to work. Until you got me started on quilting again, I had forgotten that work is a cure for many ills."

"Or at least it makes us forget them for a while," Katie said, thinking how often that had been true for her. She glanced at the pieces she'd cut for the Lancaster Rose quilt. The challenge of making it might be a cure for her, too.

She caught Naomi's gaze on her face and managed a smile. "Well, this is a box that my mamm packed, and I have no idea what's in it. I should have unpacked it long ago, instead of leaving it in the basement."

"At least no harm was done." Naomi's words were practical. "Let's see what it is." She pulled off tissue paper. "Ach, another quilt. Sunshine and Shadows, one of my favorite patterns. This should be out for sale."

Katie couldn't find an answer. All she could do was stare at the quilt that had been unearthed, her stomach twisting in rebellion.

"Katie?" Naomi's voice was filled with concern. "What is wrong?"

She shook her head, trying to think through the shock of seeing the quilt. "I . . . I didn't know this was here. I thought it had been left at home."

"It means something to you," Naomi said gently.

"Ja." She cleared her throat. She didn't have to say anything. She didn't.

But Naomi was looking at her with caring and concern, and the need to unburden herself was suddenly too strong to resist. "I made this . . . I made it for my wedding."

Naomi was silent for a moment, probably filling in all the things she didn't say. "I'm sorry, Katie. What happened to him? Did he die?"

"No." She would not let herself think that her situation might be easier if he had. That would be evil. "Eli and I . . . we had intended to wed since we were hardly more than children. I never imagined a future without him. We had set the date. Our families were planning the wedding. And then he came to me and said that he couldn't marry me. That he loved someone else."

She felt as if she hadn't breathed in a long time, and she sucked in a breath.

"I am so sorry." Naomi's hand tightened on hers. "Who was it? Someone you knew?"

"Jessica. My best friend." She felt her lips twist on the words. "I never dreamed of such a thing. Maybe I was blind, not to see it coming."

"They must have been very careful. Very ashamed, too, if no one else knew about it."

Oddly enough, that had never occurred to her.

"If they were really ashamed—" Katie stopped before she could say something really mean-spirited. "Well, I would not want Eli to marry me if he loved someone else, after all."

"No, you wouldn't, but that doesn't mean it wasn't hard to forgive."

"I forgive. Really." She shook her head. "But I can't forget. It still hurts. And now . . ."

"Now this quilt has surfaced to remind you." Naomi put her hand on it.

"Not just that." Katie tried to swallow the lump in her throat. "My mother has written that Eli and Jessica are expecting their first baby. She thinks I should be happy for them. I know that I should, but I can't. I must be a terrible person."

"Just a normal person, I think." Naomi's voice was soft and comforting. "You said that I should not be ashamed of my reaction to George's passing. And I think that you should not be ashamed of your reaction to this hurt. We must chust each go on and do the best we can, ain't so?"

Katie searched Naomi's face, finding nothing there but caring and sympathy. This conversation had started with her comforting Naomi and ended with Naomi comforting her. Oddly enough, the words eased her heart.

"Ja," she said finally. "I'll try."

"Gut." Naomi patted the quilt. "Maybe you should start by selling this. What do you think?"

Her heart hurt, but she nodded. "Ja. I think that would be best."

CHAPTER TEN

The cleanup was finally done to his satisfaction, but Caleb took a few extra minutes in the cellar to measure for shelves. He would build those for Katie, and he certainly wouldn't take any money for them. The very idea was ferhoodled.

Katie's trying to insist on paying him—well, that was just an example of her way of doing things. Independent. Determined to stand on her own two feet.

He wasn't going to cooperate with her on this one. She would have her shelves, just like his. He and William would see to that.

Caleb stood for a moment, looking around the cellar. Was he ever going to come down here without reliving the moment when he'd kissed her? Maybe not. But that didn't mean he had to dwell on it.

Since what had happened with Mattie Weaver, he'd steered clear of getting too close to anyone, at first because it was just too painful. Eventually . . . well, he'd realized it was safer that way, safer not to let anyone in, especially not another woman.

Besides, most of the community thought the worst of him for what had happened with Mattie. He couldn't entangle someone else in that gossip, even if he found a woman he wanted.

He started up the stairs. Funny. From the moment Katie Miller had rented the shop, he'd thought that having a woman sharing the space would cause problems. He sure hadn't figured on this kind of problem.

Caleb went through to his shop. Everything was quiet and in order, the front door locked, the shade down. Becky had taken care of that before she left. She'd done some rearranging, too, he noticed. He studied the way she'd grouped some of the pieces, putting a small table between two rockers, as if they invited a person to sit down. Nice, that was. Better than the way he'd lined pieces up in rows.

All was quiet on Katie's side, as well. Looked as if he wouldn't be talking to her again today, and maybe that was best. Give the memory of those moments in the cellar a chance to fade for both of them.

He pulled the back door shut behind him and stepped onto the porch. The crew Bishop Mose had brought in must have finished for the day. They'd left an open trench, and were probably planning to lay pipe in it tomorrow. Katie's mare would have to stay in the stable until that was finished.

The bishop stood by the plastic tape that blocked off the area, gesturing as he talked to Katie, who stood next to him. He must be explaining the work, judging by the gestures. Katie nodded, and the breeze that had come up after the rain lifted a loose strand of her hair. She smoothed it back into place with her hand. For an instant Caleb's palm tingled, as if he had done it, feeling the silky texture of her hair against his fingers.

It would definitely be better if he'd been able to avoid seeing her for a few days. With most women in the community he felt that there was an invisible barrier in place between them. They knew about him, about Mattie. Whether they still blamed him or not, the knowledge was in their eyes when they looked at him.

Katie was different. Of course, she'd been told what most folks believed, but it didn't seem to affect her. Maybe that was why . . .

He snapped that thought off before it could go any further. Sure, there was plenty to admire about Katie. He liked the obvious pleasure she took in running her shop and the interest she showed in every person who walked through her door. That interest was genuine, and people could tell. He'd never succeed in talking to folks that easily, even if it did lead to more sales.

He'd been standing here too long, and they'd be wondering about him. He couldn't just leave without stopping to talk. He started toward them, the ground still soggy under his feet.

"Caleb, gut. What do you think of the work so far?" Bishop Mose gestured toward the trench.

"I can't say I know much about it." He studied the trench in preference to looking at Katie and maybe having the bishop's wise eyes detecting his feelings. "It seems like it would keep the water from pooling close to the building, though."

"Ja, that's the idea. I was just explaining to Katie." Bishop Mose shook his head. "I wouldn't have had this happen for the world. If there's anything that was damaged, you chust tell me, and I'll make it gut."

"No need for that," Katie said quickly. "It was the push I needed to get the rest of my boxes sorted, that's all. And everyone has been so helpful."

There was something—a quick flash of what might have been sorrow—in her eyes. Then it was gone, and Katie was smiling.

"Ja, for me as well," Caleb said. "Nothing was damaged. When I got here, Katie and Rhoda were already moving my things up on the shelves."

He paused, but maybe saying it in front of the bishop would seal the plan so Katie would stop arguing. "William and I will build shelves on Katie's side of the cellar. I've got some pine boards in the attic that will work fine for that."

"I'll pay—" Katie began, of course.

"Indeed you will not," Bishop Mose said. "The responsibility is mine, and I will pay to have shelves put in."

"Nobody will pay," Caleb said, exasperated. "The wood is free, and so is our work. It's a simple thing to do for a neighbor."

Bishop Mose studied Caleb's face for a moment, and it wondered him what the bishop was thinking.

Then Bishop Mose nodded. "Gut. That's settled, then. And we'll all be plenty busy these next couple of weeks if Lisa Macklin's idea goes well."

"Lisa Macklin?" Caleb knew the Englisch woman, of course, just like he knew all the merchants in Pleasant Valley. But what was the bishop talking about?

"Ja, the idea to have special sale days the beginning of June. Didn't she stop by to see you two yet?"

Caleb shook his head, but Katie nodded. "I knew a little about it," she said. "Lisa asked if I would go in on an ad she was planning. I said I would, as long as Bishop Mose didn't object, and he said it was all right."

"Ja, I told Mrs. Macklin I thought it was a fine idea, so long as she didn't use the word *Amish* to advertise. I've seen enough of that in places like Lancaster County, where they get a lot of tourists. And you can be sure that any shop that puts Amish in its name isn't run by Amish folks."

"I've seen that, too," Caleb said, thinking of the trip he'd made to visit Daad's distant cousins in Lancaster after Mattie left.

"Well, that's not going to happen here," Bishop Mose said, his tone brisk. "But like Mrs. Macklin says, we all need people to buy things from us if we're going to stay in business."

"Ja, that's what I think." Katie's face grew animated. "Lisa says that advertising the special sale days in those tourist papers they put out in Lewisburg and Mifflinburg will bring shoppers in. And if they like what they see, maybe they'll return."

"We can all use that." Bishop Mose nudged Caleb with his elbow. "Don't you agree?"

"I guess so." He managed a smile. "I'm not so gut a salesperson as you two are, I think."

Bishop Mose chuckled, turning toward the lane. "That little niece of yours is coming right along, though. I asked her about the nice display she made in your window, and she said Katie gave her the idea."

"Ja?" He'd have to go and look at his own window. "I guess I hadn't noticed that, but she has been keeping the place sparkling, and she even rearranged pieces so the shop looks more homey and friendly."

Maybe that idea of Becky's had come from Katie, as well. He wasn't sure how he felt about that.

"I didn't tell her what to do," Katie said quickly. She walked alongside the bishop, but her gaze flickered to Caleb. "She was watching me arrange a display in my window, and we talked about what makes an appealing one. The idea for Caleb's window was hers."

"Gut for her." Bishop Mose's eyes twinkled. "Our Caleb needs someone to freshen up that shop of his."

Maybe so, maybe not, but Caleb wasn't going to discourage Becky from taking an interest. "I'm glad to see Becky so excited about the shop."

"Gut, gut." Bishop Mose lifted his hand in good-bye. "I will stop by tomorrow to see how the work is going." He went on out the lane.

"I must be on my way, too." Caleb headed for the stable, only to find that Katie was beside him.

"I wasn't trying to interfere in your shop," she said, her smooth brow furrowing. "I just wanted to encourage Becky."

He stopped, his hand on the harness he was about to lift down. "I know. That doesn't upset me."

Her lips curved in a slight smile, but her eyes still looked a bit worried. "I thought that something did. Upset you, I mean."

"Nothing." He wrenched his gaze away from her, staring at the harness. There was something that should be said, and maybe then things would be easier between them. "I wasn't upset . . . I was just thinking about what happened between us. I mean—"

"I know what you mean." She rushed the words, as if to keep him from spelling it out. "It's all right."

"I should apologize," he said, although he had a suspicion he didn't really regret that kiss. "I shouldn't have—"

"It's all right," she said again, her cheeks flooding with color that made her so pretty he wanted to kiss her again. "We should just pretend it didn't happen, ain't so?"

"Ja, we should."

But he didn't think he'd be forgetting anytime soon.

In Pleasant Valley, Wednesday was an early closing day for shops. No one quite seemed to know why, as far as Katie could tell, but everyone did it. So she flipped her sign to CLOSED, pulled down the shade, and tried to ignore the fact that Caleb was doing exactly the same thing.

They'd agreed to forget what had happened between them. She knew that was for the best. Unfortunately, she was finding it more difficult than she'd have believed possible.

Spending the afternoon with Molly making rhubarb and strawberry jam was just the distraction she needed. And since the shop was closed, she didn't have to worry about leaving Rhoda in charge.

"Is Rhoda about ready to go?" Caleb asked. He didn't seem to have had any trouble getting back to normal toward her, and for a fleeting moment she resented that.

"Ja, here I am." Feet clattered on the stairs, and Rhoda rushed across the shop. "Denke, Caleb."

Rhoda was spending the afternoon with Becky, so Caleb had said he'd drive her there when he went home. The plan was for Katie to pick her up after supper.

"Have a gut time." Katie bit her lip to keep from adding Mamm's usual warnings to behave properly and not embarrass the family.

"I will." Rhoda sparkled at the prospect of a break in routine. "And you, too. Say hello to Cousin Molly for me."

"Ja." Katie gave Rhoda a quick hug, and then watched as the two of them walked out the back. Silly, maybe, but she'd let them get on their way before she went out to harness the mare. It would mean one less conversation with Caleb.

She busied herself putting a bag of sugar in a basket along with jars and jar lids. Molly was providing the rhubarb and strawberries. The least she could do was supply some of the sugar they'd need.

In a few more minutes, she was on her way. The steady clop of the mare's hooves combined with the warm breeze and the scent of growing plants to ease her heart. It was foolish to be anxious when God had given her so many blessings. The hay looked near ready for a cutting in the fields, and dogwood blossoms brightened the woods. A dairy herd grazed, contented, in a pasture near the road.

By the time Katie reached Molly's, the stress of the past few days had slipped away, and she was glad to see it go.

Molly, her sleeves turned back, was busy at the sink washing the long pink stalks of rhubarb. Sarah Mast stood nearby, chopping the stalks.

"Ach, you are way ahead of me already." Katie set her basket on the table. "Sarah, I'm ser glad you are here. So, no babies decided to arrive today?"

"Not yet," Sarah said, the knife pausing in its chopping. "But tomorrow night is the full moon, so it wouldn't surprise me to see a spate of them in the next few days."

"At least it's not snowing, like it was when our Jacob was

born. I will never forget that." Molly sent a fond glance toward the playpen where young Jacob was pushing himself up on chubby arms.

"Ach, look at that fine strong boy." Katie knelt to smile at him. "He'll be crawling all over the place before you know it. Molly, he has dimples just like yours."

Molly grinned, her own dimples showing. "His daadi says the girls will be chasing him, for sure."

"They grow so fast," Sarah said, and Katie thought she caught a twinge of sorrow in her tone. And that was definitely a wistful look in her face.

"You and Aaron might..." Molly began, but she let the words trail away. Sarah would marry Aaron, Molly's oldest brother, come November. It was common knowledge that Sarah's first marriage hadn't produced any children.

"Ja. Maybe." Sarah moved over so that Katie could join the assembly line, putting the chopped rhubarb into a bowl and stirring in sugar.

"I try not to think about it too much," Sarah continued. Her lips trembled for a moment, and she pressed them together. "I would like to have Aaron's boppli, but it will be as God wills."

"I understand." Katie tried to concentrate on the movement of the wooden spoon in the heavy earthenware bowl, but it was no use. Sarah's words spoke too much to her own heart. And she knew these two as well as she knew anyone in Pleasant Valley—well enough to feel sure she could say anything to them. "I think about that sometimes. I don't regret not marrying, but it sorrows me to think of never having a child."

"You could still marry," Sarah said. "Look at me. I surely

thought marrying again was out of the question. Who would want to wed a midwife and put up with all the crazy hours? And one who was probably barren, besides? But Aaron changed my mind." Her face softened, seeming to glow with an inner joy.

"I have to admit that my cousin Aaron is a special man. But . . ." Katie paused for a moment. Funny, that she hadn't spoken of Eli to anyone in such a long time until she came to Pleasant Valley. Now, it seemed, she kept finding reasons to talk.

"But?" Sarah glanced at her, and then she shook her head. "I'm sorry. I don't mean to pry. I know how much it hurt you when Eli married your friend, but that doesn't mean you can't be happy again."

"How can I? I loved Eli. I promised to love him all my life. How can I just stop loving him?" Katie gave the spoon such a turn that pieces of rhubarb flew out of the bowl, landing on the counter. She managed a shaky laugh. "Ach, you see how foolish I am."

"It's never foolish to love." Sarah clasped Katie's hand, sticky from the rhubarb. "I don't regret loving my husband, even though that love turned to sadness when I couldn't give him a child. I thought I could never love anyone else. But the heart heals, in time. I found my heart had room enough to love again. I pray that you'll find that, too."

"Denke, Sarah." Katie whispered the words, grateful that Sarah cared.

Molly sniffled and wiped her eyes with the back of her hand. "Stop it, you two, or we'll be crying all over this jam."

"Ja, you're right." Katie managed a smile. "But that's the joy of a work frolic, ain't so? With no men around, we can say things we'd never say when they are here."

"They probably do the same when they're together, don't you think?" Sarah said.

"Ja, but they're not talking about us." Molly smiled. "At least not about love." She set the water and pectin to boil on the stove. "About engines and horses and jokes they couldn't say in mixed company, I bet."

Sarah chuckled. "You might be right about that. And they for sure wouldn't want to hear us when we start talking about having babies. Trust me. More than once I've had to stop helping the mother long enough to push the daadi's head between his knees so he wouldn't pass out."

"You wouldn't want to name any names, would you?" Molly's eyes sparkled with amusement.

"The midwife never tells," Sarah said solemnly.

They all laughed, and Katie was relieved that the mood had lightened. She needed time to think about what Sarah had said.

She thought she knew herself too well to have any doubts. She'd settled here in Pleasant Valley to get away from Eli and Jessica. How odd that being here had made her think about them even more. If Sarah was right . . .

But Katie knew herself too well for that, didn't she? How could she offer anyone second place in her heart?

She was probably a little more silent than usual for the rest of the afternoon, but the other two women more than made up for it, chattering their way through cleaning, mixing, boiling, ladling, until rows and rows of jars glowed with their ruby contents.

Then came the usual argument about how many jars each one should take. Katie and Sarah finally won that battle, insisting that Molly keep the largest share.

"It's not as if I have a family to use up the jam," Katie pointed out, arranging a dish towel over the jars that filled her basket. "Rhoda and I can't eat more than this."

Sarah and Molly exchanged glances. "About Rhoda," Molly said, and came to a stop, as if not sure how to go on.

Katie's heart grew heavy in her chest. This was not something good, she could tell. "What about Rhoda?"

"I know it's not true," Molly said quickly, "but someone in the church got a letter from a relative who lives near your parents with a ridiculous story about Rhoda running around and getting into trouble with some Englisch kids." She held out her hand toward Katie. "I'm sorry, but I thought you would want to know."

"Ja. I do." Katie let out a breath. She'd known this would happen, sooner or later. "If folks are talking, it's best that we know."

"There's no denying that some women are blabbermauls," Molly said fiercely. "To go around repeating something like that, probably exaggerating it at every turn—well, it's unfair and unkind, and that's what I said to the person who repeated it to me."

"Denke, Molly." Katie clasped her cousin's hand. "But I don't want you getting upset about it. The truth is that Mamm was a bit worried about Rhoda's rumspringa, but it's nothing all that bad."

Now that she'd heard Rhoda's story, Katie could say that with all confidence. Mamm, with her secrecy, had made Katie imagine all kinds of things. And Rhoda had too much common sense to make the same mistake again.

"That's why your parents wanted her to stay with you." Sarah's voice was warm with sympathy. "To give her a fresh start. And now the gossip has followed her here."

"Well, we all know how the Amish grapevine works." Katie managed a smile. "She'd have to go to the moon to get clear away from it. But I hoped she'd have a little more time to make friends and get settled before it came out. She's a gut girl, and she deserves a chance to show it."

"For sure she is," Molly said firmly. "And so I'll say to anyone I hear talking differently. I just hate to see Rhoda hurt."

Katie's heart winced. "So do I." She turned away, not wanting anyone to see the tears in her eyes, and picked up her basket. "I'd best get on home. If Rhoda has learned any of this . . . well, I need to be there for her."

It wasn't far into the village from Molly's, but it felt like forever as Katie drove, her thoughts twisting and turning. She prayed that Rhoda hadn't already heard this tale from someone else. Better for her to be forewarned, wasn't it? Let her get all her anger out at Katie, if need be.

Katie's heart quailed at the idea of trying to tell her little sister that people were talking about her. She'd had enough of that herself, when she and Eli broke up. People had been sorry for her. She'd hated that, but how much worse to have people condemning you.

Should she head straight for the Brand place? That was her immediate instinct, but they weren't expecting her anywhere near this early. Rhoda would be upset, having her time there cut short, and Katie would be forced either to tell her right away or to give some false reason for picking her up early.

Katie clucked to the mare, who had slowed down thanks to her driver's distraction. No, neither of those choices was suitable. She'd have to wait until six o'clock, at least, and pray that no one said anything to Rhoda in the meantime.

Katie was still worrying at it when she pulled into the lane and up to the stable. The men had finished their work in the back, but the area was still a bit wet. Maybe by tomorrow they'd be able to let the horses out.

A few minutes later Katie was unlocking the back door. She'd go upstairs, heat up some soup for her supper, and try to calm her thoughts before she went to pick up Rhoda.

But when she reached the top of the stairs, she knew it was already too late. Rhoda sat stiffly in the rocking chair, her face tight, her eyes suspiciously red. Katie held out her arms. For an instant Rhoda didn't move. Then she bolted across the room and flung herself into Katie's embrace.

Katie held her, rocking her back and forth a little, murmuring soothing words. It was as if this little sister of hers was four or five again, crying because she'd tried to climb the apple tree after Louise and fallen.

The words weren't important to Rhoda, probably. Just the sound of love and the feel of caring arms mattered. They were all Katie could offer. She prayed they would be enough.

Finally the crying ebbed. Rhoda drew back a little, trying to wipe her face with her hands. "I . . . I'm sorry. I wasn't going to cry, but . . ."

"Hush, now." Katie smoothed Rhoda's hair back from her face. Her heart twisted. Rhoda had looked so happy, so settled, when she'd left with Caleb. Now . . . "It's all right. We cry when someone has hurt us. It's all right to cry."

Rhoda nodded, choking on another sob.

"Komm." Katie guided her toward the sofa. "We'll sit here

together, and you'll tell me all about it. And we'll figure out how to make it better."

Rhoda sat down beside her, but she shook her head, tears spurting out again. "Nothing will make it better. Nothing."

"Tell me what happened." *Please, dear Father, guide me to say the right words to my sister.*

Rhoda sniffled, shook her head, and choked back a sob. "At first everything was fine. Becky and I helped her mamm with the dishes, and she said why didn't we make some fudge or maybe fix some chips and dip. So we did."

"Sounds like fun." It had been a long time since Katie had made fudge with her little sisters. They'd always let the smallest one spread butter on the oval platter where they'd pour the fudge to cool.

Rhoda nodded. "I always have fun with Becky. She's not so quiet when you get to know her. But then . . . then two of her friends came over, and when they saw I was there, one of them said her mamm wouldn't like her to be there with me. Because . . . because . . ."

Katie was tempted to fill in the rest, but maybe it was better to let Rhoda tell it the way she wanted. She patted her sister's hand and waited.

"Her mamm had a letter from Anna Hirsh, back home." Rhoda sniffed with contempt rather than tears. "You know what a blabbermaul she is. She gave some garbled story about all the trouble I got into. She made it sound so much worse than it was. And Becky's friend said they shouldn't stay if I was there."

Anger burned through Katie . . . an emotion she'd have to repent of, for sure, but at the moment it felt good. "Is that why you're home early? Did Becky . . ."

"No! No, Becky was great." Rhoda's eyes flashed. "You should have heard her. I didn't think she could, but Becky told that girl off and said that if she didn't want to be around me, she could just leave. So they did."

"It sounds as if Becky is a gut friend. So why did you leave, then? Did her mamm or her onkel say something?"

Rhoda shook her head. "Everybody was nice. But I could see that they were looking at me and wondering. It was just like when it happened, knowing people were talking about me and making the story worse with every telling."

"Not all people," Katie said quickly. "Not Becky."

"Not Becky." Rhoda's expression eased. "But I just felt like I couldn't sit there and pretend it didn't happen. I wanted to be home. With you. And when I said that, Caleb went and harnessed the horse and brought me."

Caleb. Well, he'd probably been eager to get her out of his brother's house. "Did Caleb say anything to you?"

"That I shouldn't mind what those girls said. That nobody would pay attention to them, and having Becky as a friend was better than having ten of them."

That surprised Katie into an involuntary chuckle. "He's probably right about that."

"Ja, I guess so. But I thought . . . I hoped . . . nobody in Pleasant Valley would find out about what I did. Now they'll tell everyone and it'll be just as bad as it was at home."

"Maybe not." Katie put an arm around Rhoda's shoulders. "And even if they do talk for a while, they'll get over it. I think most people will judge you by what they've seen since you've been here, and not some garbled story they've heard about what happened somewhere else."

"Do you think so?" Faint hope appeared in Rhoda's face.

"I hope so. I pray so." Katie hugged her. "Whatever happens, you have a gut friend. And you have a sister who loves you and trusts you. Is that enough for a while?"

"Are you sure you don't want me to go back home? If it's going to hurt your business . . . well, you could tell Mamm, and she would take me back." Rhoda lifted her chin a bit, but her lips trembled.

"I want you here with me." The words were firm, and a little surprising, even to Katie. But they felt right. "This is where you belong, as long as you want to stay."

CHAPTER ELEVEN

Maybe this was the wrong thing to do, but Caleb couldn't get Rhoda's tearful face out of his mind. So here he was at the back door of the shop, hesitating, not knowing whether to stay or go.

He shouldn't just unlock the door and walk into the shop, for sure. Katie would be alarmed, hearing someone down there in the evening.

He should leave. He was the last person Katie would want to see now. She might even be thinking that he was the one who'd told about Rhoda.

He took a step back, but before he could turn away, he realized someone was coming down the stairs. In a moment the door swung open.

"Caleb. I thought it was you." Katie sounded friendly enough. "Komm in."

"I won't stay. I just wanted to be sure that Rhoda is all right."

Katie glanced up the stairs. "She seems to be feeling better now that we've talked it over. It's hard for her to bear the idea of people gossiping about her, and probably exaggerating the story every time they repeat it." Katie had lowered her voice. She stepped out onto the porch and pulled the door behind her, leaving it ajar.

"I'm sorry." That wasn't enough. "I wasn't the one who—"

Katie touched his arm, silencing him. "I know you well enough to know that, Caleb."

Her words set up an echo inside him. That was how he felt, as well. How was it that they'd grown to know each other so well in such a short time?

"She told me you were ser kind to her, bringing her home and talking to her," she said. "Denke."

"It's nothing. I would have done much more to keep this from happening." He shook his head, determined to get the words said, even if they came out wrong. "I know I didn't like Becky's friendship with Rhoda at first. But I've seen how much it means to Becky."

"It's important to Rhoda, as well. She told me how Becky stood up to those other girls for her."

"She did? I hadn't heard that part of it." He felt a smile tug at his lips, despite the situation. "I wish I'd seen our little Becky being that brave."

"That was the only bright spot for Rhoda, Becky defending her like that." Katie looked up at him, her face a pale oval in the fading light. "And your kindness."

He was silent for a moment, but the words pushed at his lips. "I knew how she felt. I know what it is to have people thinking the worst of you, not wanting to listen to your side, even if you could tell them."

He stopped, aghast at what he'd nearly revealed. He didn't talk about Mattie. Not to anyone.

"You went through it," Katie said gravely. "You do understand, don't you?" She looked at him, and it was as if she could see past the barriers he had put up, past the front he'd built to hide his feelings. "You . . . It wasn't true, was it? What people said about you?"

His jaw tightened almost to the breaking point. "Mattie and I were sweethearts. She went away. She was pregnant, but she wouldn't marry me."

He tried to turn away, but Katie held him there, her hand on his arm. He could have pulled loose, but he didn't.

"That's what I was told," she said slowly. "That's what people believe. But that's not all of it, is it?"

"I don't know what you mean." He had to armor himself against the caring in her face.

Her breath seemed to catch. "I've tried and tried to make sense of it. Out of you being here while your child is out there someplace in the world. But I couldn't, because it's not true, is it? The baby was not yours."

He could only stare at her. How could she know the one thing he'd never said to a living soul except Mattie?

He should deny her words. He should walk away. But he couldn't. Everything . . . the very air he breathed, pressured him to say the truth, just this once.

"It was not my child." Pain mingled with relief. "How did you know?"

"Because if it were, you wouldn't be here."

So simple. If Mattie had carried his child, he would not be here, whether she'd married him or not.

He blew out a breath that wasn't quite steady. "Ja." He shook his head. "You can't talk about this, not to anyone."

"But why?" Distress filled her face. "You have a right to be free of the past, don't you?"

"Not at the cost of hurting someone else." He nearly choked on the words, but he forced himself to go on. "Mattie made her choice, but her parents still live here. Her brothers and sisters, too. They went through enough grief already. How could I bring it all up again? It would be unkind, and would do no gut, anyway. People will believe what they want."

"But you . . . You live as if you were guilty. You always seem apart, even when you're with the rest of the church. That isn't fair."

"That's the way it is."

"But it doesn't have to be." Her grip tightened. "Caleb, you know you didn't do anything wrong. Even if other people never know it, you don't have to stand back, looking at life as if you can't be a part of it."

He shook his head, suddenly exhausted, as if saying it out loud to her had taken everything out of him. "Maybe you're right, Katie. But I've been living this way for so long that I don't know any other way."

He turned away, feeling her hand drop from his arm, and walked to the buggy.

It was nearly one o'clock the next day, and Rhoda still hadn't come down to the shop. When Katie had rushed upstairs for an early lunch in anticipation of the quilting group's arrival that afternoon, Rhoda's bedroom door had been closed.

Katie glanced at the stairs. Should she go and check on her? Or would Rhoda resent being looked in on as if she were a child?

If Mammi were here . . . Katie stopped that line of thought. Mammi was not here. Mammi had shifted responsibility for Rhoda to Katie, and all Katie could do was follow her instincts.

Unfortunately, those instincts didn't seem to be telling her much, either about Rhoda or about Caleb. Katie's heart ached for each of them, but she didn't see what she could do to help.

That lay at the core of her frustration, she knew. She shoved a bolt of fabric into place with a quick movement. She wanted to do something, anything, that would ease their pain.

Caleb was in his shop. She'd felt his firm footsteps vibrating through the floorboards in the stillness. But he hadn't so much as nodded to her. After letting her see his pain, he'd withdrawn from her, just as he withdrew from life.

Perhaps she'd seen that withdrawal all along, but she hadn't recognized it until the words had come out of her mouth. Amish were called to live in the world but not be a part of the world. Even if he didn't intend it, Caleb lived a life in the Amish community but was not part of it. He pulled back from the very people who would help him.

Or would they? Katie's thoughts worried at the question even as she prepared the back room for the quilters. In the immediate aftermath of Mattie's leaving, people may well have given him reason to feel he wasn't welcome. But he was forgiven, even though that forgiveness was mistaken. He could take part in life again, but he'd chosen not to. No one could change his role but Caleb himself.

The sound of light footsteps brought her hurrying to the front room. It was Rhoda carrying a tray with coffee and cups, and Katie's heart gave a little leap at the sight of her. Rhoda was maybe a bit pale yet, but she was forcing herself to act normally, and Katie was glad.

"Should I bring some cookies down as well?" Rhoda set the coffee tray down on the small table.

She was making an effort to sound as if nothing was wrong, and all Katie could do was the same. "Let's wait until folks start to arrive, ja? Do you think I have the sewing machines in the best place?" She had set up two treadle machines in the back room for those who wanted to machine piece their quilt tops.

Rhoda moved to the door to look. "Ja, there's plenty of light from the windows." She seemed to make an effort to think of something else to say. "Do you think everyone will come back?"

"I hope so." Katie had already seen an increase in the number of Englisch customers, maybe because of Lisa and Donna talking about the shop.

She hesitated. Should she tell Rhoda she didn't need to stay downstairs when the quilters began to arrive? Or was it better for her sister to be around other people right now?

Before she could make up her mind, the bell over the front door jingled.

Rachel, Molly, and Myra came inside in a chattering group, each of them with a baby. Before Katie could react, Molly was calling to Rhoda.

"Ach, Rhoda, gut. I hoped you would be here. You're so gut with the kinder . . . can you give us a hand?"

Katie didn't know whether to laugh or cry. Molly, with her usual quickness, had decided that involving Rhoda with the little ones was a cure for a bruised spirit. Well, maybe Molly had it right, because Rhoda's face lit with a smile when Myra's little Anna Grace held out chubby hands to her.

"Komm here, you sweet girl." Rhoda scooped the boppli into her arms, the strain leaving her face. "Give me a kiss."

Katie felt her own tension melting away at the sight. With the two younger babies asleep, Rhoda could devote herself to Anna Grace and be soothed by the child's loving spirit. God seemed to give His Down's syndrome children that extra measure of sweetness, maybe to reward those who cared for them.

Katie hurried forward to greet everyone. "So we will have a houseful of babies today. Rhoda, you'll have your hands full if they all wake at the same time."

Rhoda's smile flashed, and it seemed she'd regained some of her sparkle. "That will be fun."

Rachel chuckled as she moved little Josiah's carriage along the aisle. "Fun, ja. Much as I love my four, some days are not so much fun."

"Ach, you know full well you love every minute of it," Myra said. "And your Gideon is such a gut daadi."

"You are fortunate to have him no farther away than the shop most of the time," Molly declared. She led them into the back room and pushed little Jacob's buggy into the corner, setting down the basket that held her work. "I thank the gut Lord every day that Jacob doesn't have to work away any longer, now that he has such a fine job with the construction company in Fisherdale."

There was a murmur of agreement. Everyone knew it became harder each year for the young men to find work that kept them close to home. Thank goodness Molly's Jacob worked nearby now.

The bell announced another arrival. Katie turned to see Donna and Lisa coming in, talking together. She breathed a sigh of relief. There had been that bit of antagonism between them over Lisa's plans to bring more shoppers to Pleasant Valley, and Katie was glad to see it seemed to be forgotten.

"Katie, I was just telling Lisa she ought to do an easier design for her wall hanging," Donna said. "Help me convince her."

Donna, it seemed, liked to have a say in what others were doing. This would take careful handling, Katie feared.

"There's no convincing about it." Lisa's tone was a little tart. "I want to do this leaf pattern in fall colors. If I can find the time to work on it, I should have the table runner done by autumn, you see."

Donna was right, in a way. There were simpler patterns for beginners, like the one-patch she was doing, but the choice was Lisa's.

"I've already mentioned to Lisa that the leaf pattern is a bit complicated." Katie ushered them toward the back room. "But it is her project, so she must decide." She nodded toward Donna's handwork bag, done in a lovely crewel design. "Have you made up your mind on the fabric for your one-patch? That print material you were looking at is so pretty."

Distracted, Donna began talking about the colors she'd picked. Katie relaxed slightly. Keeping these two happy was going to take an effort.

"We are not late, I hope." Naomi and Emma came through from Caleb's shop, with Becky right behind them.

"Not at all. We're just getting started." Katie was relieved to see Becky head straight for Rhoda and the babies. In a moment the two girls were spreading a hooked rug on the floor and sitting down with Anna Grace between them.

Katie breathed a silent prayer of thanks. Time with her friend was just what Rhoda needed right now.

With everyone there, work got going quickly. No, not everyone, Katie corrected herself. Melanie hadn't arrived yet. The young woman had seemed so enthusiastic—surely she hadn't decided to drop out already.

In a few minutes, Emma had taken over one of the sewing machines. Katie stopped to admire the patches she was chain stitching.

"Sunshine and Shadows," she said. "That is one of my favorites."

"I have not made a quilt other than the ones we make for the sales in"—Emma's foot eased off the treadle—"goodness, I don't know how long."

"You were too busy with the midwife practice." Naomi sat near her friend, working on the patches for her Tumbling Blocks quilt by hand. "It's nice you have more time now that Sarah is working with you."

"Ach, I'm not used to having time, and that's the truth of it," Emma said. "I like being useful."

"You are useful," Naomi said placidly. "Sarah could not do without you in the practice. I've heard her say so more than once."

"Making a quilt is useful, for sure," Katie added. "Is this one to keep or for a gift?"

"I haven't decided." Emma's brows drew together in her strong face. She looked like a woman who was seldom undecided about anything. Maybe her uncertainty was a result of the mini-stroke that had caused Emma to turn catching babies over to her niece. It must be hard for a woman like Emma to feel she was no longer contributing.

"Sunshine and Shadows," Naomi said softly. "The patterns of life. I have been in the shadows for a time, Emma, with my life turned upside down. I'm starting to komm into the sunshine. You will, too."

Katie slipped away, her eyes stinging with tears. It sounded as if Naomi was just what Emma needed now.

She moved to the table to help Lisa cut out the final pieces for her leaf design. "Be sure the edges are exactly even," she cautioned before Lisa could make a too-hasty snip. "The cutting is the most important part, I think. If the pieces are not true from the beginning, there will be trouble later."

Lisa flashed her a smile and lined the fabric up more carefully. "I'm always in a hurry, it seems."

"You are making this for the pleasure it gives you," Katie said. "There's no need to hurry."

Donna chuckled at Lisa's expression. "The Amish don't live by the clock, Lisa."

"Well, why should we? It will all get done." Katie wasn't sure whether the woman had meant that in a derogatory way or not, and she cautioned herself not to read meaning into a casual comment. "The old saying is true enough. The hurrier I go, the behinder I get."

A gentle wave of chuckles greeted that, some more rueful than others. Maybe hers was the most rueful of all, Katie realized. How often was she guilty of thinking she had to manage everything—her shop, the sales, Rhoda's happiness? It was in the gut Lord's hands, not hers. She must simply do the best she could with what He had given her. She glanced at the pieces for her Lancaster Rose quilt, laid out on the table. What difference did it make whether she worked on it today or tomorrow?

"Is Melanie not coming today?" Myra asked, her tone gentle. "I thought she was enjoying herself last week."

"I haven't heard anything from her," Katie said. She'd thought Melanie had enjoyed herself, too. Maybe she'd been wrong.

"Young people are always busy," Donna said. "My kids have such hectic lives I don't hear from them from one week to the next."

"Your children don't live here?" Rachel asked.

"Scattered across the country," Donna replied. "Well, it's only natural. Their professions take them away. My son is a heart surgeon in Dallas, and my daughter manages a big advertising agency in Chicago."

"You must be proud of them," Lisa said, with perhaps a little wistfulness in her tone. Lisa didn't have children, Katie remembered. And with her husband gone, she seemed very alone. Maybe that was why she threw herself into her business so much.

"Very proud," Donna said. "Very."

She seemed to mean that, but Katie couldn't help but think that, in her own way, Donna was lonely, too.

"I stopped by the hardware store this week," Donna said abruptly. "It seems like that fiancé of Melanie's keeps her working pretty hard. We were just passing the time of day when he butted in and gave her something to do. I can't say I liked that."

No, Donna wouldn't. Of course, from what Katie had seen, Melanie and her fiancé ran the hardware store by themselves.

"Maybe something came up that Melanie couldn't leave work this afternoon," she said.

"Mike, most likely," Donna muttered.

Katie turned that over in her mind. Surely the man . . . Mike, his name was . . . didn't object to Melanie's joining their group. Maybe he'd felt that Donna was wasting Melanie's time with her talking.

If so, he needed to understand a bit more about running a store in a small place like Pleasant Valley. Chatting with customers was never a waste of time. Even if they didn't buy anything today, they might well be back to buy tomorrow.

Melanie herself put an end to the speculation by rushing in, carrying her wall hanging materials in a shopping bag with the name of a department store emblazoned on it.

"Sorry I'm so late, everyone." She was breathless, her face flushed with embarrassment. "We got busy in the store."

Katie ignored a snort from Donna. "We understand. It's not a problem at all. Show me how you're coming with the wall hanging." Melanie had decided on a Crazy Quilt pattern, saying maybe her mistakes wouldn't show so much then.

"I haven't had much time to work on it this week," Melanie said, hurriedly getting out her supplies. "We've been so busy."

"Your store must be doing better than anyone's then," Lisa said. "I don't mind admitting trade's been pretty quiet for me this week."

"Oh, well." Melanie's flush deepened. "Everybody needs things from the hardware store, I guess."

"Komm, I'll help you," Katie said, intervening. "We'll figure out the matching, and then it will be easier to work on."

Beginners sometimes thought they understood, only to find themselves at a loss when they tried to follow the instructions on their own. Perhaps Melanie just didn't want to admit that.

The afternoon seemed to pass too quickly, making Katie aware of how much she enjoyed these get-togethers. The women's soft voices, the whirr of the sewing machines, the flash of needles . . . this was her favorite part of the week.

If she and Eli had married, would she have carried on at the shop? Probably not. She'd have been busy having babies, running the home, spending her sewing hours on clothes for the children. Maybe, as they grew, there would have been time to be busy with the quilts again. That was the cycle of life for a woman.

For most women. She made the correction. Her life was not like most.

"Well, when you Amish get married, it's for good." Melanie's words, spoken to Molly, were loud in a moment of silence. Melanie glanced around, flushing a little, probably because everyone had heard. "I mean, I guess you Amish don't believe in divorce."

"When two people make vows before God, it is forever," Rachel said. "That doesn't mean we don't have problems, just like other folks. But we try to work them out."

"Most people go into marriage thinking it is forever," Lisa added. "Amish or English. I'm sure Mark and I had our share of disagreements, but we never considered ending things." A shadow crossed her face, and Katie knew she was missing her husband.

"But if you find out you've married the wrong person, maybe it's better to get out of it." Melanie said the words almost to herself.

Katie and Lisa exchanged glances. How did one answer that? Melanie wasn't even married yet. If she was having doubts already . . .

"People don't have to be married to be happy." Donna's tone was assertive. "But it's unusual to see an Amish woman Katie's age who isn't married." She looked at Katie expectantly.

A flash of anger startled Katie. It wasn't any of Donna's business why she wasn't married.

"I'm sure Katie has her reasons." Lisa hurried into speech to cover the awkward moment. "I don't think we should put her on the spot."

Donna's cheeks grew mottled. "No offense," she muttered. "I just wondered."

"It's all right." Katie took a firm hold on her temper. "I was engaged, but he married someone else." She shrugged, trying to turn it off lightly. "It was better to know that before we took vows rather than after."

"It certainly was." Lisa's tone was emphatic. "Now, about these pieces, how did you say they should fit together, Katie?"

Katie bent over the table, her gaze fixed on the quilt patches, glad to hide her face for a moment. Goodness knows she should be able to talk about Eli naturally after all this time.

Realization hit her, so sharp and clear it was like being hit by lightning. She'd told Caleb he was hiding his pain by avoiding other people, but wasn't she hiding, too? Wasn't she immersing herself in the shop, in the people who came into it, to hide her own pain?

She didn't want to think that, but she had to face it. She'd told herself that coming here would be a new start for her, but the truth was that it was just a new way to cover the same old pain.

"Are you certain-sure you'll be all right minding the shop this afternoon?" Caleb had a feeling he was the one who wasn't all right, but he wasn't going to let Becky see his apprehension.

"It will be fine, Onkel Caleb." Becky's face shone with excitement, as if he had given her a gift by letting her watch the shop while he went to a meeting that he didn't want to attend anyway.

"That's all right, then. If you are not sure of anything, just tell the person he'll have to wait until I return, ja?"

"I will, for sure." Becky gave him a gentle push. "Go now. Katie is waiting for you."

Sure enough, Katie was standing at her shop door, obviously confident in Rhoda's ability to watch the shop while she was out. Just as obviously, it would be rude to set off down the street to Mrs. Macklin's shop without her, since they were going to the same place. It wasn't Katie's fault that he found himself tongue-tied around her these days.

"All ready?" He tried to manage a smile as he approached Katie, but it probably looked more like a grimace.

"We'll be just in time for the meeting," Katie said, opening the door.

He followed her out to the sidewalk. Mrs. Macklin had asked all of the Main Street merchants to attend a meeting about the sale days plans. His immediate response had been that meetings didn't interest him. He was willing enough to put some items on sale, but that was all.

However, Bishop Mose had gotten involved, and if the bishop asked you to go somewhere, you went. Besides, Caleb's instant refusal would only serve to prove that what Katie had said about him was true.

So he'd go. But that didn't mean he'd do anything. Or say anything. He'd be there. Let that be enough.

He caught the movement of Katie's head as she turned to look at him. "I'm sure the girls will be fine." Her tone was reassuring. "If Becky has any problems, Rhoda will be right there."

"Ja, I know. I'm not worried."

Katie's eyebrows lifted. "Then your black look must be because you feel obligated to walk with me. You don't have to, you know. If it makes you uncomfortable—"

"Ach, Katie, stop putting words in my mouth. The fact is that I'm not much of a one for meetings."

"I know," she said quietly.

And there, he'd as much as told her that what she thought about him was true. "It's not—not because I feel uncomfortable around people. This meeting, Mrs. Macklin's plans—we haven't done anything like this before."

"Bishop Mose says we haven't needed to before."

"I know. And that's why I am going." Just going, that was all. Let other people volunteer to be on committees and such.

"I'm glad." Her words sounded a little stiff.

And now that he took a close look, it seemed Katie wasn't her usual confident self. Was she still worrying about that upset with Rhoda?

The only way to find out was to ask. "Is something else wrong then?"

"No." The answer came so quickly that he knew it wasn't true.

They had already reached Mrs. Macklin's shop, and there was no time for him to say anything else, even if he could have thought of something.

CHAPTER TWELVE

*M*rs. Macklin's gift shop, like most of the shops along Main Street, had a back room, and that was where the meeting was being held. Caleb followed Katie down the rows of shelves filled with candles, wreaths, baskets, and such-like. Lots of stuff there, but he had to admit that Mrs. Macklin had it arranged in a way that made you want to stop and look, even if you weren't in the market for any of the things the woman sold.

The back room was fairly large, as such rooms went, and Mrs. Macklin had arranged folding chairs in a circle so that there was no back row to hide in. A table at the door was laden with a heavy coffee urn and platters of baked goods that he recognized as having come from Paula Schatz's bakery. Paula herself, round and rosy-faced, presided over the food, urging people to have just one more sticky bun or slab of apple walnut cake.

"That's enough," he began, but Paula plopped a cinnamon bun on his paper plate.

"Ach, you have room for a little more, for sure." Paula, like most Amish and Mennonite women, it seemed, loved to see people enjoying their food.

"If I eat all this, I won't be gut for anything but taking a nap," he told her.

"Get on with you, Caleb Brand." She waved a dish towel at him, pleased with that response for some reason. "Everyone knows you work as hard as any two men."

If they did, it was news to him, but he accepted the plate and coffee. Katie had already taken a seat next to Alma Gluck, who helped her husband run the candy shop. Bishop Mose sat a few chairs away, so Caleb took the seat next to him. He spotted a few people who, so far as he knew, didn't own shops in town, and that puzzled him.

"There are folks other than storeowners here," he said quietly.

Bishop Mose nodded. "Some of the volunteer organizations want to be involved, too. Just watch," he murmured. "All the Amish women will sit together, and all the Amish men."

"That's natural enough, isn't it?" Caleb wasn't sure what the bishop was driving at.

"Natural," Bishop Mose said. "But I would not like our Englisch neighbors to think we are standoffish."

Caleb didn't bother to say it, but surely the Englisch merchants thought that already. And weren't the Amish to live in but not of the world? Maybe the bishop was trying to find the line between doing so and offending their non-Amish neighbors. Caleb was sure he didn't know where that line was.

Which was why he'd let himself be guided by the bishop in attending this meeting. It wasn't a matter of not thinking for himself. It was a question of trusting someone as mature in the faith as Bishop Mose whenever one was in doubt.

Mrs. Macklin started the meeting once everyone was satisfied with plenty to eat and drink. He had to admit that the woman had a nice way about her. She was enthusiastic but not threatening or overly bossy, and she kept hold of the reins of the meeting, not letting it stray from its purpose . . . to plan what each of them would do for the Summer Sale Days.

When Mrs. Macklin used that expression, the first ruffle arose in the meeting from Mike Sullivan, who managed the only hardware store in town.

"If we're going to do this, it seems to me that we could come up with a better name than Summer Sale Days," Sullivan said, "especially if we want to pull people into town."

Mrs. Macklin didn't skip a beat. "What would you suggest, Mike?"

"Well, how about calling it Amish Days? Seems like that's good publicity."

Several people separated Caleb from Katie, but he had the impression she grew tense. Certainly the bishop had.

"That would be something to consider," Mrs. Macklin said smoothly. "But I think our Amish colleagues would not like to have their faith used as advertising."

Sullivan looked as if he didn't like being disagreed with. "Why not? Lancaster County is filled with businesses that are called Amish this and Amish that. And they've sure got plenty of tourists coming there."

"I think you will find that places that advertise that way are not Amish-owned," Bishop Mose said. He didn't raise his voice, but it seemed to dominate the room.

Sullivan scowled. "I'm not Amish, but I don't mind using the word if it brings in business."

"And that would be as offensive as calling it Catholic Sale Days or Episcopal Sale Days." Cliff Wainwright, who owned the bookstore, shoved his wire-rimmed glasses in place and looked at Sullivan as if he were studying him. "I for one would not be comfortable trading on someone else's faith to make a few dollars. What about Pennsylvania Dutch Days? That might work."

There was a murmur of agreement from the other merchants, Amish and Englisch alike. Katie darted a quick smile at Caleb, as if wanting to share her pleasure in the quick resolution with someone. With him.

He met her gaze for a moment and then looked away. And found himself looking straight at Ruth Weaver, Mattie's mother. The unexpectedness of it shocked him, and it took a moment to gain his balance. Ruth had quite a little business in hooked rugs, selling them out of her home, so maybe that was why she was here. But that didn't explain why she was looking at him.

He didn't see any of the Weaver family often, managing to sit in church where they weren't in his line of sight and steering clear of coming too close. For their part, they usually did a fine job of looking right through him when they did happen to meet. But now . . . well, maybe it was because Ephraim, her husband, wasn't with Ruth, but she sat there, her gaze on him, almost as if she wanted to say something.

"Well, that sounds like a majority," Lisa announced briskly, pulling Caleb's attention back to her. "I've already volunteered to handle publicity, and if anyone would be willing to help me or has any ideas, do please get in touch with me."

"Is anyone else going to be selling food?" Paula Schatz put the question. "I'll have baked goods and coffee, of course, but it seems to me this is an opportunity for more than that. A hot dog stand, maybe, or some other sort of sandwiches."

"And soup," someone else put in. "Especially if it's not a real hot day, homemade soup goes real good."

That opened the flood gates. It seemed everyone was willing to talk about food, and soon folks from the Volunteer Fire Company to the Ladies Circle at the Methodist Church had offered to set up food stands.

Caleb leaned back in his chair. This wasn't so bad. Folks were really getting involved, and that would be what it took to make something like this work. Whatever awkwardness had remained after the discussion of the name was swamped in a flurry of ideas.

He glanced at Katie. She'd been in on the plan from the beginning, thanks to her friendship with Lisa Macklin, and she looked pleased. More than that—glowing, lit up with enthusiasm. Sometimes he forgot how pretty she was when that light was in her face.

He sat back again, forcing himself to focus on the meeting. He had no right to be thinking about Katie that way.

But who was he trying to fool? Himself? If so, it wasn't working. He had feelings for Katie Miller. He might not know what to do with them, but they were real, and growing stronger all the time.

"Well, I think that's about it," Mrs. Macklin said after the last detail had been ironed out. "There is just one other thing. A few merchants couldn't be here today. Would someone be willing to call on them and try to get their support?"

Cliff Wainwright raised his hand. "I'll be glad to touch base with people," he said. "But I think the Amish would respond better to another Amish person."

Silence fell for a moment. Bishop Mose nudged Caleb. He kept his gaze in the other direction. Whatever the bishop thought, he wasn't the one to take on this job.

Unfortunately, looking away from the bishop meant he was looking straight at Katie. The appeal in her deep blue eyes was far more potent than the bishop's nudge. She wanted him to do it. He could read that in her face.

He didn't want to. But he raised his hand, because she was just too hard to resist.

Caleb was very quiet as they walked back toward their shops. Katie glanced at his face, searching for some reaction on his part to the meeting. His lips were set, his eyebrows drawn down slightly, giving nothing away.

Well, she was not one to be silent, was she?

"Denke, Caleb. It was ser kind of you to offer to help."

He blinked, as if that were not at all what he'd been thinking. "It wasn't exactly my idea."

Now it was her turn to be surprised. "But . . . you offered. You must have wanted to, ain't so?"

"I knew . . ." He paused. "Bishop Mose nudged me. I knew that was what he thought was best."

She was conscious of a vague sense of disappointment. Surely she hadn't been thinking he'd done it for her, had she?

"Ja, it is not easy to turn down the bishop. Of course you would do it for him. I just thought you looked unhappy about something."

"Ruth Weaver was at the meeting. Mattie's mother." He chopped off the words.

She tried to read through the words to the feeling behind them, wanting him to say more. "You must see her from time to time, don't you?"

He jerked a short nod. "Ja. But she always acts like I'm not there. I don't blame her for that. But today . . . today she was looking at me almost as if she wanted to say something."

"Maybe she does." Katie prayed she wasn't saying the wrong thing. "Maybe you should give her the chance."

They'd reached her shop door. He grasped the knob to open it and then paused, hand on the knob, looking into her face. Then he shook his head and opened the door.

Before he could cross to his own shop, they were set upon by both of the girls, bubbling with enthusiasm.

"Katie, at last you are here." Rhoda's eyes danced. "I can't wait to tell you. I'm so excited."

"Ja, tell her." Becky looked almost as exuberant as Rhoda. "Tell her."

"Tell both of us," Caleb said, clasping his niece's hand. "So far all Katie knows is that you are both babbling."

Becky giggled. "It's the best thing."

"Well, what is it?" Katie took off her bonnet, amused by the girls' reactions. "Don't keep us in suspense."

Rhoda took a deep breath. "I sold a quilt!"

"You did?" Her surprise was surely all that Rhoda could wish. She hadn't expected that on such a quiet Friday afternoon. "Rhoda, that is wonderful gut. Which one? Who bought it?"

Rhoda clasped Katie's hand and swung it, reminding Katie of her sister's smaller self on the first day of school. "I don't know who she was. Englisch. A stranger, I think. Not anyone I'd seen around town."

"Someone driving around who saw your sign," Caleb guessed.

"Ja, or maybe someone I talked to at the Mud Sale," Katie said. "A couple of women said they'd stop by one day. So which quilt did she buy?" It was good news anytime a quilt sold, and especially nice that Rhoda had been the one to make the sale.

"It was the one . . ." Rhoda hesitated. "You know, the one that was in the box we brought up when the cellar flooded."

The one Katie had made for her marriage. That was what Rhoda was trying not to say—the quilt that had represented her broken dreams was gone now.

Well, Naomi had advised her to sell it, and she'd been right. Now Katie would not look at it and remember.

"That's fine, Rhoda." She tried to sound as if that quilt meant nothing more than any other. "I'm ser glad you sold it."

The faint worry in Rhoda's face was wiped away. "Me, too. I never made such a big sale before. She was looking and looking, and I tried to find out what colors and patterns she was interested in, like you taught me, but it seemed like she just wanted me to let her alone, so I did. I figured she was just a looker, but then she brought the quilt to the counter and said she'd take it! I was so surprised. Becky will tell you."

Becky giggled. "Rhoda's eyes got all round. I'll bet the woman knew it was the first quilt she'd ever sold."

"I thought you were supposed to be watching my shop." Caleb flicked her cheek with his finger, smiling.

"I was, honest, Onkel Caleb. I just stepped over to see what Rhoda was doing. I'd have been back the minute the bell rang, honest."

"I know. I'm teasing, that's all."

"When the woman handed over the money, all in tens, my hands were shaking," Rhoda confessed. "Two hundred dollars, just like that."

Katie stared at her, feeling the color drain from her face. "Two hundred? Rhoda, that quilt was priced at six hundred."

"Six—no. No! The price tag was right on it. I peeled it off myself." Rhoda whirled, running to the counter where the quilt book was kept. "Look, here, here is the tag. I took it off just like you showed me, and I stuck it to the cover because I thought you'd want to enter it yourself."

Katie could only stare numbly at the tag stuck to the front cover of the notebook in which she kept careful notes, a page for each quilt, who made it, a description of the quilt, and any other information she had about it. The tag said two hundred dollars, but that wasn't the price she'd put on the quilt.

"Maybe . . ." Becky's voice was very small. "Maybe you were thinking six hundred, but you wrote two by mistake."

"No." Katie tried to soften that with a smile at the girl. "It's a gut thought, Becky, but I know it was correctly marked."

"Was there anything else in the shop that was marked two hundred?" Caleb asked, in the tone of one determined to get to the bottom of the situation.

"Ja. Some of the bigger wall hangings, and the crib quilts."

"But . . . but how could they get mixed up?" Rhoda was on the verge of tears, all her earlier happiness wiped away, and Katie realized she minded that even more than the loss of the money.

"I doubt it was a mix-up." Caleb's expression was grim. "I think the woman probably switched the tags herself. Komm, let's see if we can find a piece without a tag." He gave the two girls a gentle push.

Gratitude pierced Katie's hurt. Caleb was helping the girls by giving them something to do. While they were busy playing detective, they wouldn't be grieving about what had happened while they were in charge. She went quickly to join the search.

"It has to be one of those two things." She knew exactly what the price was on every item in the shop, but she could hardly expect Rhoda to be that well-informed, could she? "A baby quilt or a wall hanging."

The two girls started on the baby quilts, while she went through the wall hangings. But each one seemed to have the original tag she'd put on it. "Nothing here," she said. "These are all right."

"The baby quilts all have their tags, too," Becky said. "I don't understand."

"I do." Rhoda fairly flew across the shop to the archway, where Naomi's baby quilt hung on the quilt rack. She shook the quilt out, looking in every corner. "The tag is gone from this one. I saw her looking at it. She must have taken the tag off."

Katie found she didn't want to believe it. "Maybe we're wrong. Maybe the tag just fell . . ."

"And then it ran across the room and attached itself to the quilt?" Caleb was bending over the bed where the quilts were displayed. He straightened, something in his hand. He held it up. "Here's the proof, I think. The price tag from the quilt, stuck to the back of the bed post."

Katie stared at the tag, accepting the truth. "She planned it. She deliberately switched the tags."

"She wouldn't have gotten away with it if you'd been here," Rhoda said, her eyes filling with tears again. "She probably figured I was just a dumb kid who wouldn't know the difference. And she was right!" The tears spilled over.

"Hush, now." Katie put her arms around her sister. "It's not your fault."

"You'd have known," Rhoda said, her voice choking.

"I would have, ja." Katie put her palms on Rhoda's cheeks, so that Rhoda was forced to look into her face. "But I never expected you to know that much. How could you? I was the one who priced everything. It's not your fault."

"She was a bad woman." The words, coming from sweet Becky, startled all of them. "She ought to . . . to go to jail."

Katie's gaze met Caleb's, and she knew he was thinking what she was. This was one of those moments an Amish parent used to teach the difference between the world's ways and the Amish way.

"I will not go to the law over this," Katie said gently. "It is only money, and at least the quilt was one of mine, not one on commission. No one is hurt." Except Rhoda, but the law wouldn't fix a sixteen-year-old's feelings.

"We don't go to the law," Caleb said. "We live separate, remember?"

"Ja." Becky still looked a little rebellious. "But the woman was Englisch. So the Englisch law . . ."

"The Englisch law will catch up with her sooner or later," Caleb said. "And if not, God still knows what she has done."

"We forgive." With one arm still around Rhoda, Katie drew Becky close with the other. "God forgives us, and we forgive others. That's what God offers us, ain't so?"

"Ja," Becky said, perhaps a little reluctant still. Rhoda nodded, wiping tears away with the back of her hand.

"Gut. Now why don't you two go upstairs and have a snack. There are some Whoopie Pies that Molly made waiting to be eaten."

The two girls started toward the stairs, but Rhoda turned back and seized Katie's hands. "I will learn the price of every single thing in the shop," she said fiercely. "I promise."

Katie nodded, her throat tight, and watched as they ran up the stairs. Then she glanced at Caleb. His face was filled with sympathy.

"That was the best way to handle it, I think." His forehead furrowed. "But I do wonder . . ."

"Wonder what?" Katie asked, when it appeared he wouldn't finish.

"I wonder if the quilt will eventually show up in one of Bennett Hargrove's shops."

"Surely he wouldn't do that." She hated to think anyone would stoop so low.

"There are people who think the Amish are easy to cheat," he said. "Either because they think we are dumb or because they know we are reluctant to go to the police."

"Ja, I know." It would be foolish not to be aware of that. Even the Amish could not be isolated from the wrong that some would do. "But I still wouldn't like to think that about someone I've met." She shrugged. "Anyway, there is nothing to be done about it. Except forgive."

"Ja. But sometimes forgiveness is hard, especially when the one hurt is someone you care about."

Katie could only stare at him. Did that mean that he cared about her? Or was he thinking of the two young girls, their happiness shattered by a mean act?

Caleb didn't explain. He just nodded and headed back to his shop.

Caleb and William started on the new shelves in the cellar first thing on Saturday morning.

"I thought we'd get going on these shelves before this." Caleb measured the upright, and then measured it again just to be sure before cutting.

"B-b-best to know the cellar was d-dry first." William bent over the board with the saw. He glanced up and grinned before making the cut. "S-sure this is right?"

"I'm sure." It was a joke between them, with William teasing Caleb a little, maybe, for his caution with measurement.

He watched William making the cut at a precise angle. He could trust William to do things right or admit he couldn't . . . a valuable trait in a woodworker. Or in any worker, for that matter.

This was going well, having William help him in the shop. Good for William, too, maybe, to be out from under his brother's wing a bit.

And with William, Caleb didn't have to talk. They worked together in companionable silence. Caleb was in a mood to appreciate that.

Not like with Katie. Her words challenged him to consider how he'd chosen to live his life. Her enthusiasm got him volunteering to do something he didn't enjoy. And seeing her hurt made him long to protect her. Worse, he'd come close to letting her see that.

William cleared his throat, and Caleb realized he'd been standing there staring at nothing. "R-ready to d-do the other one?"

"Ja, sure." Caleb bent to measure the second upright, annoyed with himself for letting thoughts of Katie distract him from the job at hand. Well, no more.

They worked without any but necessary words for the next hour, by which time the uprights and top were finished, and they were ready to start on the shelves.

Caleb stood back for a moment, looking at the unit to be sure everything was true. He bent, checking the angle once more.

William grinned. "M-m-must be important to g-get it r-right for K-Katie."

"I don't build anything that's not my best work." Caleb frowned at William. Was he that obvious? He hadn't figured anyone, least of all William, would be connecting his name with Katie's.

"S-sure thing," William said, his tone saying he thought the opposite.

It didn't help that Katie came down the stairs just then, carrying a jug of lemonade and a couple of glasses. "I thought you two might be ready for a drink about now." She set the things on the bottom step, along with a paper bag. "And here are fresh-made donuts, too."

"Denke." Caleb couldn't help but take a step closer to her, even though he knew William was watching and wondering. "We should have the shelves up before it's time for the girls to leave for the mall."

Becky had talked Rhoda into going to the mall this afternoon, insisting that she couldn't let what a couple of girls said make her hide. That, he thought, was pretty mature thinking for his little niece.

He'd arranged a ride for them himself, not wanting to make them depend on others. Ben was an old friend who often drove the Amish, and he'd see the girls safely there and back.

"That's fine, but it doesn't have to be finished today," Katie said. She glanced from him to William. "Denke. Let me know if you want anything." She went lightly back up the stairs.

He turned back to the work, knowing William was watching. Caleb wondered how long it would take him to bring it up.

"K-K-Katie's plenty n-nice."

Not long, it seemed. "Ja. She's a nice woman."

"You l-like her."

"We're friends, that's all." So much for thinking that with William, he didn't have to feel any pressure. "Nothing more."

"There c-c-could be." William, it seemed, was not easily discouraged.

"What are you—a matchmaker? Find a girl of your own, why don't you? There are plenty around." He bent to his work.

"They d-don't want s-s-somebody who t-talks like me."

"That's foolish," he said sharply, looking up at William. "There are plenty of girls who would like you if you gave them a chance."

"Isaac s-says—"

"Ach, don't bother with what Isaac says." Caleb clapped William's shoulder. "Isaac doesn't know everything. Just give the girls a chance. There is someone out there who is just right for you."

William flushed a little. "D-denke. B-but shouldn't you g-give yourself a chance, t-too?"

"That's different." Wasn't it? "What folks think I did is a lot worse than stammering. Nobody wants to see their daughter settle for me."

"K-Katie's different."

William might not say much, but he had a way of getting to the heart of the matter. "Ja," Caleb said slowly. "Katie is different."

With Katie, he didn't have to pretend. She'd known the truth because she'd really looked at him, not letting her view be colored by the past.

Maybe William had it right. If the past didn't matter to Katie, then it might be he could risk making a fresh start.

Or, at least, risk taking a first step.

CHAPTER THIRTEEN

Katie stood at the shop door, waving as Rhoda and Becky got into Ben's car. The geraniums she'd planted in pots on either side of the door seemed to smile up at her, lifting her heart with the beauty of the spring day. To her surprise, Caleb came and stood next to her.

"They are so excited that Ben will wish he had earmuffs on by the time he gets them to the mall," Caleb said, a slight chuckle in his voice.

"Rhoda has some money in her pocket, and it will be burning a hole until she finds something to spend it on."

Caleb's brown eyes twinkled as he turned to look at Katie instead of at the departing car. "I think I can guess. You paid Rhoda for her work this week, and maybe you didn't save out quite so much as your mamm and daad would have."

"True," Katie admitted. She'd felt a bit guilty, knowing perfectly well Daad would not have let Rhoda have so large a share of what she'd earned. "But how do you know that?"

He grinned, and his engaging look made him seem younger and gave her heart a little bump. "Because I did the same with Becky."

She couldn't help laughing. "Ach, you don't think we're spoiling them, do you?"

"If we are, that is what onkels and big sisters are for," Caleb said. "I'm not going to worry over it." He paused. "Although I do wonder what they will buy. Not something that will get us in trouble, I hope."

Get us, he'd said, as if they were a pair. "I can tell you that exactly. I was a sixteen-year-old girl myself, a long time ago."

"Not quite that long ago." Caleb's voice seemed to soften.

Her heart skipped a step, but she rallied quickly. It wouldn't do to let Caleb think he had an effect on her when his voice went low like that.

"Long ago," she said firmly. "But I'm sure some things haven't changed. They will look at a dozen different items at the cosmetics counter, and they will end by each buying a tube of pink lip gloss."

Caleb leaned his broad shoulders against the door frame, appearing ready to stand there all afternoon talking to her. "Whatever is pink lip gloss? I don't know."

"I should hope not," Katie said with mock severity. "It's pink sticky stuff that a girl smoothes on her lips to make them look pinker. They will do the same thing I did—hide them away and try the effect when no one is around to see." She couldn't help a chuckle, remembering. "Once Mamm and Daadi came home earlier than I expected, and I went running downstairs, forgetting I had it on."

"Did you get a scolding for that?"

She shook her head. "Mamm saw it first, and she motioned for me to wipe it off before Daadi turned. And she never said a word about it afterward, so I imagine she'd done the same herself once or twice."

She expected Caleb to laugh at that, but he seemed to be staring at her lips.

"I don't think you need any such thing to make you look any prettier."

Her heart gave a little thump. Caleb, paying her a compliment? For a moment she thought her hearing had misled her. Glancing at him, she thought by his expression that he had disconcerted himself.

"And, so what things do boys spend money on during rumspringa?" It took an effort to keep her voice steady. "I don't have brothers, so I don't know."

"Not lip gloss, for sure," he said. "Silly gadgets. I remember a plane that had an engine. I hid it in the barn and scared the horses when I tried to fly it. And then there was the rocket Andy and I went in on together." He shook his head ruefully. "That didn't work out so well."

"What happened?" Katie was enjoying this look into the person he'd been before Mattie hurt him so.

"Andy was sure he'd found the perfect place to set the rocket off, out in the field behind the barn. We decided to try it one Saturday when Mamm and Daad had gone to market."

"I take it something went wrong."

Caleb smiled, his expression rueful. "Andy was so sure he knew how the rocket worked, but he couldn't get it to go off. So he got mad and lit the fuse without stepping far away, and didn't the thing catch that time. Caught his pants on fire as well. I was so busy trying to get the fire out that neither of us even saw the rocket. We were just lucky it didn't hit the barn."

"Did your parents find out?"

"Ja, for sure. We never did succeed in putting anything over on them. Andy got the worst of it, because he was older and supposed to be responsible, but I had my share as well. We both ate our meals standing up for a few days."

Caleb was smiling, obviously enjoying the memory of the whole misadventure. Boys were different creatures, for sure.

"Andy will be watching those boys of his extra careful, ain't so?"

"Ja, and they're up to plenty already. He'll have his hands full."

Was there a trace of regret in Caleb's voice? Maybe grief that his brother had such a large family while he had none? But it wasn't too late for Caleb, if only he could move past his feelings about what had happened with Mattie.

He took a step back, seeming to shake off the memories. "Ach, I'm forgetting to tell you something. William and I finished the shelves. Maybe, since it's pretty quiet right now, we can get your things carried down and stowed away."

"Denke, Caleb. It was wonderful kind of you and William. But I can take things down myself. There's no need to put you to any more trouble." And she surely didn't need to spend any more time alone with him in the cellar, remembering that kiss.

"It's no trouble. And two can do it twice as fast." He turned toward the back of the shop. "Komm. We'll leave the cellar door open so we'll hear if anyone comes in the front."

Katie tagged along after him, giving in to the inevitable. She could hardly prevent him from picking up the plastic bins she had stacked in the back hallway.

And Caleb was right, of course. In a matter of minutes they'd taken all the bins down the stairs.

"This is a big improvement over the cardboard cartons," he said, hefting the largest of the bins.

"Ja, I certain-sure wasn't going to risk making the same mistake again." She turned the bins so that she could read the labels she'd put on them.

"Where do you want this one?" Caleb still held the largest of the bins.

"Ach, I'm sorry, letting you stand there and hold that. Let's put it on the middle shelf, where it doesn't have to be pulled down."

He slid it effortlessly into place and picked up another. "All neatly labeled, I see. You are an organized woman, Katie Miller."

"That's how I like things," she admitted. "If I see a shop where things are in a jumble, my fingers itch to straighten it out. Unless it's put that way on purpose, of course."

He paused in the process of sliding another bin into place. "Why would anyone do that?"

"My onkel Jacob has what he calls a junk shop. All kinds of little odds and ends of things that he picks up at sales. He says folks come to him because they think they're going to find a treasure, and looking for it is part of the fun. He'd never let me straighten up a thing, but he always knows exactly where everything is."

"He sounds like a smart man."

"Onkel Jacob says nobody bests a Dutchman in a deal. They

just think they do." She could hear his voice saying it, and a wave of missing the cantankerous old man went through her.

"You miss him," Caleb said, with an insight that unsettled her.

"Ja. We'll go back for a visit, maybe this fall, once the shop is better established."

Caleb put the last box into place and stood back, seeming to admire the neat arrangement. "That's important to you, having the shop go well, ain't so?"

"Ja." She hesitated, but she'd said so much to him that it hardly seemed to matter if she told him a little more. "Mamm didn't understand why I couldn't be content staying put and working in her shop, but Daad . . . well, if he didn't understand, at least he thought I should have my chance. He put up the money to get me started and signed the first year's lease on the shop. I have that long to be supporting myself."

Caleb studied her face, his gaze intent. "So that's why the Pennsylvania Dutch Days are important to you."

"Ja, for sure. If sales don't pick up soon . . ." She let that thought trail away. Caleb understood.

He reached out, taking her hand in his. His work-roughened fingers brushed the pulse that beat in her wrist. Did he know how crazily it was thumping?

"You're going to make it," he said, his voice deep and gentle. "I am certain-sure of that." His fingers caressed her wrist, and her skin seemed to warm where they touched.

He drew her a little closer, and her heart pounded. In a moment he would kiss her. It wasn't too late to step back, to avoid it. But she didn't want to.

The bell on the door upstairs rang, breaking whatever had been between them. She stepped back, drawing her hand free. "I'd best take care of the shop."

"Ja." But Caleb caught her hand again as she turned toward the steps. "One thing . . . will you go for a drive with me after church tomorrow?"

She shouldn't. That would be like an announcement that they were seeing each other. But she wanted to.

She let the impulse carry her. "Ja, Caleb. I would like that."

It had been a surprisingly good Saturday afternoon in the quilt shop. Katie straightened the quilt on the bed, disarranged by a woman who'd wanted to look at every single one and then gone away without buying a thing. She had, however, asked about the Pennsylvania Dutch Days next week, and Katie considered that a good sign.

Today's receipts didn't quite make up for the four hundred dollars she'd lost yesterday, but she was determined not to dwell on that.

When the door opened she turned, but it wasn't another customer. It was Melanie.

"Hi, Katie. I had to drop a deposit off at the bank so I thought I'd pop in and say hello."

"This is a nice surprise for sure. Do you have time for a cup of coffee? It won't take me a minute to run upstairs and get it."

Melanie glanced at the leather-strapped watch on her wrist. "Better not. Mike will be wondering why it's taking me so long."

Katie leaned against the counter, ready to enjoy a chat, no

matter how brief. "Stop by some other time when you can stay longer, then. My cousin Molly keeps me supplied with baked goodies, you know."

"Molly's sweet, always so cheerful and smiling," Melanie said. She fidgeted with the strap on her watch. "You know, I really just wanted to say . . . to apologize, I guess."

"Whatever for?" Melanie certainly hadn't done anything wrong.

"I guess Mike spoke out of turn at the meeting yesterday." Melanie's color deepened. "I'm sorry. Sometimes he just doesn't seem to understand that words . . . well, words can hurt people."

That almost sounded like personal experience speaking. "Ja, they can, but what Mike said isn't your fault. Anyway, nobody was offended. We're used to Englisch folks not understanding. I'm just glad you and Mike are participating in the sale."

"Yeah, well, anything to bring in business, Mike says. But I . . . well, especially after what Donna said on Thursday, I thought you might be feeling fed up with us English."

"Ach, no." Katie smiled at her. "Besides, I know all Englisch are not alike, any more than all Amish are."

"Donna can be nice, but she scares me a little," Melanie confessed. "You never know what she's going to say."

"She'll say what she thinks, that's for sure." A thought hit Katie. "Donna is like her quilt design—all straight lines. You know where you stand with her."

"But to ask you why you weren't married!" Melanie's eyes rounded. "Honestly, that was the end. I'd have told her so, except, like I said, she scares me."

"I wasn't offended. In a way . . ." Katie paused, feeling her way. "I think having her bring it out into the open was gut. It made me think about what happened in a different way."

"You must have been terribly hurt, to have the person you loved do that." Melanie's face filled with sympathy. "I'd think that would just be the worst thing in the world."

Katie considered. "I'd have said that once, but now . . . well, now I know that there are worse things all around us. What happened with Eli and Jessica is in the past, and I have to get over it."

"Yeah, but that's not so easy to do. I mean, you can't just tell yourself to get over someone." A spasm of pain crossed Melanie's face.

"Maybe not, but I can try. In fact, I think I'll write a note to Jessica." Now that she'd said it, Katie realized that thought had been lurking at the back of her mind since she'd read Mamm's letter. "I'll tell her how happy I am that they have a baby on the way."

"Do you really feel that way?" Melanie looked at her suspiciously.

"Not entirely," she admitted. "But I think writing the note will help me get there."

"You're a brave person." Melanie gripped her hand for an instant and then turned away. "I wish I were. I . . . I'd better get back."

"I'm not," Katie began, but Melanie hurried to the door, leaving her to wonder just what Melanie found so brave about her.

She'd said she would do it, so she'd better write the note now, before she changed her mind. She pulled a tablet and envelope from the box under the counter.

Don't think about it too much. Just write.

She grasped the pen. *Dear Jessica*—that was the easy part. *My mamm passed your news on to me. I just wanted to say that I am happy for you, and that I wish you well.*

It was just a few lines, but Katie felt as if she'd run a mile. Quickly she signed her name, folded the paper, and stuck it in the envelope.

Writing Jessica's married name cost a pang, but Katie forced herself through it, addressed the envelope, sealed it, and stamped it. Without pausing, she went quickly to the front door and put the letter in the mail box, shoving the flag up.

There. It was done, and she couldn't change her mind.

She lingered on the doorstep for a moment, enjoying the afternoon sunshine. The maples along the street were fully leafed out now, tracing shadows in the sunlight. A car came down the street, slowing as it approached the shop. That was Ben's car, surely. The girls were back earlier than she'd expected.

The car stopped. Rhoda got out, slammed the door, and rushed past her. Katie heard a muffled sob and then the pounding of her sister's feet as she ran upstairs.

Shaken, Katie glanced back at the car, but Ben was already pulling away from the curb. She hurried inside, hesitated a moment, and then shut and locked the door, flipping the sign to CLOSED. Whatever had brought Rhoda back in tears, she obviously needed Katie's attention.

Katie went up the stairs slowly, giving Rhoda time to realize she was coming. Time for her, too, to petition the Lord for wisdom and patience. Lots of patience.

Rhoda had run straight for her room. Katie followed, and found that her sister had flung herself on the bed and was weeping into the pillow.

Katie sat down next to her, patting Rhoda's shaking back. "Komm, now. It can't be that bad, can it? Sit up and tell me about the problem, and I will help you."

That brought on a fresh outburst of weeping. Even as she hurt for Rhoda, Katie couldn't quite control a spurt of exasperation. She surely hadn't been so dramatic when she was sixteen, had she? Still, it was a dramatic age, when joy seemed brighter than the sun and sorrows the end of the world.

"Rhoda," she said firmly. "Stop now. You can if you try. I cannot help you if I don't know what's wrong."

"Nobody can help me." Rhoda shoved herself up on her elbows and turned a streaming face to Katie. "Nobody. I wish I'd never come here. I wish I were dead."

"Schtoppe that now." Katie grasped her by the shoulders and pulled Rhoda up so that she sat on the bed. She gave her sister a little shake. "You must not say that. It is a sin. Control yourself."

Harsh words, maybe, but they seemed to work. Rhoda's sobs lessened. "I'm sorry. I didn't mean that."

"I should hope not. Now tell me." Katie handed Rhoda a tissue, then gave that another thought and plopped the whole box in her lap. "Now."

Rhoda sucked in a shaky breath. "We . . . We went to the mall. The other girls—they didn't want to talk to me, but I heard what they were saying. Awful things—that I'd stayed out all night with an Englisch boy, that my parents shipped me here because they were so ashamed."

"I'm so sorry." Gossip was a sin, but somehow it seemed more tolerated than most sins were. Those who gossiped could tell themselves they were only repeating what they'd heard.

Rhoda sniffled a little. "But I was okay, because I was with Becky."

"That's gut." So far there was nothing to account for tears, but apparently more was coming.

"We went to the food court, you know. And the boys talked to us. They didn't seem to care what anyone was saying."

"Ja." Katie wasn't so sure about that, but right now she needed the whole story. "And then what?"

Rhoda wiped her eyes with her fingers. "I went to the restroom, but Becky didn't go with me. So I was walking back by myself, and Tommy Esch . . . he . . . he was waiting at the corner and he grabbed me and kissed me, just like I was the kind of girl anyone could do that to. And Becky was there, and she saw, and now she hates me!" That brought on a fresh burst of tears.

Katie held her sister, patting her, trying to think this through. From the sound of things, it was the Esch boy who was at fault, not Rhoda, but things were not always what they seemed.

"Rhoda, listen to me. When Tommy kissed you, what did you do?"

"Well, I . . . At first I was just surprised. And then I pulled away and I smacked his ear for him." She looked indignant. "I know you'll say I shouldn't hit anyone, but he deserved it."

"Never mind that now." Actually, Katie found she was applauding the act. Apparently her pacifism didn't extend that far. "Sounds as if Tommy was behaving like a bad little boy, and if his parents had been there, they'd have done worse."

"Ja." Rhoda seemed to brighten for an instant, but then the tears started again. "But I don't think Becky saw me do that. She thinks I was trying to steal the boy she likes, and she'll never forgive me. I didn't mind so much what the other girls said. But I've lost Becky, and now I don't have anyone."

It all sounded so familiar. So sad, and so familiar.

"I don't know, either," Katie said. "But we'll figure it out, Rhoda. I promise."

Katie woke even earlier than usual on Sunday morning. Not that she'd had much sleep to speak of. Most of the night had been spent praying and worrying. She could only hope she'd done more praying than worrying.

But the answers she'd sought didn't come. She had no idea how to deal with this situation. Assuming Rhoda was telling the truth, and she was convinced that she was, that didn't mean anyone would believe it. Tommy had been born into this community, after all.

She couldn't fool herself. The way news flew around Pleasant Valley, no doubt half the church had already heard what had happened. And the rest would hear some garbled version at worship today. Katie cringed at the thought.

The first thing to do was check on Rhoda. Brushing her braid back over her shoulder, Katie went quickly across to her sister's door.

"Rhoda?" She opened the door. "It's time to get up."

Rhoda groaned and pulled the quilt up over her head. "I can't."

"Komm now." Katie sat on the edge of the bed and patted her sister. "It's not as bad as that. You'll feel better once you're up and dressed."

Rhoda pulled the quilt down to show a horrified face. "Katie, I can't go to worship today. I can't. I'll throw up if you make me. I know I will. Please."

Katie knew perfectly well what Daad would do. The same thing he'd done when news of Eli's dumping her came out. They'd gone to church just as usual, trying their best to show nothing at all on their faces. Those might have been the hardest three hours she'd ever been through, sitting there, knowing everyone knew . . .

Daadi was stronger than she was. She just couldn't do it to Rhoda, not when she knew from experience how it hurt. Maybe things were different for the Englisch, but for the Amish, one person's sin mattered to the whole church. And having the church family look down on you was about the worst thing that could happen to a person.

"All right. I'll make some oatmeal. Just try to sleep a little until it's ready."

Tears welled in Rhoda's eyes. She bit her lip, nodded, and closed her eyes.

Katie went back to the kitchen and started breakfast, trying not to think about anything else. She could only pray she was doing the right thing for her sister. Certainly Rhoda looked sick, with that pale face and red-rimmed eyes. Even her hair had lost its usual luster.

The oatmeal smelled good enough to waken her taste buds. She added brown sugar and milk to the tray, along with a wedge of walnut streusel coffee cake and a dish of sliced peaches, and carried it into Rhoda's room.

"I can't eat all that," Rhoda groaned. But she sat up and pushed the pillows into place behind her so that Katie could put the tray on her knees.

"Just eat what you can." She'd like to add that it would make her feel better, but she suspected this trouble was too big to be solved by a gut breakfast.

After they'd both eaten and dressed, she and Rhoda sat in the living room for devotions. She read the Psalm for the day slowly, praying that Rhoda would understand the psalmist crying out for God's help and be comforted.

The day dragged on. She couldn't help but think about what was happening in the service now. It should be easier when noontime passed, only then she could imagine people talking while they ate.

Talking about them, most likely. Well, it had to be faced.

Two o'clock. Caleb wouldn't come now for their prearranged buggy ride. She knew that. Whatever had begun between them was wiped out, completely erased.

When she heard the clip-clop of hooves and the creak of a buggy in the lane, her heart nearly stopped. He wouldn't—

She ran to the window. No, he hadn't. It was Molly and her family. Trying to swallow the lump in her throat, Katie hurried down the steps and reached the door as Molly did.

She opened the door, stepping out into the sunshine and into Molly's embrace, which was even warmer than the sunshine.

"We heard at church." Molly pressed her cheek against Katie's.

"It didn't happen like folks are saying," Katie said quickly. "It wasn't Rhoda's fault. Tommy just grabbed her and kissed her."

"Hush now, you don't have to defend her to us. We love

Rhoda, too. I don't doubt Tommy was put up to it by the other boys. Probably that Gordy Schultz. He's always one to start trouble and then sit back looking angelic." Molly appeared as angry as someone with her soft, dimpled face could.

"I didn't think about that, but it makes sense." A hint of relief eased Katie's tension. "It might make Rhoda feel better to think that it wasn't Tommy's idea."

"Tommy sat in church this morning looking as white and miserable as if he had a belly ache. Serves him right."

Katie found, to her surprise, that she could smile. "Forgive him, Molly."

"Have you?" Molly gave her a shrewd look.

"Well, not yet. But I will." She hugged Molly again. "Denke. You've made me feel better, knowing you understand."

Molly glanced at the stairs. "Will you and Rhoda come for supper? We'd like that."

"You are ser kind. But I think Rhoda is better to stay quietly at home today. I'll tell her what you said, for sure."

Molly nodded. "Give her a kiss for me, ja?"

Little Jacob gave the cry of a boppli waking from a nap, and Molly hurried off the porch and went quickly to the buggy.

Katie waved. She'd have gone back upstairs, but another buggy was turning in and drawing up at the barn. Bishop Mose climbed down and went to the head of his horse to fasten it to the hitching rail.

Her stomach sank. She'd expect a visit from someone after missing church, but not necessarily the bishop. And not so soon.

She waited, knowing she must speak to him first, before he saw Rhoda. He walked toward her steadily, looking like an Old

Testament prophet with his long white beard flowing to his chest. A kindly one, though, with gentleness in his eyes.

"Katie, I see that Molly already stopped to inquire about you. I hope you are well. We missed you at worship this morning."

"I'm well, denke. Rhoda is . . . She doesn't . . ." She decided to abandon that sentence. She put her hand on the sleeve of Bishop Mose's black cloth coat. "Will you listen to her story? Please?"

Bishop Mose patted her hand. "That is why I'm here, ja?"

Katie nodded, blinking back tears. "Denke," she whispered.

She led the way up the stairs. Rhoda bolted up from her chair at the sight of the bishop, her face paling. "Katie . . ." Her voice wobbled.

"Komm now, Rhoda," Bishop Mose said. "There is no reason to be upset at the sight of me. We will sit down here together, and you will tell me what happened. And we will see what must be done."

"You'll think I should go home, but—"

Bishop Mose pulled up a chair. "I have not heard your story yet." His tone was gently chiding.

"I'm sorry." Rhoda sank onto the seat, her eyes downcast.

"Now then," he said.

Rhoda nodded. Her voice choking a little, she told the story exactly as she had told it to Katie. As she reached the end, she glanced up at the bishop, coloring.

"Maybe Becky and I were playing up to the boys a little bit, just 'cause the other girls wouldn't talk to us. But nothing to make Tommy think he could do something like that." Her cheeks flamed. "And now Becky is hurt because of it, and that's not right."

"I'm glad your thought is for your friend," Bishop Mose said. "She was not at worship today, either. Thomas was there, looking as if he wished he wasn't. Who were the other boys?"

"Gordy Schultz, Adam Mast, and Joshua King." Rhoda had obviously expected a stern talking-to, and she eyed the bishop cautiously, as if wondering if it was still to come.

Katie bit her lip. Should she mention what Molly had said about the Schultz boy? No, she would not be a tale-bearer. Bishop Mose knew his flock well. If what Molly said was right, he would know that.

Bishop Mose held out his hand, gesturing Katie closer. "We must pray that we see God's will in this situation, and ask for His guidance and comfort. And you will then go about your daily work, continuing to pray that, ja?"

"Ja, denke," Katie said, and Rhoda nodded.

Afterward, Katie walked back down the steps with the bishop, trying to find words to express her feelings.

"Stop worrying so, Katie." He smiled at her. "You are doing all that can be done. Now you must be calm and trust. Just trust."

He went out. She closed the door and leaned her forehead against the glass for a moment. *Please,* she prayed. *Please.*

CHAPTER FOURTEEN

Caleb leaned against the side of the cow he was milking, finding the creature oddly comforting. He'd volunteered to do the milking, deciding he had to get away from the tension in the house for a bit, at least.

Nancy was angry, of course. Someone had hurt one of her young, and she didn't forgive that easily. She would subside for a while, but then she'd spurt up again. She'd taken to calling Katie and Rhoda "those Miller girls."

She'd even tried to get Mamm to say she wouldn't go to the quilting. But Mamm, who usually didn't disagree with Nancy, had been unexpectedly firm. It was foolish for grown-ups to get involved in their kinders' quarrels.

Nancy hadn't liked that. Caleb felt sure that Andy was going to get an earful once he and Nancy were in the privacy of their room tonight.

Ja, Caleb had been glad to escape to the barn. It was not so easy to escape from his guilt, though. He'd known Rhoda's reputation from the beginning, and he'd let Becky get close to her.

He'd like to believe that wasn't because of Katie, but just the thought of her was like a knife in his side. She'd have been expecting him this afternoon, and he hadn't come. Well, no, after what happened, she probably hadn't expected him, but that didn't make him feel any better. He ought to have sent word, somehow, that he wasn't coming.

Someone slipped into the barn through the open door, silent as a shadow. Becky. She put on a milking apron, got her stool and a bucket, and went to the next cow.

"I thought I would help you, Onkel Caleb."

"That is gut." He tried to find something helpful to say, but nothing came.

"Milking is comfortable, I think," he said finally. "Sabbath or not, the cows must be milked."

Becky's hands began to work. Small, capable hands. The beasts liked her better than any of the boys, to tell the truth. She was gentle and sure. And quiet.

"This is nice," she said. "You are right. It is comfortable." She hesitated. "It's not comfortable in the house when Mamm is upset."

"No, I guess not." His hands worked in rhythm with hers. "She is only angry because she loves you."

"I know. But . . . I don't like to hear her say things about Rhoda."

"You don't blame Rhoda for what happened?" He tried to keep his voice even.

"Well . . . ja." Becky's words were muffled, as if she were leaning her head against the cow's side. "But she's so much fun, laughing and talking all the time. I guess I understand why Tommy would like her better than me."

"Don't say that. You are sweet and kind, and that is more important."

A little sob broke the stillness, tearing at his heart. "I never had a friend like her before."

"I know." He got up, walked around the cow, and bent to press his cheek against Becky's head. "I know, little girl. It hurts when a friend lets you down."

Not just hurts. It tears you apart, so that you can never be whole again.

No. That wasn't going to happen to Becky. She wasn't going to be like him. This was one of the sorrows that a person could get over. She would cry a little, grow a little, and get over it.

Not like him. His idea that he could forget the past and start to live life again seemed foolish now. He couldn't, and it was just as well he'd realized that.

Katie came downstairs slowly on Monday morning, reluctant to face the day. Still, for Rhoda's sake she had insisted that they act no different from usual. One day was enough to hide away and grieve over what had happened. Besides, Bishop Mose had been encouraging, hadn't he?

She stepped down the last step into the shop, frowning a little. It must be a darker morning out than she'd thought. The shop seemed filled with shadows. She turned toward the front and froze.

Her mind seemed hardly able to accept what her eyes were seeing. Something obscured the plate glass window that displayed her quilts.

Dread pooling in her stomach, Katie forced herself to walk closer, to see what was there. Paint. Someone had splashed red paint over the outside surface of the large plate glass windows. No words, just big, ugly splotches of paint.

She took one shaky breath, then another, her stomach twisting rebelliously. She had to—she didn't know what she had to do. Her mind was oddly blank.

Footsteps on the stairs told her Rhoda was coming. She whirled, hands going out, as if she could somehow protect Rhoda from the sight.

But that was foolish. She couldn't keep her sister from seeing this, or from jumping to the conclusion that it was, in some way, payback for what had happened on Saturday.

"Rhoda—" She tried to find some word to prepare her, but Rhoda was too quick for her.

She saw, and her face crumpled. "This is my fault." She hovered on the edge of tears. "This happened because of me."

"We don't know that." Katie had to stay calm. She had to model for her little sister the behavior she expected from her.

"It's true," Rhoda cried.

"Hush," she said. "Vandalism happens, and we both know how often it's directed at the Amish. We may not be the only shop the vandals hit."

"Caleb's windows weren't touched." Rhoda pointed out the obvious. Sunlight streamed through the clean windows of Caleb's shop.

"That doesn't mean anything." Katie didn't convince herself, but somehow she had to convince Rhoda. "And even if it is because of someone blaming you, that doesn't mean that you should blame yourself. That would just be doing what they want."

"But it's not right, somebody hurting you because they are mad at me." Rhoda's eyes shimmered with tears, but she seemed determined not to let them spill over, which was good. "What will we do?"

"We will do the right thing, even if someone else chose wrong. We'll get some buckets and sponges and clean up. We'll forgive, and we'll move on." She touched her sister's arm in reassurance. "Komm. Let's fetch what we'll need."

Rhoda pressed her lips together. Then she gave a decisive nod and headed for the utility closet where the cleaning supplies were stored.

Denke, Lord. Help me to help Rhoda. And help me to forgive.

In a few minutes they were stepping out onto the sidewalk. Already people were stopping to gawk, staring or quickly averting their eyes when they saw them.

Katie pasted a smile on her face and picked up a dripping sponge, sure that her face was red with a bad combination of anger and embarrassment. This was not going to be easy—either the cleaning up or being the focus of everyone's interest.

A few minutes of work showed her just how hard the cleaning part would be. Only the wettest of the paint came off with water. Most of it was securely dried on. It would take a lot of soap and water and scraping to get the window clean, if it could be done at all.

Caleb undoubtedly had turpentine, but she couldn't bring herself to go and ask. Besides, he was there in the shop—she could see him moving about in the back. If he could ignore this, he was even angrier than she'd thought.

"Ms. Miller, this is terrible!" Cliff Wainwright hurried over to her, his glasses pushed on top of his head, making his gray hair stand on end. "I can't believe someone would do this to your shop."

"I know." She couldn't either, but the evidence was running up her arm. She wiped away the rivulet of red before it could reach her sleeve. "It is such a mess." Somehow it eased the tightness in her chest to talk to one person, at least, who shared her feelings.

"Vandals. I don't know what the world is coming to." Cliff began rolling up his sleeves. "Do you have another sponge?"

For a moment she was too startled to speak. "Ach, I can't take you away from your shop to help me."

"Nonsense." He reached a hand out for the sponge. "You would do the same for me, I'm sure."

She swallowed the lump in her throat and handed him the sponge.

Moments later, Bishop Mose came striding down the sidewalk, his white beard ruffling so that it looked as agitated as his expression.

"Katie, what a thing to happen. I came as soon as I heard. Others will be here to help, but I see that Cliff has beaten all of us."

Mr. Wainwright saluted him with a dripping sponge, apparently on good terms with the bishop. "I'm closer, so I got here faster."

"I will catch up with you soon." Bishop Mose leaned over to

study the paint. "We need some more scrapers, ain't so? Caleb will have some. I'll get him."

But before Katie could speak, before the bishop could move, the shop door opened. Caleb came out, holding a pail of soapy water and several scrapers.

"These scrapers will work better on the dried stuff," he said.

Katie wasn't sure who he was talking to—not her, since he didn't look at her. Perhaps she was being unfair to think he hadn't come out until the bishop's presence made it impossible not to.

"Gut, gut, chust what we need." Bishop Mose grabbed a scraper and set to work, red flecks flying.

"Bishop Mose, you don't need to do that." Katie felt whatever control she'd had over the situation slipping from her grasp. "I should . . ."

The bishop made a clucking sound, reproving her. "I set an example for my people of what they should do. And you show your humility by letting others help you, ain't so?"

She could hardly argue with the bishop. "Ja," she murmured. "That is so." She glanced at Rhoda. To her relief, the girl seemed to be getting over her shock quickly. She worked amicably enough, it seemed, next to Mr. Wainwright.

"I brought some extra buckets." Lisa Macklin hurried up the walk, buckets clanging in her hands. "Just show me where to fill them."

Humility, Katie reminded herself. Gelassenheit. It would not be showing that most Amish of qualities to argue with each person who wanted to help. "This way."

By the time Katie and Lisa came back out, the buckets filled with soapy water, several more people had arrived to work, and Paula Schatz was setting up a coffee urn and trays of donuts.

"Paula will have everyone in town out here when they smell her donuts," Cliff Wainwright joked.

"And so they should be," Paula retorted. "Mennonite, Amish, or Englisch, something like this hurts all of us." She leaned closer to Bishop Mose, lowering her voice. "Chief Walker is coming. He was having his morning coffee when we heard."

Katie was sure her dismay showed on her face. Bad enough that everyone in town knew . . . she didn't want to be involved with the law. And judging by the stiffness of his back, Caleb Brand had found a new reason to disapprove of her.

"It is all right." Bishop Mose seemed to understand her thoughts. "The chief is bound to ask questions about such vandalism. Just give him honest answers. No one can blame you for what someone else has done."

Before she could digest that, Chief Walker arrived. She'd seen him around town, of course, but had never spoken to him. To her eyes the stocky man in a uniform had the same lines of wisdom and authority in his face as Bishop Mose. And the two of them greeted each other as equals.

"Nasty thing to happen, Ms. Miller." Chief Walker shook his head. "There's been a rash of vandalism this spring, but none right in town before this. Kids, most likely, but that doesn't mean they can get away with breaking the law."

Discovering she had nothing to say to his words, Katie waited, hands clasped, trying for calm.

"You and your sister live over the shop, I understand." The chief nodded toward the second floor. "Any chance you heard anything?"

She shook her head. "I did not." She glanced at her sister. "Rhoda?"

"I didn't hear anything, either." Rhoda came to stand next to her. "Our bedrooms are at the back."

The chief nodded. "Natural enough. You were probably sound asleep, and they'd be careful not to make too much noise." He glanced from one to another of her neighbors. "Anybody else hear anything or notice anything odd last night?"

Silence for a moment. "Probably the same kids who painted bad words on John Mast's barn," Paula volunteered. "That was red paint, too."

"Bad words." Cliff snorted a bit. "So illiterate they couldn't spell anything with more than four letters."

"They're getting brave, bringing their antics right into town. That'll just make it easier to catch up with them." Chief Walker brought his gaze back to Katie's face. "But we don't want to jump to conclusions. Can you think of anyone who had reason to pull a trick like this on you, Ms. Miller?"

Just say the truth, the bishop had reminded her. "No. I can't."

"Well, don't worry about it too much." Chief Walker became suddenly more human with his smile. "Between us, Bishop Mose and I have a pretty good idea of who's behind any trouble like this that comes up. I'm the first to admit that if it's Amish kids, he can deal with them better than I can."

"Ja, that's so," Bishop Mose said.

"And if it's English . . . well, I'll catch up with them, and they'll be doing worse than scraping off paint for their punishment, believe me." Chief Walker strolled off, stopping to speak to a few other people as he went.

Katie looked at Bishop Mose. "I don't want to cause trouble for anyone."

"Ach, I know that fine. But Chief Walker was right. If they are Amish, I will find out." He patted her hand. "It would be worse for them to get away with their wrongdoing, you see. Komm, we have cleaning up to finish. Soon the shop will look as gut as new, ain't so?"

She nodded, trying not to feel that it would take her a long time to forget, even when the paint was gone. She must try to look at this vandalism in a different way, although that seemed impossible right now.

Caleb was here helping, cleaning paint from the windowpane with even strokes of the scraper. Whatever else he felt about her and Rhoda right now, he was being a good neighbor.

And the rest of these people, some of whom she hardly knew by name—they were good neighbors, too. Amish, Englisch, Mennonite, they were her community. Whatever happened, she belonged here.

Caleb came out of his bedroom door at the grossdaadi haus just as his mamm emerged from hers. He bent to kiss her. "Ready for breakfast?"

She nodded, patting his cheek. "I will tell you a secret." She leaned a little closer, smiling. "Sometimes I would like to have breakfast all by myself in my own little kitchen."

"If that is what you want, why don't you?"

He touched her elbow as they went down the steps, not sure she needed it, but concerned. She'd seemed so fragile this past year.

But she went down easily, with none of the hesitation that sometimes worried him.

"Men," she said scornfully. "You never see what's right in front of your noses. I can't do that, because it would certain-sure hurt Nancy's feelings."

He turned that over in his mind. "Men don't notice things like that because we would never think in that way. We would just say what we want."

"And then wonder why someone was frosty to you," Mamm said. "Ach, it's nothing. Komm, we don't want to keep them waiting."

He followed, puzzling over her words. He had never considered how Mamm felt about the way things were. He had taken it for granted that she enjoyed having Nancy assume all the chores that used to be hers.

Well, it was certain-sure he didn't understand women. One particular woman, to be exact.

Katie had behaved bravely in the face of yesterday's trouble. She was a strong woman who would deal with what came her way. As for him . . . he'd been torn between wanting to blame Katie herself for all the problems that had risen since she'd arrived and wanting to put his arms around her and protect her from any storm.

He couldn't. Not with Becky wandering around the house like a forlorn ghost, reminding him that he might have been able to prevent her pain if he'd kept her away from Rhoda to begin with.

He entered the kitchen, where Nancy was marshalling her family around the table, the wooden spoon she used to stir the oatmeal in her hand.

"Komm, Becky, wake up," she said, her tone a bit sharp. "Can't you see your daad is ready for his coffee? Onkel Caleb, too, most likely."

Becky, pale and drooping, filled coffee cups, and they sat down to the silent prayer that began the meal.

Like any morning, the boys squabbled among themselves over who had the most brown sugar on his oatmeal and Nancy dispensed justice with a firm hand. Andy ate quickly, talking to Caleb about whether the fine weather would hold long enough to get the rest of the first hay cutting in. Naomi ate quietly, not seeming to pay attention to what was going on, and Becky did the same, eyes downcast.

"So, Caleb," Nancy said once she had her family sorted, "we never did hear from you about what happened at that Miller woman's shop yesterday. Ann Schultz told me that someone told her that the windows were broken and red paint splashed all over the quilts for sale."

"Ann Schultz doesn't know what she's talking about if she told you that. No windows were broken, just some paint splashed on the glass." He couldn't help it if he sounded annoyed, what with Nancy seeming to wish the affair had been worse than it was.

"Well, whatever happened, all I can say is that it was probably well deserved if the truth were known."

Everyone at the table stared at Nancy. But before any of the adults could react, Becky was on her feet, cheeks flaming. "That is a terrible thing to say. How could you? Katie Miller has been as nice as can be to me. She doesn't deserve anything bad, and I wish I had been there to help her."

Caleb had been surprised by the ill will that Nancy had shown, but he was downright astonished at Becky for standing up to her mamm that way. She had never been so lippy in her life, and Nancy stared at her daughter, apparently speechless, her face flushed.

"Enough." Andy's voice was even, but Caleb knew the sound of his brother pushed to the end of his rope. "Becky, you will apologize to your mamm for speaking that way to her."

Becky, tears spilling over, sniffled. "I'm sorry, Mammi."

"And Nancy, I am ashamed of you, to speak the way you did about a sister. You should be on your knees asking forgiveness for such unkindness."

Nancy, cheeks flaming, sank back into her chair. The boys stared into their cereal bowls. Caleb and Naomi glanced at each other and turned wordlessly to their breakfasts. Andy seldom spoke that way to his family, but when he did, there was no doubt that they listened.

It was an awkward meal. Caleb was glad to escape as quickly as possible. He headed out to the barn.

Most of the time he liked living in the house where he'd been born, with family all around him. But once in a while he almost envied Katie her snug little apartment with only her sister for company.

He had begun harnessing the gelding when he realized his mother had followed him to the barn. "Mamm?" He looked at her questioningly. "Is something wrong?"

"I just wanted to be sure you're helping Katie with the repairs."

"I helped with the cleanup yesterday, for sure. Lots of folks did." Now, what exactly was in Mamm's mind?

"Ja, I know. But does everything look just like new? That will be important to her, not just getting it cleaned up. As long as there is any sign of what happened, she will be reminded."

Mamm again had more insight than he did. "I will check and see. If the frame needs to be repaired or repainted, I will do that."

"Gut." She patted his shoulder, smiling a little. "I did not enjoy that fuss at the breakfast table, but I was glad to see Becky standing up for Katie."

"Our Becky is growing up," he said, not sure what his mother was driving at.

"Ja. And I think she is feeling a bit guilty for judging her friend without giving her a chance to defend herself. You should not do that either, ain't so?"

"I try not to," he said, stung. "But ever since Katie moved in next to me, things have changed."

Mamm nodded, agreeing. "Changed, ja. And the biggest change is in you."

"I don't know what you mean." But he could never fool his mamm. She always saw through him.

"You have changed. The ice that Mattie put around your heart has been melting, and I think that Katie is responsible. Don't let it freeze up again."

She turned and walked back toward the house, leaving him standing there, speechless.

CHAPTER FIFTEEN

*K*atie realized she was hurrying as she came down the street to her shop from Lisa's, and she deliberately slowed her pace. Amish women didn't race about like city dwellers, even when, as today, they had much to do.

She and Lisa had been meeting about the Pennsylvania Dutch Days event, which seemed to Katie to be growing out of all resemblance to the simple sales promotion it had once been. Everyone wanted to get involved in the project now that it was up and going, and the enthusiasm threatened to overwhelm Katie.

Lisa, on the other hand, seemed to thrive on it. She was a born organizer, and her big green loose-leaf notebook, which contained details of every part of the project, was becoming famous in Pleasant Valley.

"Look in the green book," Katie had heard one of the Plain merchants say this morning, "and see who is selling funnel cakes."

Or if it wasn't funnel cakes, it was a question about what size tables could be on the sidewalk, and whether the fire company auxiliary could sell barbecue, or any of the hundreds of such answers listed within the bright green covers.

The Englisch seemed to bring their questions straight to Lisa, but Amish were more likely to use Katie as an intermediary. Like it or not, she seemed to have become, in some people's view at least, one of the organizers.

And if the event flopped? What would they think of her then? That was the question that kept her up at night.

Katie scurried the last few steps to her door, her gaze inevitably drawn to the window. The glass had been polished to a shine, but the dark green paint around the frame had suffered.

Averting her eyes, she went inside, smiling at Rhoda. "Any business while I was out?"

"Five women came in for fabric," Rhoda reported. "I think the Dutch Days has everyone making something to sell. And two more had questions for you about it, but they said they'd be back. I wrote their names on the pad."

"Gut." Rhoda was turning into quite the businesswoman. "I have the women for the beginners' quilting class coming later for their first meeting, so would you mind taking posters around to the Main Street shops for me?"

Rhoda sent a glance toward the window. For a second she looked upset at the thought, but then she gave a determined nod. "Ja, I'll take them."

Katie handed over a stack of the posters she'd picked up at Lisa's. "Lisa says to give everyone as many as they can use."

Nodding, Rhoda headed for the door. If she hesitated again at the window, Katie couldn't tell.

Rhoda had barely disappeared from view when the bell jingled again. The Amish woman who entered was vaguely familiar from church and from the Pennsylvania Dutch Days meeting, but Katie couldn't recall her name.

"Wilkom," she said. "Can I help you with anything?"

The woman sent a quick, sidelong glance toward Caleb's shop as she approached the counter. "Ja, I . . . I am chust wondering where to set up a table for my hooked rugs. For the sale, I mean."

Katie pulled out the sketch map of the street that showed where each stand would be. She spread it out between them on the counter. The woman seemed nervous. Maybe she hadn't done anything like this before now.

"There are lots of places available." Katie tapped the paper. "Here is room for another table near Caleb's shop next door. Or over here by Bishop Mose's harness shop."

"I . . . I had best take the one by Bishop Mose." The woman gripped the edge of the counter with work-worn hands.

Katie poised her pencil over the square to mark it. "I'm sorry, but I don't remember your name."

"It's Ruth. Ruth Weaver."

It was a wonder Katie's pencil point didn't break. This was Mattie Weaver's mother, then. Of course she wouldn't want a space in front of Caleb's store. Katie wrote the name on the square by the harness shop. "There. You're all set." She smiled, hoping her face didn't betray her feelings.

"Denke." Ruth Weaver turned, as if she meant to leave as quickly as she'd come, but then she hesitated. "You have a nice shop. I'll come back to look at material another day."

"Anytime," Katie said. "I hope the sale goes well for you."

Ruth nodded, but her gaze was fixed on the archway between the shops, and Katie could make nothing of her expression. It seemed to cover some deep feeling, but it wasn't anything as simple as anger.

Before Katie could find anything else to say, Ruth hurried out.

Katie let out a long breath. What had the woman been thinking as she stared so long at Caleb's shop? Well, whatever it was, there was nothing Katie could do about it. She'd best get working on having everything ready for the new quilters.

It had been a surprise when several women had stopped by the shop and asked when Katie would start a beginners' class. In each case, the woman was an Englisch person who'd heard about the quilting group from Lisa or Melanie or Donna. That original group was bearing fruit already.

Katie had decided that five was the most she could manage with women who had no idea how to quilt. They would make a simple pattern . . . a bars design on a place mat. Fast to do if they were apt learners, and then, once they'd learned the basics, they could make a whole set of place mats.

She began setting up materials in the back room. In addition to what the learners would need, she laid out several examples of quilt patterns and her own quilt in progress. That Lancaster Rose quilt had been suffering from neglect lately, she'd been so busy.

And there was the sound of someone in the shop—maybe another of their volunteers with a question. Before she could reach the door, Caleb was there, seeming to fill the opening.

She hadn't talked to him since Saturday except under Bishop Mose's eyes when they were cleaning up yesterday.

"Do you have a moment?"

"Of course." She arranged her face in what she hoped was a natural smile. Had he heard the voice of the woman who had once been his intended mother-in-law? Katie certainly wouldn't speak of it unless he did.

He came in, making the small room seem even smaller. "My maam asked about you. She wanted me to say that if you need anything, just tell us."

"Denke." Her tension eased. "That is ser kind of her. But you already helped yesterday. There is nothing else to do."

"I noticed the paint around the window looks a little dull and scratched." He moved closer, absently fingering the fabric pieces she'd laid out. "I see that the paint can is still in the basement. I'll take care of touching it up for you."

"That's not necessary. I can easily do it myself." She glanced at his face and wished she hadn't, because his eyebrows had lifted, and his lips tilted in the slightest smile.

"What was it Bishop Mose said yesterday? Some teaching about humility in accepting help, was it?"

"I think you know full well it was," she retorted. "But you ..."

She couldn't very well say that she didn't want him doing favors for her after standing her up for their buggy ride on Sunday, could she?

"How is Becky?" she said instead. Maybe that subject would remind him.

"Better today. She is actually showing a little spirit."

"Using it to vent her anger with Rhoda?"

"No, using it to defend you."

"What?" Katie could only stare at him. "Why?"

Caleb's gaze slid away from hers. "I'm afraid Nancy was being outspoken about the vandalism. Andy talked to her pretty sharp about that unkindness. But not before our Becky had her own say about how gut you have been to her."

Katie wasn't sure whether to respond to Nancy's ill will or Becky's defense. In the end she did neither. "Is that what most folks are thinking—that the vandalism is because Tommy Esch kissed Rhoda?"

Caleb's forehead furrowed. "I don't know about most folks. Nancy jumped to that conclusion. What does Bishop Mose say?"

"He . . . He seems to have some ideas." Confiding in Caleb might not be the best thing.

"Katie?" The gravity in his tone brought her gaze to Caleb's face again. He leaned toward her, hand planted on the table. "Will you tell me what Rhoda says happened at the mall?"

She hesitated. Hadn't she just reminded herself that confiding in him could be a mistake? But he was looking at her with such honest concern that her misgivings slipped away.

"Rhoda says that she and Becky were at the food court, and the other girls were ignoring them. So when the boys came to her and Becky, they played up to them a bit. You don't need to tell me that Rhoda was the leader in that, because I'm sure she was."

"She's more outgoing than Becky is," he said, his tone neutral.

"Ja, well, Rhoda went to the restroom, and when she was coming back, Tommy grabbed her and kissed her. Apparently Becky saw that. Maybe she didn't see Rhoda box his ears for him."

"No," he said slowly, "she didn't. And I guess she didn't let her friend explain, either."

"No." Katie looked at him steadily. *Any more than you did, Caleb.*

"I hope Rhoda gave him a gut hard clout." Caleb's reaction was unexpected.

"Ja, I expect she did. Molly thinks . . ."

"What?" He was sharp.

"That maybe the other boys dared him to do it."

He nodded slowly. "That seems most likely. Tommy isn't the kind of boy who'd think of a mean jest on . . ." He let that trail off, because the shop door bell had rung.

Katie hurried out, very conscious of Caleb right behind her.

An Amish boy stood looking around the shop. Katie tried to place him, but couldn't.

"Joseph?" Caleb strode toward him. "Katie, this is Joseph Auten. What brings you here, Joseph? Thinking of taking up quilting?"

The boy grinned. "Bishop sent me with notes. One for Katie Miller and one for you."

Caleb held out his hand. "Hand them over then, and get on back to work."

The boy gave each of them a piece of folded yellow tablet paper. "Bishop said not to dally." He scooted to the door and was gone in a moment.

Katie frowned at the paper. At both pieces of paper. Why was Bishop Mose writing to each of them? She flipped the paper open. It was the shortest of notes, asking her and Rhoda to come to his house that evening at seven.

She showed it to Caleb. "Is yours the same?"

He scanned it. "Ja, except that it asks me to bring Becky. If I were guessing, I would say that Bishop Mose has found out something."

"But what?" Katie's mind scampered from the vandalism to Rhoda's behavior and back again.

Caleb shrugged. "I guess we'll find that out at seven tonight." He turned away, and then back again. "About Sunday," he said abruptly. "I'm sorry. It was wrong of me not to let you know I wasn't coming. . . ."

"I understood," she said quickly, not wanting to let him guess at how his failure to send a note had hurt.

But she suspected he knew anyway. He looked for a moment as if he'd say something more, but then he turned and walked off.

Katie and Rhoda left home in plenty of time to walk to Bishop Mose's house on the edge of the village that evening. Fortunately Rhoda hadn't given her an argument about wearing her bonnet. It was one thing to dash over to a neighboring shop on a summer day wearing only the kapp over her hair, but a summons to the bishop's place called for a bonnet.

"What do you think he wants, Katie?" Rhoda asked the question for perhaps the tenth time.

"I don't know the answer to that now any more than I did every other time you asked me, ain't so? Since he wants both Caleb and Becky to be there, as well, I can only guess it has to do with what happened at the mall."

Rhoda's heart-shaped face was pinched. "It's going to be so embarrassing," she moaned. "Can't we just forget about it?"

"We must trust the bishop to know what is right."

"But I don't want to blame anybody or get anyone else in trouble. Even Tommy. I just want to be friends with Becky again."

The words squeezed Katie's heart. "I know."

She'd been making an effort to speak lightly with her young sister, but Katie couldn't rid herself of an edge of worry. She had confidence in Bishop Mose's ability to discern the truth, but what if he felt Rhoda's behavior deserved censure? How would she deal with that?

They were nearing the edge of the village, where the mix of shops and houses turned to just homes, most English but a few Amish. Children ran around outside in the long sunshine of early June. Roses were blooming with abandon, as if to celebrate the warmth and light, and people were out mulching flower beds and mowing the grass.

A group of boys played basketball in a driveway while a couple of small Amish girls tried to master roller skates under the watchful eyes of a slightly older sister. Beyond the houses farmland stretched in a carpet of pale green to the wooded hillsides that enclosed Pleasant Valley.

A peaceful scene . . . It was small wonder that those first settlers who'd crossed the Susquehanna to establish homes here had named it Pleasant Valley.

Pleasant, ja. But envy and malice existed everywhere, even in these peaceful surroundings. Gossiping tongues caused heartache here as in every place where people tried to live together. And someone had slipped through the night to vandalize other people's property.

Only God is truly good, Katie reminded herself. The rest

of us borrow what goodness we can from Him, always praying that we're doing what He has for us to do.

Bishop Mose's small, unpretentious house was in sight now. He had lived there alone, she knew, since the death of his wife, but the rest of the community would have made sure that he was well taken care of.

A low fence surrounded the yard, and a climbing rose bloomed on an arbor over the gate. Katie pushed it open. If only Daadi were here . . .

But he wasn't, and this situation was her responsibility. She had changed in the short time she'd lived here in Pleasant Valley. Grown, maybe. She could only hope she'd grown enough to deal with whatever was about to happen.

Several buggies were parked in the lane behind the house. Her heart gave a little jump. If the ministers and deacon were here, too, that was a sure sign that action would be taken against someone.

Please. Her heart murmured an incoherent prayer.

Rhoda slipped her hand into hers. Katie squeezed it. Together they walked to the door.

Bishop Mose must have seen them coming, because he opened the door before she could knock.

"Komm in, komm in." His smile was as welcoming as always. "Komm and have a seat. We are all here now, I think."

She and Rhoda followed him from the tiny hall into the living room, furnished with a bench, two rocking chairs, and a table under the window on which lay a Bible, in High German, no doubt.

Katie's gaze skipped quickly across the people who sat, ill at ease it seemed, waiting for them. Becky, her parents, and

Caleb sat close together on straight chairs. Tommy Esch, bony hands dangling between his knees, sat a short distance away between his father and mother. One of the congregation's ministers stood behind them.

Katie and Rhoda took the two remaining seats, avoiding the big chair by the table, which was clearly Bishop Mose's.

Katie glanced toward the Brand family from under her lashes. She'd have given a lot to see Naomi's kind face with them, but she wasn't there. What were they thinking? Caleb caught her gaze, and his firm lips relaxed in a slight, reassuring smile.

Why something so simple should make her feel better, she didn't know, but it did.

Bishop Mose turned his chair to face the rest of them and sat down. "Now then." He planted his hands on his knees. "Let us get on with this."

Katie took Rhoda's hand again. A quick glance at her sister's face told her that Rhoda was suffering an agony of embarrassment at having her troubles discussed by the adults.

"I would not ordinarily find it necessary to talk to parents about a disagreement among sixteen-year-olds." The bishop's first words seemed to echo Katie's thoughts. "But in this case, the disagreement may have led to an action that has brought in the police . . . a serious bit of mischief directed against a sister who has done nothing wrong."

He paused, shifting his position a little in the heavy wooden chair. No one else moved, perhaps even breathed.

"I discussed the situation with Brother Joseph, and we feel this is the proper step to take."

The minister nodded solemnly.

"I will begin by saying that I have talked with Rhoda Miller about the incident that occurred before she came to this community. I am satisfied, as was her home bishop, that while she may have acted foolishly, her behavior was nothing more than what might be expected of any of our young people embarking on their rumspringa years."

A wave of relief moved through Katie, and she felt as if Rhoda experienced the same. Bishop Mose had checked on what had happened back home, and he was satisfied, as he said. Word of that would get around, maybe, and folks would feel more lenient toward Rhoda.

Bishop Mose silently looked from one person to another. "Of far greater concern to me is the sin of gossip, which seems to have flared like a fire in our community. The tongue truly is an unruly member, and those who embark on speaking ill of a sister are in need of confession and repentance."

Rhoda's lips moved, but Katie could not hear the words. Maybe she didn't need to. She could sense Rhoda's fear ebbing. She didn't dare look toward Nancy, after what Caleb had revealed about her.

"Now, for the current situation. It is my understanding that at the mall on Saturday, Thomas Esch kissed Rhoda Miller in a public place. According to Rhoda, that kiss was unwelcome." He fixed an intimidating stare on the boy. "Well, Thomas?"

Thomas stopped staring at the toes of his shoes and looked up. His blue eyes swam with tears.

"I'm sorry," he said, his voice breaking. "I am so sorry. I shouldn't have. I know that."

"You will tell us exactly what happened." Bishop Mose's tone was like the voice of God cracking from the heavens.

"We . . . we . . . Some of us guys were talking to Becky and

Rhoda. The other girls were acting silly, and gossiping about Rhoda. Then . . . Then Rhoda left the table, and Becky went to the counter to get a soda. I didn't think of kissing her," he said hurriedly, glancing from his father's forbidding face to that of the bishop. "One of the guys dared me. He said Rhoda would like it. But she didn't. She smacked me a gut one."

A growling rumble from his father suggested there might be worse to come for the unfortunate Thomas. Katie tried to feel sorry for him, but she couldn't forget all the hurt he'd caused.

"That was what you deserved, ain't so?" Bishop Mose was uncompromising.

"Ja," the boy muttered miserably. "I was wrong. I ask God's forgiveness."

"And that of Rhoda and Becky, who were hurt by your foolishness," Bishop Mose said.

"Ja." Tommy cast a quick glance at the two girls and then studied his shoes again. "I am sorry, Becky. I am sorry, Rhoda."

Becky nodded. She was blinking back tears as she looked at Rhoda, but Rhoda's face was turned away.

Forgive, Katie said silently. *Forgive, little sister, or it will grieve you forever. I know that too well.*

"Now." Bishop Mose wasn't finished. "Who was the one who dared you, Thomas?"

Tommy hesitated, and Katie could practically feel the universal adolescent code battle with his reverence for his bishop.

"Speak." Tommy's father grabbed his shoulder and shook him. "Answer the bishop."

"It was Gordy Schultz," Tommy muttered, his face flaming. "But I should not have listened."

"No, you should not. I'm glad you realize that. But there is more." Bishop Mose paused, and the air in the room seemed to spark with tension. "What do you know about the vandalism to Sister Katie's shop?"

Tommy looked up, mouth dropping open, eyes wide. "Nothing. Nothing. Honest. I would never do anything like that."

Bishop Mose leaned forward, hands on his knees, looking more than ever like some Old Testament prophet confronting Israel with its sins. "This is more serious than a prank, Thomas Esch. The police are involved. A sister has been injured. If you know anything, have any idea who did this thing, you must speak now."

"I don't, I don't." Tears spurted from Tommy's eyes. "Really, I don't have any idea."

Bishop Mose stared at him for a moment longer. Then he nodded. "I believe you."

Katie found that she believed him, too. But if the damage to her shop hadn't been caused by someone angry over Rhoda, then by who, and why? Who had reason to do such a thing to her? She couldn't see an answer.

Bishop Mose stood. "We will pray now for forgiveness and understanding."

Every head bowed. In the silence, Katie asked for forgiveness for any thoughtless anger or resentment she might hold, trying to release it all, knowing that only in forgiving could she find forgiveness.

The bishop raised his head, and the prayer ended. Becky jumped up from her chair and then stopped, waiting for a sign from Rhoda. The moment seemed to last forever.

Then Rhoda choked back a sob and darted toward Becky. In

an instant the two girls were in each other's arms, crying and laughing together.

The young ones could cry and hug and come back to their friendship again easily. It was a bit harder for the grown-ups. Katie had to listen to uncomfortable apologies from Thomas's parents and even more uncomfortable ones from Becky's parents.

Bishop Mose turned from consulting with the minister. "Brother Joseph and I will call on the others who are involved. I trust that all this will be quickly forgotten." He smiled at the two girls. "Forgiveness is only real when it lets the past slip away. We each of us, every day, do something in word or thought for which we should be asking forgiveness."

The two girls nodded soberly, and Katie thought that he didn't need to worry about them, at least not at the moment.

But the bishop's words took painful root in her heart. How often had she given lip service to forgiveness while holding on to the pain?

Caleb stopped in front of her as his family moved toward the door. "Forgive me, Katie Miller?" His eyes were serious.

"It's already done," she said, knowing it was true. "I will see you tomorrow, ja?"

"Tomorrow," he said, and there seemed to be a promise in the word.

Chapter Sixteen

Caleb took a step back on the sidewalk, looking at the work he and William had done on Katie's window frames this morning. Good work, though he shouldn't think it. Still, surely there was nothing prideful about being pleased with the help he'd given his neighbor.

Neighbor. And something more? After last night, he had the sense he and Katie had passed a milestone of some sort. Bishop Mose had taken care of his flock as he usually did. The innocent had been cleared, the wrongdoer identified and hopefully brought to a properly penitent frame of mind. No Englisch judge could have done better.

There was still the matter of who had committed an act of vandalism against Katie. Had it been directed against her personally? That wondered Caleb the most, and he'd guess Bishop Mose felt the same.

Well, he couldn't stand here admiring his handiwork. He'd

barely seen Katie today. She'd been rushing around taking care of last-minute details about Pennsylvania Dutch Days.

He was just as glad he'd finished up his part in the project. He'd dutifully contacted the rest of the Amish merchants in town, and most were eager to participate, though maybe a bit doubtful about how many customers they could actually expect.

Katie was back now; he'd seen her go in. He didn't need an excuse, did he, to go have a word with her?

He stepped inside to find that Rhoda and Becky, who were supposed to be watching the shops, had found a compromise. They sat in the archway, heads together, chattering away sixteen to the dozen. Caleb couldn't help smiling at the sight.

"Rhoda, is Katie around?"

"Ja, she just got back." Rhoda gestured with a handful of envelopes. "She took her lunch out on the back porch since it's so nice today. If you're going out, would you take the mail to her?"

"For sure." He took the envelopes, smiling at her. "You two are watching the shops now, aren't you?"

"We won't ignore a customer, Onkel Caleb." Becky took his joking comment seriously. "We think everyone is too busy getting ready for Pennsylvania Dutch Days to shop much today."

"I'm sure you're right," he agreed, tickled with her air of being a serious businesswoman. "I'll give these to Katie."

Waving the letters, he walked back through the shop to the rear door. And discovered that his heart was beating a bit fast at just the prospect of seeing Katie.

Careful, his cautious side warned. *Don't jump into anything. You don't know how she feels.*

But when he stepped outside and Katie looked up and smiled, it seemed to him that he did know.

"Having a busy morning?" she asked. "You did a wonderful-gut job on the front window frames. No one would ever know they'd been damaged."

"That's the aim of the work."

He pulled a chair over next to her. She had a sandwich and a glass of milk on the small table, but they looked untouched. She must have been poring over the notebook she held, which was probably all about the sale days.

"You should be eating, not working," he pointed out.

"I'm trying to do both." She shook her head. "Who would imagine there were so many details involved in something like this? And I didn't get much done on it yesterday."

"But you did get one big problem cleared up. I'm wonderful glad to see those two girls talking and giggling together again."

"And here I thought you were always trying to get away from females chattering and giggling." Katie had a teasing glint in her eyes.

"Ach, well, I'm finding I've gotten used to it, what with my neighbor having groups of women in practically every day. Having only two girls talking makes this a quiet day."

"Don't count your chickens," Katie said, smiling. "The quilting group is meeting this afternoon instead of tomorrow, because tomorrow everyone will be getting ready for the sales."

"I might have known it," he said with mock dismay.

Katie's expression sobered. What was she thinking? Surely she didn't think he was serious.

"Last night," she said, "I was sorry for Tommy in the end, despite the trouble he caused."

"I think it's safe to say his father will make sure he doesn't take any foolish dares in the future. Tommy is not a mean boy. Just heedless of consequences, as so many of us are at that age."

"I suppose." Katie still looked concerned. "Do you think he was telling the truth about what happened to the shop?" She tilted her head as if gesturing toward the front windows.

"I think so," Caleb said slowly. "I think he was too appalled by the trouble he'd caused to think of lying at that point."

"Ja, that's what I thought, too. But if it didn't have anything to do with Rhoda, then . . ." She looked at him, eyes troubled. "Then why my shop?"

"It may have been random." He wasn't sure he believed that himself, but he didn't want her to feel as if she had a target painted on her. "Our section of the street is fairly dark. Maybe they were taking advantage of that."

Her eyebrows lifted. "They were careful not to get any paint on your windows, ain't so?"

It was no use trying to protect a woman like Katie from something unpleasant. She'd always rather know the truth. Still, he hesitated.

"Komm, Caleb," she said. "You are thinking of another answer. I can see it in your face. Just tell me."

He leaned toward her, elbows on his knees. They were very close, knees almost touching. It seemed to him that he could feel the warmth that came from her.

"Most of the merchants are pleased about Pennsylvania Dutch Days," he said slowly. "But not everyone in town feels that way."

Her expressive face told him she'd already considered that answer. "I didn't want to think it was because of our plans. No one has said anything to me directly, but . . . well, there's been a feeling."

"Ja." He gave in to the urge to put his hand over hers. "Some think the attention may bring trouble along with the increased business, but it's hard to imagine they'd do the very thing they're afraid of. And there are some who feel it's all for nothing and will fail."

Katie seemed to shiver. "That's what keeps me awake at night. What if we've gone to all this trouble and no one comes?"

His fingers tightened over hers almost without his intending it. "You can't think that way. Most of Pleasant Valley is buzzing, and not just the village, but the rest of the valley as well. William says that Rachel Zook is bringing plenty of plants from her greenhouse."

"Ja." Katie brightened. "She'll set up a table next to the quilt shop. But if people don't show up to buy . . ."

"Well, then we'll know that doesn't work. No one will blame you." He hoped that was true.

"I'm not so sure." Her hand seemed to clench in his. "I'm new here, ain't so? I want to belong. But if this doesn't work, that might not be possible. And if it does, but a lot of people don't like it or think it causes trouble, the answer is the same."

"Katie, stop. You already fit in. You have lots of friends." *And something more in me.* But Caleb couldn't quite bring himself to say the words. "All the women from the quilting groups, and the people you've met through the Dutch Days, and . . ."

And him? How could he let himself get serious about Katie? She'd tried to assure him that people no longer blamed him for what had happened with Mattie, but he couldn't quite accept that. And what had been wrong with him, that he could have been engaged to marry Mattie and not have even suspected that there was someone else in her life?

Whether Katie believed it or not, he still bore the taint of what had happened. He couldn't expect someone else to join him under his cloud, could he?

He sensed Katie drawing back even before she pulled her hand free.

"I'm sure you're right." Katie's voice was brittle, and he felt as if he had failed a test. "I'll try not to be so foolish. You just caught me in a weak moment."

"Not you." He tried to smile, tried to regain the easy, teasing spirit between them, and knew he couldn't.

"What is this?" She nodded toward the envelopes he'd dropped on the table.

"Sorry, I'm forgetting. The mail. Rhoda asked me to bring it out."

Katie picked up the envelopes, maybe glad of something to distract her from Caleb. She leafed through them quickly and then stopped, staring. She put the others down, caressing one envelope.

"What is it?" He couldn't help asking the question, even though it was none of his business.

"I had sent a note to my friend Jessica," she said, her voice slowing. "I thought it was time—past time—that I showed her I am over what happened between us. Here is her answer."

"Aren't you going to open it?" Or maybe she was waiting to be alone. "I should leave anyway—"

"No, stay," she said quickly. She looked a little embarrassed. "I wouldn't mind having some moral support right now."

"Courage," he said, gripping her shoulder briefly. "It will be all right. Like Rhoda and Becky."

Katie smiled a little at the reminder. She ripped open the envelope. Its contents dropped onto the table, and she stared. He did, as well. The woman had sent Katie's note back, unopened.

"I'm sorry," he began, taking a step closer, longing to comfort her and not knowing how. "She didn't mean it. I'm sure she regrets it already."

"I don't think so." Katie picked up the envelope, her fingers shaking a little. "She doesn't forgive me. I left it too late, and now Jessica can't forgive me."

"Katie—" His heart overflowed with pity and concern for her. "You can't . . ."

She shook her head, holding up her hand as if to silence him. "Don't, Caleb."

She rose, seeming a little unsteady for a moment. Then she turned and fled inside, leaving her lunch lying on the table. And leaving him with nothing to do about the pain he felt in his heart.

Katie had put the envelope out of sight in a drawer, but she couldn't put it out of her mind. *Forgiveness.* The word kept echoing in her heart as she replayed everything she'd heard Bishop Mose say about it.

She'd recognized that she was doing wrong. She'd tried to change. But Jessica had thrown her effort right back in her face. Katie felt as if she'd been slapped.

She automatically set up the room for the quilting group. She knew the church's teaching on forgiveness was right. But what did you do when your forgiveness wasn't accepted?

It was a relief when the quilters began to arrive. She couldn't think of herself when she was busy with them.

In just a few meetings, they'd settled into a routine—some working on the machines while others pinned and cut, stopping to help each other almost before she noticed that help was needed.

Donna came in right on time, but with a discontented expression on her face. She held up her forefinger, looking at Katie accusingly. "I have paint on my hand from your new window frames."

"I'm so sorry." Katie hurried to get her paper towels. "I'm sure it will wipe right off. If not, I'll get some paint thinner." But she couldn't help reflecting that it looked as if Donna had touched the paint to see if it was dry.

"That's funny," Lisa said innocently, glancing up from her work. "I was sure there was a Wet Paint sign out there."

For a moment the two adversaries glared at each other. Katie held her breath. How could this group become what she wanted if these two were always fratching?

Suddenly Donna threw back her head with a hearty laugh. "All right, you got me," she said, shaking her head. "I'm the person who can never resist testing a Wet Paint sign for myself."

The others chuckled, perhaps with relief.

"Ach, I do that as well," Emma admitted. "Some of us are just made that way."

Donna had barely settled to her work when Melanie came rushing in, a bit late as always. Surely the hardware store couldn't always become busy just when she had to leave, could it?

"I'm sorry," Melanie said, her cheeks bright pink. "Don't let me interrupt you."

"It's fine," Molly assured her. "We are just getting started. You are all flushed, Melanie. Are you all right?"

"I'm ... I'm fine," she said, her color deepening still more. "I didn't want to be late so I ran, that's all."

Wanting to draw attention away from Melanie, Katie began demonstrating the technique of chain sewing, a shortcut most experienced quilters used when working on the machine. She'd taken to demonstrating a different technique each week, hoping that would keep things interesting, even though it was old stuff for the experienced quilters.

Soon everyone was deep into her work and just as deep into conversation. Katie loved hearing that—it was the sound of a quilting circle that was melding the women so that they were becoming friends even as they worked.

And then she realized that Donna's voice had risen. "I'm sure you mean well," she said to Lisa, "but the last thing we need in Pleasant Valley is a lot of outsiders. Tourists. We live here because we like it the way it is. Of course, you are a relative newcomer."

And what did that make her? Katie wondered. Lisa had been here for several years.

"That's rather shortsighted," Lisa said tartly. "There are plenty of people in town who are struggling to keep their businesses open. If they all have to close down for lack of business, what will Pleasant Valley be like then?"

Donna flushed dangerously. "I know a little more about this community than you do. Things will even out. They always do. In the meantime—"

"In the meantime, people are hurting," Lisa snapped.

Katie had to intervene before the argument escalated, but how? Before she could think of an answer, Melanie did it for her. Across the combatants' voices, she spoke to Molly.

"I love that pattern you're doing, Molly. What is it?"

Molly jumped in right away, holding up her work almost in Donna's face. "This is a Log Cabin, an old, old design. There are as many variations of it as there are quilters, ain't so, Naomi?"

"Ach, ja," Naomi said. "It means something different to everyone, I think. That's the way it is with the old patterns."

Melanie looked intrigued. "How can a quilt pattern mean something different?"

Molly smiled, touching her fabric. "I picked this pattern because my husband had to work away for so long. Now that he is settled in a gut job here, this quilt will remind me how happy I am that we have a home."

"Ja," Naomi said softly. "It was hard on you, on any married couple, to be separated that way. It's not how things are meant to be."

Melanie leaned forward, her expression serious. "You Amish get married awfully young, don't you?"

"Not always," Molly said. "But often we are ready by the time we're twenty or twenty-one."

"That means you're going to be together for a long time. I mean, I know you don't believe in divorce."

"Marriage is forever," Emma said. "When you have troubles, you just have to work them out." Her eyes twinkled. "My husband was the most stubborn man in the world, and there were times I didn't speak to him for days. But we always made up."

"*He* was stubborn?" Naomi looked fondly at her friend. "You are every bit as stubborn as he was, that's certain-sure."

"Well, maybe so. He put up with a lot, all those years I was catching babies." Emma seemed to glance into the past and smile at what she saw there.

"You must know your heart," Naomi added. "That's what I told my children. Know this is the person for you, because you are married forever."

"Ja," Myra said softly. "You want to marry someone who is a gut friend, like my Joseph. That's important."

Melanie stared at her, a mix of emotions on her face. Katie realized that the Crazy Quilt pattern was crumpled in her hands.

"Melanie? Is something wrong?"

Melanie wiped tears from her cheeks. She smoothed out the fabric. "I just . . . Maybe I have prewedding jitters." Her smile was a little wobbly. "Everybody says that's natural."

To Katie's surprise, it was Donna who came and put her arm around Melanie's shoulders. "I'm sure it is. But if you have doubts, there's nothing wrong with waiting."

"That's right." Lisa put her hand over Melanie's. "There's no need to rush into anything."

"I shouldn't have said that." Melanie seemed to realize just how much she'd confided in them. Her cheeks flushed. "Really, everything is okay. Please, forget what I said."

She looked so distressed that Katie hurried to reassure her. "We won't say anything. It's all right."

Murmurs of agreement came from the others.

"Lots of secrets are shared at a quilting frolic," Naomi said, her voice gentle. "That's as it should be. When we work together, we share our thoughts, but everyone in the group will keep them private."

Melanie's smile trembled just a little. "Good. Because really, everything's fine."

Was it? Katie hoped so. Despite her hopes for the group, she hadn't anticipated that the quilting circle would lead to that sort of sharing, especially from an Englisch person.

But Naomi was right . . . women became close over a quilt, and maybe it didn't matter whether they were Englisch or Amish.

Everyone on Pleasant Valley's main street was busy, it seemed to Katie, getting ready for Pennsylvania Dutch Days. The volunteer fire company even had its ladder truck out, hanging a banner welcoming visitors. Lisa had procured the banner, Katie wasn't sure how, but it certainly did seem to make the project official.

Across the street and down a bit, Katie could see Melanie setting up tables in front of the hardware store. She watched the girl for a moment. Her bright green shirt and blue jeans were her usual cheerful attire, but she hadn't been so cheerful yesterday.

Katie's broom paused as she thought of that conversation. Melanie had brought up the subject of marriage a couple of times, almost as if she needed to talk about it. Was Melanie's upset just prewedding jitters? That could happen to any bride, surely, no matter how happy she was.

Or was Melanie's emotional display a sign of something more serious? Judging by Lisa's and Donna's reactions, they thought it possible.

Well, she couldn't offer any advice. She certain-sure wasn't an expert on the subject of engagements.

Melanie turned, saw her, and waved, smiling. Katie waved back, relieved at the smile. Whatever had caused Melanie's mood yesterday seemed to have cleared up today.

One less thing to worry about. As for Caleb's drawing away each time she got too close and Jessica's rejection of her peace offering . . . well, she could do nothing about either of those, it seemed, no matter how much they hurt her heart.

She finished sweeping the sidewalk where she intended to place folding tables and paused again, looking down the street with a smile. Even those who had doubts about the success of the project were making an effort. As for those who were outright opposed . . . well, here came Donna now, probably intending to give her another lecture on the subject.

"Looks as if you're getting ready, Katie. Like everyone else in town." Donna glanced down Main Street with an expression of distaste.

Katie's heart sank. "Ja, I'm doing what can be done today." She tried to sound positive. "Much of getting ready will have to wait for morning."

Donna nodded. Frowning a little, she looked at the folding tables that leaned against the building. "I just wanted to tell you something about tomorrow."

Here it comes. Katie braced herself.

"If we do get a crowd of people tomorrow, or more likely on Saturday, I'll be around most of the time. If you get rushed, you may need an extra person here to help."

Katie was so surprised that it was a moment before she could speak. "Denke, Donna. That is ser kind of you."

Donna waved that away. "I wouldn't want to see anyone ripping you off when you were busy. You know, taking something without paying while you were tending to another customer. That's the danger of an open-air sale like this."

"I don't . . ." Katie paused. There was no point in getting into an argument about people coming to the sale to steal. It did happen. Or cheat, like the woman who'd cheated Rhoda. Still, Katie didn't ever want to reach the point where she'd expect that sort of behavior. "I don't know how to thank you," she said. "Your help would be very wilkom."

Donna gave a short nod. "Least I can do," she said gruffly, and walked off.

"What did she want?" Lisa, who seemed to be here, there, and everywhere today, came up to Katie as soon as Donna had gotten a little distance down the street. "To give you another forecast of doom and gloom?"

"She came to offer her help, anticipating that there might be vandals around. I'm ashamed to say that I feared another lecture, too."

Lisa looked suitably surprised. "I guess we both shouldn't jump to conclusions about Donna. I suspect you've had a good effect on her. And on me."

Katie shook her head, disclaiming any influence. "I know that people do bad things. But how sad it must be to always expect the worst of others."

"You have a point there. It's no way to live." Lisa smiled, gaze straying to the clipboard she carried. "I just stopped to see if you need anything for tomorrow."

"We are fine, I think. Rhoda is inside organizing the things we'll put out in the morning. Otherwise, we're all set."

"Good, good." Lisa checked something off the list she carried. "I'd better keep on going if I'm going to finish on time. I'll see you later."

Katie nodded, watching Lisa stride off briskly. The woman certainly seemed to thrive on busyness. Was she, maybe, trying to fill the hole left in her life after her husband's death?

Carrying the broom, Katie went inside, to be pounced on by both the girls. "Komm, schnell." Rhoda tugged her hand. "We want to show you what we've done."

"Ja, komm," Becky echoed, her eyes dancing.

"Are you sure I want to see?" Katie said, teasing. "What are you up to?"

"Look." Rhoda propelled her to the archway between the shops.

The entire area was filled with quilt racks, maybe a dozen of them, their wood polished to a gleam, all hung with table runners and baby quilts.

"Isn't it great?" Becky was practically bouncing with excitement. "I brought down all the quilt racks that Cousin William has finished and polished them."

"And once they were dry, we sorted out the quilted items to hang on them," Rhoda said. "And everything is clearly marked, so there won't be any mistakes," she added. "So, do you like it?"

"I love it," Katie said. "But maybe Caleb doesn't want—"

"What doesn't Caleb want?" Caleb asked, surfacing from behind the back counter.

Katie's breath caught, and she felt her heart beating somewhere in her throat at the sight of him. "I just . . . I just wanted to be sure you approved of this."

"Ja, Becky and Rhoda asked me before they did anything. They wanted it to be a surprise for you."

"It's a wonderful-gut surprise," Katie said warmly, smiling at the girls. "Denke. We'll put them out first thing in the morning, and I'm sure they'll attract buyers."

"That's what we thought," Becky said. She glanced out the window and squealed. "Rhoda, look, there's Rachel, and she's brought the baby. And Myra, with little Anna Grace. Let's go help them."

The two of them rushed outside, and Katie waved through the window at Rachel and Myra. Surrendering babies to the two girls, they set about unloading tables off the wagon.

"I should go and help them." But Katie didn't move. Somehow she couldn't, not when Caleb was standing so close, looking at her with such affection in his eyes.

"It seems they've brought their husbands to help." Caleb's hand closed around her wrist. "You can spare a little time for yourself, you know. You've been rushing around for days, getting ready for the sale. Have you taken care of everything you need?"

She gave a breathless chuckle. "Seems like those two girls have done that. I do have to get a few more small items down. They're gut to draw people in and get them looking at the more expensive quilts."

"Ja, teacher, I remember that from your lecture. We are doing a display of bookends and such-like outside just for that reason." Caleb seemed so relaxed today, smiling down at her, that she couldn't help but smile back.

Once again her breath caught. Once again their gazes met. But this time Caleb didn't flee. This time he looked deep into her eyes. And then he bent and kissed her, heedless of anyone who might be looking in the shop window.

And she was even more shameless, because her arms went around him as if it were the most natural thing ever, and the world slipped away until she didn't care if all of Pleasant Valley stood outside the window looking at them.

Finally Caleb drew back. To her dismay, she saw the caring in his gaze replaced with that familiar denial.

"I shouldn't. I'm sorry." He turned away.

"No," she said, before she lost her courage. She caught him by the arms so firmly that he couldn't pull away without hurting her, and she knew he wouldn't do that. "Stop, Caleb. This is ridiculous. We are both of age, and if we want to kiss . . ." She knew she was blushing, and she didn't care. ". . . well, then, it's nobody's business but ours."

He shook his head, his eyes darkening. "I'm not free."

"You're not married," she snapped back. This was about Mattie, of course.

He shook his head, misery in his face. "Katie, you don't know what it's like, everyone looking at me and knowing. Or thinking they know, which is just as bad. I can't pull you into that."

"Caleb, that's not true." She took a breath, trying to find the words for what she wanted to say. "I don't know if we are meant to be together, but I would like the chance to find out."

She only realized when she said the words how true they were. She had loved Eli, but losing him didn't mean she could never love anyone else. She was ready now for a real new life, and it was being here and getting to know Caleb that had made her so.

"You don't understand," he said again, and she wanted to shake him.

"Stop it," she said, astonished by the tartness of her voice. "You are a smart man. You must know, surely, in your heart, that no one condemns you." Tears stung her eyes, but she wouldn't let them fall. "But I think it's true that you can't move forward. Not until you know why it is that you condemn yourself."

Before the tears could fall she turned and walked quickly away from him.

CHAPTER SEVENTEEN

*B*y noon on Friday, Katie knew the Pennsylvania Dutch Days had met their hopes and expectations. Through the shop windows, she could see people wandering up and down Main Street . . . so many that Chief Walker had made a hasty decision to close off two blocks to cars and buggies.

The vendors adapted quickly, with many of the stands moving onto the street to provide space on the sidewalks. It was wonderful, seeing so many people working together to make this event happen so quickly.

Katie brought her attention back to the customer she was trying to help. "Now here is the Log Cabin Star pattern in blue, yellow, and white." She turned back a quilt to expose the next one.

"Oh, it's beautiful."

Katie would be more encouraged by the words if the woman hadn't said the same thing about every quilt she'd looked at so far.

"Ja, it is," Katie agreed. "I made this one myself, with a little help from my mother and sisters on the quilting. It's one of my favorite patterns. If you look very closely, you may be able to see a few differences in the quilting stitches, since they are all put in by hand."

"Hal!" The woman called to her husband, who stood at the window looking out at the food stands. "Come and see this one. I think it's the one."

"You thought that about at least six of them." The man smiled good-naturedly at Katie and dutifully admired the quilt. "Hurry it up, sweetheart. I want to get something to eat."

Katie's stomach growled in sympathy. She hadn't eaten anything in hours. She didn't mind letting Rhoda or Donna or Molly handle other sales, but she preferred to show the quilts herself.

Besides, it kept her mind occupied enough that she didn't obsess about Caleb. The moment she told herself that, she knew it wasn't true. Caleb was always there, lurking at the back of her mind, so that it seemed he was taking up residence there.

"Let me look at that one with the shades of brown and yellow in it again," the customer said. "What did you call that design?"

"Sunshine and Shadows." Katie dutifully flipped back to the quilt made by Caleb's mother. "This was made by an older lady, a widow, in our community. She's a very skillful quilter."

"Lovely," the woman crooned, stroking the pattern.

Naomi would be pleased if her quilt sold. She probably wouldn't be pleased to know what Katie had said to her son.

Or would she? Surely Naomi wanted Caleb to come back to life again.

Still, Katie shouldn't have said what she did. It had been hurtful, and even if Caleb needed to hear it, he certain sure didn't need to hear it from her. They didn't have the kind of relationship that would allow her to speak so. Two kisses didn't make a close relationship.

But she and Caleb weren't seventeen-year-olds, trying out falling in love and choosing a mate. They were older; they'd both experienced tragedies in love. Anything that happened between them had to be more serious.

"I just can't decide," the woman moaned.

"Sweetheart, lunch," her husband pleaded. "Maybe we could go eat and then come back. That might help you make up your mind."

And it might make her walk away without buying anything. Katie tried to resign herself. That was all part of running a quilt shop.

"I know what I'll do." The customer's face lit up. "I'll get both of them. One for our bedroom and one for the guest room. They'll be perfect. You don't mind, do you, Hal?"

Katie held her breath. Two quilts? Surely not.

"Anything that will get me to lunch." He grinned at Katie again, getting out his wallet. "They are both real pretty."

In a few minutes the transaction was done, and Katie still felt a bit dazed as she watched the couple walk out the door with the wrapped quilts. Two quilts in one sale. That in itself was enough to make this day worthwhile.

Donna, who'd been helping another customer, hurried over to her. "I thought that silly woman would never make up her mind. Go get some lunch before you fall down. No arguing, now."

If Donna helped out in the store much, Katie suspected the woman would soon forget whose store it was. Still, Katie did feel as if her belly was bumping her backbone.

"Ja, denke. I will. I won't be long. Shall I bring you something?"

"I'll pop out for a minute when you get back." Donna shooed her to the door.

Katie stepped outside into warm sunshine and a jostling, cheerful crowd. The mixed scents of funnel cakes, barbecue, sticky buns, corn chowder, and who knew what else assailed her. Every group in town, from the Volunteer Fire Company to the Methodist Ladies Circle to the PTA from the public school, had gotten in on the project. Like volunteer groups everywhere, they were old hands at raising money. Each group had its specialty, and none of them infringed on anyone else's.

"Katie, this is a wonderful-gut turnout, ain't so?" Rachel leaned over the counter of her stand, beaming. "It's so much fun to do this right here instead of traveling to a Mud Sale. We'll probably have even more folks tomorrow, it being Saturday."

"Ja, I hope so." Katie was about to ask Rachel how her sales were going when several women who'd been picking among Rachel's herb plants came up with their selections, and Rachel turned to them.

Tempting as it was to stop and visit, Katie had better get her lunch and return to work. She slipped through the crowd and stopped at the Catholic Women's Guild stand. Everyone said their sausage and pepper sandwiches were the best.

Moments later, holding a paper plate with an overstuffed roll in one hand and a can of soda in the other, Katie began navigating her way back to the store, taking care lest she drop sausage and peppers on someone's clothing.

And then she saw him. Caleb, moving straight toward her. Her breath caught in her throat. He was looking down, frowning, and he hadn't seen her yet. She waited until he was within a few feet of her. They couldn't talk, not in this public place, but she could say two words. *I'm sorry.* He would know why.

"Caleb."

He stopped dead, staring at her.

"I—"

His face was closed, as if a door had been slammed shut on everything he thought and felt. "I must go." He turned and elbowed his way through the crowd, moving so fast she couldn't possibly follow.

And even if she could, what good would it do? Caleb was in there, someplace, but she would never be able to reach him.

Saturday was the busiest day his shop had ever seen, and as far as Caleb was concerned, that was fine for several reasons. He was pleased about the sales, of course, and it did his heart good to see Becky darting from customer to customer, forgetting her shyness in her role.

Most important, though, was that the busyness could keep him from thinking about Katie. Or at least, if not that, from glancing at her and listening for the sound of her voice. He'd come to work the outside tables for that very reason.

"Ja, those are traditional Pennsylvania Dutch designs." He handed the set of bookends to a customer. Smaller things were most popular, that was certain. Things folks could fit into their trunks and bring home easily.

"I'll take these. And the pair with the birds on them, as well. I'll put them away for Christmas gifts."

He started to reach for them, but Becky beat him to it.

"I will be happy to ring this up for you," she said.

Caleb nodded his thanks as Becky took over the customer. She understood that waiting on people was not his favorite thing to do. Now, if he were upstairs in his workshop . . .

Running away from people, Katie's voice said accusingly in his mind. *That's what you do.*

Well, maybe so. But that was his business, wasn't it? Katie didn't understand.

From the corner of his eye he caught the movement of Katie's shop door and a flash of blue dress. She was coming out to the sidewalk, maybe to take over from her friend Donna, who'd been handling customers at the outside tables for the last hour or two.

He headed for the door, raising his hand to Becky. "I'm going upstairs for something. Will you take over out here?"

"Ja, for sure. Do you think I could run and get some lunch soon?"

"In a bit," he said shortly, and escaped inside.

William, showing a cabinet to a customer, gave him a questioning look as he hurried to the stairs and started up. Why was everyone looking at him that way? His irritation edged upward, accompanied by a growing sense of guilt.

Becky didn't deserve a short response from him, and William was doing his best to deal with customers despite his stammer. Neither of them was to blame for the fact that he felt raw and exposed every time Katie looked at him.

They'd already carried down most of the furniture from the workroom, but there were a few more carved wooden items that might be put out for sale. He began filling a box with pairs of bookends and some wooden toys he'd experimented with. He'd begun to think tourists would buy almost anything as a souvenir of their trip.

Footsteps on the stairs had him turning around. It was William, running a hand through his shock of yellow hair.

"Andy and your m-mamm came in to h-help. I'm g-glad to g-get away."

"Gut." Caleb was ashamed of himself, hiding away up here when it was so difficult for William to be talking to strangers. "Sorry I rushed off. I wanted to take a few more things down." He gestured with the box.

"N-no problem." The tension eased out of William's voice now that they were alone. "Things are really g-going gut, ja?" He leaned against a half-finished jelly cabinet.

"Guess so."

"That K-Katie, she d-deserves the credit, ain't so?"

Caleb's fingers tightened on a duck decoy, and he forced them to relax. "Ja." The last thing he wanted was to talk about Katie. He picked up the box. "I'll go down and price these. Why don't you take a break for a while?" He went back downstairs before William could reply.

If he'd expected a moment's respite, he hadn't gotten it. Everything about this day only served to remind him of Katie. Of Katie's words. Of the expression on her face when he'd pulled away from her.

He set the box down on the counter and began methodically putting stickers on the items. Andy was dealing with a customer, and he could see Mamm out on the sidewalk, helping Becky. No one to talk to him right now, to sing Katie's praises.

That wasn't fair. Katie had worked hard and done a fine job. It was his fault that—

"Caleb." The soft voice was the one that had haunted his dreams last night. He looked up from the box to find her standing at the counter.

"Katie." He fought to sound natural. "Busy day, ain't so?"

She gave a slight gesture, as if to dismiss the activity as unimportant. "I saw you were having a bit of a break. I just need to say—"

"You don't need to say anything." He hurried the words out. "The fault is mine."

She shook her head, lips pressing together. "I had no right to say what I did. I'm sorry."

He sucked in a breath, trying to find a way to say the words without hurting her. "I was wrong. I should not have . . ."

Kissed her? He shouldn't have, but he couldn't regret it.

"It's all right," she said quickly. "That's all I wanted to say." She spun and went back to her shop, but not before he caught the glint of tears in her eyes.

This was no good. He had to talk to her, in private. He couldn't let her blame herself, and the only way was to try to be honest, both with her and with himself.

The opportunity to talk to Katie didn't come until evening, when the tables had been removed from the sidewalks, the banners taken down, the CLOSED signs put on the doors. Only a few last stragglers were making their way out of town, and peace settled over Pleasant Valley again.

Katie had sent Rhoda off with Becky at Nancy's invitation to spend the night. Nancy was, he supposed, trying to make amends for her harsh words.

He could hear Katie moving around in the shop, probably

trying, as he was, to put things back in order before the Sabbath. It wasn't church Sunday tomorrow, so they'd have a quiet day after today's busyness.

He set a quilt stand back in its proper place, took a deep breath, and walked through the archway.

Katie looked up from the place mats she was folding, and her expression seemed to tell him that she had been listening to him, as well.

"I have to tell you this," he said abruptly, before he could lose his courage. "You know about Mattie. About what happened between us." He shook his head when she seemed about to say something. "I know what you will say. That it is in the past, that everyone has forgotten about it except me. But you don't know everything."

"Tell me." She reached across the counter, as if she would touch his hand, and then seemed to think better of it.

The store was so quiet . . . as if it, too, needed to recuperate from the noise of the day. Its warmth and color, so like Katie, seemed to enclose him. But he couldn't accept the comfort it offered.

"After Mattie left, when folks found out about her, I went to the city to find her. To tell her . . ." He let that trail off, not wanting to remember the boy he'd been. But the memories were there, whether he wanted them or not.

"I was nineteen. I'd never been in a place bigger than Mifflinburg in all my life. Neither had Mattie, but there she was, living in the city, sharing an apartment with some Englisch friends I didn't even know she had."

"I'm sorry." Katie's murmur was soft with distress.

"When she opened the door, I didn't even know her at first, she looked so different. But then she seemed glad to see me. She asked me in, and I told her what I'd come to say."

He took a breath, his throat tight. "I said I still wanted to marry her. I said if she was determined to leave the Amish, I would leave, too. Even though I knew the baby wasn't mine, I would love it anyway."

His throat seemed to close entirely. He remembered saying the words, the feel of them on his lips. The way Mattie had shaken her head, her newly short hair swinging out from her face.

"She said no. She had been meeting an Englisch boy in secret the whole time we were engaged. When she realized she was pregnant, she thought she would marry me, but when the time came, she ran away instead."

"You did all you could," Katie said. "No one could have done more. How can you reproach yourself?"

He shook his head. She didn't understand. "I never knew. How could that be, that I never even suspected there was someone else?" He had to make her understand. "Mamm says my heart's been frozen for a long time. That you started it thawing. But I can't be sure, Katie. I just don't know if I have it in me to give my heart to someone again."

Katie automatically slipped the straight pins into the bodice of her dress, hardly needing to think about the fastening after all these years. She stepped to the window as she settled her kapp in place, glancing out at the street. Sunday morning was sunny and also very quiet, after all that had happened yesterday.

Everything that had happened, from the success of Pennsylvania Dutch Days to the truth she'd heard from Caleb. Pain pierced her heart as if she'd driven one of the pins straight into it.

Faced with the pain of Mattie's rejection, he'd followed his natural instincts and withdrawn. She understood that. It was his way of coping. But he'd withdrawn so far that he doubted his own heart.

He had been honest with her. That was all she could expect. Only now that the dream was over, she knew she had begun to hope for more.

She brushed a hand down her apron, straightening it even though it already hung perfectly even. She should be happy. Everything she and Lisa had planned had worked out well, and the crowds had been even better than they'd expected. Some of those people would surely come back to Pleasant Valley to shop, meaning good things for all of them. Perhaps she could even stop worrying about the shop.

She wandered out to the living room, feeling vaguely unsettled at being alone on a Sunday morning. Rhoda had spent the night at Becky's, and since it was an off Sunday, there was no rush to get ready for church.

Katie sank down in her rocker and reached for the Bible on the table next to it. Ordinarily on an off Sunday Daad would read the Scripture out loud, his deep voice making the High German words resonate. When she was a child, she'd thought that must surely be what the voice of God sounded like.

Well, today she would have devotions on her own. Independence could be a fine thing, but it could also be a bit lonely.

She opened the Bible to the passage they'd reached in Isaiah and began to read aloud, even though there was no one to hear.

"'Remember ye not the former things, neither consider the things of old.'" Her voice shook a little. "'Behold, I will do a new thing; now it shall spring forth; shall ye not know it? I will even make a way in the wilderness, *and* rivers in the desert.'"

Her eyes filled with tears as she reached the final line. That was how she felt, and she couldn't deny it. Like a desert that would never blossom.

But God promised a way in the desert, streams in the wasteland. She sat for a long time, her hand on the page, pondering those words. Somehow, she must try to hold on to that promise.

Finally, her prayers over, she stood. She set the Bible back in its place, and looked around the tidy rooms. The sunshine seemed to be calling her outside. Perhaps she would take a walk down Main Street. By then it would be time to go and fetch Rhoda from Becky's house. Somehow she suspected Caleb would make himself scarce when he saw her coming. They had nothing left to say to each other.

Katie went down through the shop. She unlocked the front door and stepped outside, tilting her head back to feel the sunshine on her face.

Denke, Father, she prayed silently. She would be content. She must be content.

A buggy came down Main Street . . . a family on their way to spend the off Sunday with relatives, no doubt. Once she'd picked Rhoda up, they'd go out, also, to Sarah Mast's to have dinner with her and the rest of the Miller family.

The buggy drew closer, and her stomach clenched. That was Caleb's buggy. He was driving, and Rhoda sat beside him.

Katie pressed a hand against her heart, as if that would ease the pain she felt there. Nonsense. She had to lecture herself. It was nonsense to think she'd gotten over Eli and fallen in love with Caleb in little more than a month.

Unfortunately, she didn't quite believe herself. His face grew clearer as they approached, and she struggled to accept the truth. Caleb had made her see how foolish she'd been to think that she could never love anyone but Eli. Unfortunately, the end result had been to discover that Caleb was trapped just the way she had been, and he didn't seem to see, or even to want, a way out.

She forced a smile to her face as the buggy drew to a stop. "I did not expect to see you this morning," she said.

Rhoda scrambled down, carrying her duffel bag. "I promised you I'd be home early to go to Sarah's."

"Ja, you did." Katie hugged her. "But I expected to come for you."

"Caleb said he'd drive me." Rhoda scurried to the door. "I'll go and pack up the cookies I made to take to Molly's." The door banged behind her, leaving Katie alone with Caleb.

She forced herself to look up to the buggy seat. "Denke, Caleb. This was ser gut of you."

"It made no trouble to bring her." He stared for a moment at the horse's ears, and then seemed to yank his gaze away to look at her. "Besides, I . . . Well, I thought maybe I sounded harsh yesterday. I didn't mean—"

"It's all right." It was hard to keep her smile in place when her heart seemed to be crying. "I would rather know the truth."

"Ja." He took a deep breath. "Gut. I just want us to be friends."

For an instant she thought of Myra's words about loving someone who was also your best friend. Katie's smile wavered, and she stiffened it until she feared her face must look like a mask.

"Ja," she said. "Friends."

Caleb glanced away, as if he could not hold her gaze any longer. His eyes narrowed. "There is Cliff Wainwright. He looks as if something is wrong."

Katie turned, raising her hand to shield her eyes from the sun. Caleb was right. Cliff was hurrying toward them, his white hair standing on end as if he'd just gotten out of bed. As usual, his glasses were pushed on top of his head, but his shirt collar was open and his tie dangled.

She was suddenly chilled. "Cliff, is something wrong? You don't look well."

"Neither will you when you've heard." His face was grim.

Caleb slid down from the buggy, and Katie felt him come and stand next to her. "What is wrong?"

"Vandals again, that's what." Cliff spat out the words. "They hit a bunch of merchants last night, but Lisa Macklin got the worst of it. Her shop has been trashed."

"Lisa." Katie's numb lips formed the name. "I must go." She rushed down the street, her heart pounding in her chest. Trashed. That sounded bad. Poor Lisa. All her pleasure in what had happened yesterday would be turned to ashes.

CHAPTER EIGHTEEN

*K*atie moved through the small knot of people who had gathered in front of Lisa's shop, talking in low, tense whispers. She reached the front of the crowd and stopped, staring. Shocked.

She had imagined something bad, but nothing like this. The front windows had been smashed, all the candles and knick-knacks broken or trampled almost past recognition. Beyond, the shop itself was a mass of overturned shelves and broken displays. It was as if a malevolent giant had crashed through, swinging a massive club at everything in his path.

She took a breath that caught on a sob. Caleb gripped her elbow. "Komm away. There's nothing you can do."

She pulled free of him, shaking her head. He was just being kind, she understood that, but at the moment she couldn't handle his kindness.

"I must talk with Lisa."

Lisa stood with Chief Walker, staring numbly at what was left of her shop. She huddled inside a sweater despite the warmth of the sunshine, and her face looked pinched and old.

Katie moved, and Lisa looked over and saw her. For an instant she just stared, but then she walked toward her stiffly, trying to smile even as she blinked back tears.

"I am so sorry." Katie put her arms around Lisa, feeling the woman lean against her as if needing the support. "So sorry."

"I know." Lisa's voice was choked. "You know what it's like, don't you?"

"Ja," Katie said softly. She moved her hand in gentle circles on Lisa's back. "Why don't you come with me and have some coffee? You don't have to stay here."

Lisa drew away, making an effort to compose herself. "Thanks, but I'd rather stay. I . . . I can't seem to take it in. All that destruction—it's so hard to look at."

"I'll help you clean up. Everyone will help."

"No, we can't." Lisa put her hand on Katie's arm, as if to stop her from moving. "I can't touch anything until Chief Walker is done with his investigation. And the insurance adjuster, too. He's supposed to be on his way."

Katie nodded. She hadn't thought of that. Being Englisch, Lisa would naturally have insurance. Amish folks didn't, relying on God's providence and each other in times of trouble.

"You will be able to rebuild, then," she said. "You'll put everything back the way it was."

"I don't know." Lisa sounded defeated. "I just don't know if I have the strength to do that. Mark's dream . . ." She stopped on a sob.

Chief Walker beckoned Lisa, and she returned to him. He gestured, seeming to ask her something about the door.

"I've been talking to some of the other folks," Caleb said, his voice low in Katie's ear. "Several businesses had spray paint on them, but nothing as bad as Mrs. Macklin's place."

Katie's breath caught. "I just don't understand it. Why would anyone do this to her?"

"Maybe . . ." Caleb began, and then he shrugged. "Most likely it was just a random choice. Maybe they liked the idea of breaking all those fancy things."

Katie nodded, but she had a sense that Caleb had been going to say something else and changed his mind.

Melanie came hurrying through the crowd to Katie. "I just heard. This is awful. Who could have done it?" Her voice was shaking, and she looked nearly as bad as Lisa. Poor girl. She had probably never seen destruction like this before.

Katie patted her arm. Melanie grabbed her hand and hung on tightly.

"We don't know," Katie said. "Most likely the same kids who damaged my place." She tried to sound matter-of-fact in the face of Melanie's distress.

"Kids? You think it was kids?" Melanie shot the question at her.

"Usually that's the case with vandalism, I think."

"It looks like someone just charged in there with a baseball bat and started swinging," Cliff said, running his hand through his hair, making it stand up still more. "Someone would have to be really angry to do that."

Melanie's lips trembled. "I can't stand to think about it. I can't."

Before Katie could suggest that she go home, Melanie had rushed off through the crowd.

"Poor kid," Cliff said, looking after her. "I suppose she still thinks the world is all cotton candy and lollipops."

"Was that Melanie?" Lisa came back to them, looking a little more like herself. "Why did she run off?"

"She was upset," Katie said. "I know she wanted to say how sorry she is."

"Everyone's sorry." Lisa's voice went flat. "So much for my new life. First Mark, now the shop. I guess this wasn't meant to be."

"You can't look at it that way. You're still shocked." Katie hated hearing Lisa sound so defeated. She was always so full of life and enthusiasm.

"Things will look better tomorrow," Donna said, having elbowed her way through the crowd, and hearing those final words. She pressed her cheek against Lisa's for just a moment. "You'll see. In the meantime, you come home with me. We'd love to have you, and you shouldn't be alone at a time like this."

"That's a wonderful-gut idea," Katie said, relieved. Brisk, no-nonsense Donna wouldn't let Lisa brood over what had happened. "You'll feel better staying with someone for today, at least. I'm sure Chief Walker will catch these people quickly, and then you won't have to worry."

Donna's eyebrows lifted. "Quickly? Somehow I doubt it's going to be that easy. How is he going to track down a gang of outsiders?"

"Outsiders?" Katie stared at her blankly.

Donna pulled a tissue from her bag and handed it to Lisa. "Outsiders," she repeated firmly. "I hate to say I told you so, but if you do something that brings a lot of attention to Pleasant Valley, this is the sort of thing you have to expect."

The sidewalk was unsteady beneath Katie's feet. "But, Donna, how can that be? My store was hit before the celebration took place."

"The publicity had already gone out, hadn't it?" Donna was unmoved. "Mark my words, you've opened a Pandora's box, and—"

"That's ridiculous." Lisa's voice had recovered its strength, and color came into her cheeks. "Everyone knows there's been vandalism in this area for years. Chief Walker told me it peaks in spring and again in late October. The only difference is that usually it's been directed against the Amish." Lisa's glance swept the circle of bystanders, her voice rising. "And we've all said how terrible it is, but nobody ever did anything. Well, now it's hitting us, and you can't blame Pennsylvania Dutch Days for that."

Nobody said anything, although there was some shuffling of feet. Even Donna seemed silenced by Lisa's reaction.

But silence didn't necessarily mean they agreed with her. If people blamed Lisa they'd blame Katie, as well. And if she didn't have the support of the community, her days here would be numbered.

It was an uneasy time in Pleasant Valley. Caleb set the newly finished blanket chest against the wall, adjusting its position to catch the afternoon light, liking the way the grain of the wood showed up. Even his pleasure in the completed piece couldn't erase the tension he felt . . . the same tension that seemed to pervade the community, Englisch and Amish alike.

He understood the feeling. After what had happened on Sunday, he'd had to battle a sense of dread when he approached his shop yesterday morning and again this morning.

So far, nothing else bad had happened. Maybe the vandals, aware of the response they'd created, had decided to lie low.

"That's a lovely piece." Katie approached from her shop, making an effort to sound normal but not quite succeeding.

Caleb ran his hand along the neatly fitted corners. "Turned out okay," he conceded. They'd both been making an effort, he realized. An effort to be friends. Neighbors. Nothing more.

That was his choice, and he'd made it. So why did he find his path so difficult?

Katie rubbed her arms. "I feel as if we're waiting for something to happen. When I lock the shop at night, I feel . . ."

"Ja, I know. Me, too." He straightened. "It's going okay, staying with your cousins?" Considering the recent violence, Katie's cousins had insisted that Katie and Rhoda stay with them for a bit.

Katie nodded. "Rhoda loves helping take care of baby Jacob, so that's keeping her happy. And I'm enjoying the company. But I worry about the shop when I'm not here. I know I shouldn't, but I do."

"I know. I feel the same. I think everyone in town does. How is your friend Mrs. Macklin?"

"She is having a hard time, I think." Tears welled in Katie's eyes. "That shop was her husband's dream, and since he died, she felt it was all she had left of him. I'm not sure she has the heart to come back from so much trouble."

Caleb tried to picture his own shop smashed with such violence, but his mind recoiled from the image. "I understand how she feels. If everything I worked for had been destroyed, I don't know if I could do anything but walk away."

Katie adjusted the position of a rocking chair by a quarter of an inch, as if she couldn't be still. "What are other people saying, do you know?"

He wasn't sure it would do Katie any good to hear everything folks were saying. "I stopped for coffee at Paula's a couple of times and listened to the talk. Folks say Chief Walker is on the warpath. He's had people patrolling the streets all hours of the night, and he even called in the lab from the state police, they say."

"Amish shouldn't be involved with the law." A shiver seemed to run through Katie, despite the warmth of the afternoon. "I'm sure folks will be thinking that my actions brought this on."

Caleb couldn't deny that he'd heard something like that expressed by a few Amish, but it wasn't necessary to say so to Katie, was it? She needed comfort now, not more bad news.

Comfort he couldn't give her. He didn't have the right. He'd told her what he knew was true about himself—that he didn't have that kind of love left to offer a woman.

Still, he had to fight the longing to put his arms around her, draw her close, and smooth his hand down her back. . . .

"How was your quilting class today?" he asked, in a desperate effort to send his thoughts in a different direction.

Katie's lips tightened. "Only two people showed up. The others didn't even stop by with an excuse."

"They might have a gut reason," he began, but saw she wasn't believing that.

"Ja. And that reason is their sense that I am somehow responsible for the trouble. Or that it might rub off on them, from just being around me." She said the words bravely, but he saw the pain behind them.

His heart twisted in sympathy. Katie had worked so hard to make a go of her business, only to see it at risk because of something she couldn't control.

"Chief Walker is a gut man. He'll find out who is doing these things, and then everything will go back to normal."

She looked at him steadily, her gaze questioning. "Do you really believe what you are saying, Caleb?"

He risked touching her hand. "Ja. And you must as well. Trust, Katie. That is all we have."

Trust. They could have had more, but he couldn't change who he was, and Katie would never accept being second best.

Who was pounding a hammer in the middle of the night? Katie fought her way up from sleep, struggling to open her eyes and focus her thoughts.

Reality washed over her in a chill wave. She'd been asleep in the bed she shared with Rhoda at the Miller farmhouse. Rhoda still slept, but from below, Katie could hear knocking. Someone was knocking—pounding, even—at the front door.

She swung out of bed, grasping the robe that lay across the footboard and pulling it around her. Something was wrong. No one aroused an Amish household in the middle of the night unless something bad had happened.

Reaching the hallway, she closed the door softly behind her. Her cousin Aaron was already headed down the stairs, with Molly's Jacob right behind him. Molly peered from the door of their bedroom, her eyes wide and frightened in the glow of the gas lamp someone had lit.

"What is it? Should I go down?" Molly's voice was a whisper.

"You should get back into bed before you wake the baby." Katie turned her cousin around, giving her a little pat. "I will go and see what it is and come back and tell you."

At the mention of the baby, Molly gave in, retreating into the bedroom. "Tell me right away," she whispered.

Katie nodded and hurried down the stairs, feet bare against the boards, hand sliding down the banister. Trouble, she thought. It had to mean trouble.

Aaron stood at the door, open now, with Jacob beside him. Standing in the doorway was a young man in a police uniform. All three of them turned and looked at Katie.

The chill wrapped around her heart. "What is it? What is wrong?"

"Katie, there has been some trouble at the shop." Aaron, the oldest, took charge matter-of-factly. "Officer Caruso was just telling us. Chief Walker wants you to come."

She clutched her robe, needing to hold on to something. "How bad is it? What has happened?"

"I'm just supposed to bring you, ma'am." The policeman looked very young and a little embarrassed. "I'll take you in the patrol car. If there's someone who can come with you . . ." He looked uncertainly from Aaron to Jacob, probably not knowing what their relationship was.

"I will come with my cousin," Aaron said promptly. "It will only take us a few minutes to dress." He came to Katie, taking her elbow. "Komm, now. You must dress."

"But—" Her mind whirled with unanswered questions.

"We will find out everything when we get there." Aaron

urged her up the steps. "Do you want me to send Molly to help you?"

Katie took a firm hold of herself. She must look upset, for Aaron to offer that.

"No, no, I'm fine. I'll try to get ready without waking Rhoda." She went the rest of the way quickly, her bare feet making no sound on the wooden treads.

She slipped into the room, found the small flashlight she kept on the bedside table. Rhoda still slept. Gut.

Katie took her clothing from its peg and began to dress. *Hurry, hurry. The faster you go, the sooner you will know what has happened.*

In moments she was back downstairs. Aaron opened the door, and they followed the policeman out to his car, a dark bulk in the lane that led to Aaron's machine shop.

She'd ridden in cars often, of course, but never in a police car. The lights of the dashboard were a confusing mixture, and a radio crackled intermittently with words she couldn't grasp.

"Sorry about this, folks." The officer sped up when he reached the main road. "Nobody wants to get wakened in the night by a cop at the door, I know."

"What time is it?" Katie still felt a bit disoriented, as if her mind couldn't quite decide whether this was a dream or real.

"A little after two, ma'am. The incident happened about an hour ago."

"The shop was vandalized, ja?" That was the only thing she could think of that would bring the police out.

"Chief Walker will tell you all about it." Obviously he wasn't supposed to talk. She would have to be patient. And pray.

They drew up in front of the shop in what seemed record

time. Katie got out, Aaron right behind her, and stood staring for a moment, trying to understand what she was seeing.

Two police cars stood in front of the shop, turned so that their lights shone blindingly into it. The colored lights on top of the cars whirled, turning the surroundings different colors. She took a step forward. The shop—

Seeing Lisa's place after the vandals had hit it had prepared her a little. The windows were smashed, and the door hung askew. Inside, she could see—

She started to run toward the shop, but Chief Walker was there to catch her, stop her. "I can't let you go in yet, Ms. Miller. I'm sorry. Once the officers are finished gathering evidence, then you can go inside."

But she didn't need to go in to see the worst of it—the callous, wicked vandalism. Someone had sprayed paint over the quilts. Quilts that had taken women hundreds of hours to finish, ruined in minutes, seconds, maybe.

She swayed, and Aaron was there to grasp her arms.

"It will be all right, Katie. It will. Maybe they are not all ruined. Maybe . . ." His voice ran down. Maybe he couldn't think of anything else to say.

True, perhaps they were not all ruined. But the shop, her cozy shop into which she'd poured her love and enthusiasm, was battered almost beyond recognition. She didn't think it could ever be the same again.

Nausea gripped her, so fierce it was all she could do not to throw up. She'd told Lisa she'd understood, but she hadn't, not really. The paint on the window had been nothing compared to this.

But there was worse. The vandals had raged into Caleb's

shop, as well. His front window was broken, and quilt racks and chairs looked as if they had been smashed against the wall. The red paint was there, too.

She choked on tears. Caleb would never get over this. Wasn't that what he'd said just yesterday? And he would never forgive her. How could he?

"I'm as sorry as I can be." Chief Walker patted her shoulder awkwardly. "One good thing, though. We caught him. The neighbors heard him and called in, and I already had a car out on patrol. I'm sorry we didn't get here in time to prevent the damage, but at least we caught him."

Him, the chief kept saying. She'd assumed what everyone had, that it was a gang of kids.

"Who?" She was almost afraid to hear the answer.

"Mike Franklin. Manager of the hardware store." A note of satisfaction tinged Chief Walker's voice. "I always did think the culprit wasn't the usual gang of kids."

Katie could only stare at him. "I don't understand. Why would he?"

"It was my fault." Melanie stepped hesitantly from the small knot of bystanders. "I'm so sorry, Katie. So sorry. It was all my fault." She burst into tears, huge racking sobs that shook her whole body.

Katie put her arms around the girl, holding her close, patting her as if she were Rhoda. "Hush now, Melanie. Just because Mike did this thing, that doesn't mean it was your fault. It will be all right."

"It won't." Melanie shook her head so hard that her hair whipped her face. "It's my fault. Everyone will blame me. You'll hate me."

"No one will hate you." Katie kept her voice calm with an effort. All she wanted to do was run away and bury her face in a pillow, but she couldn't. This poor child needed help, and already Chief Walker was backing away, obviously relieved to leave her to Katie. "Don't talk so foolish. Komm, now. This crying is not doing any gut. We must face things."

Except that she didn't want to face anything. She wanted to hide.

But her words seemed to have an effect on Melanie. The young woman straightened, wiping tears away with her hands. Her body still shook with intermittent sobs, but she seemed to be gaining control of herself.

Katie held her, looking around the small crowd for someone else who could help. To her relief, she saw Lisa and Donna, standing together, looking as if they were holding each other up. Katie nodded to them, and they came through the crowd to join her.

"Melanie is blaming herself for what Mike did," she said softly.

"That's foolish," Donna said, her voice brisk. "Now, Melanie, stop the crying and tell us what is going on. Why did Mike do such a thing?"

That brought a fresh onslaught of tears. "It . . . It was because of me," Melanie wailed. "He didn't want me to have any friends or to do anything without him. He kept saying if I loved him I wouldn't want to do anything without him."

"That's what you were so upset about at quilting class," Katie said. "He didn't want you to come."

Melanie nodded, sniffling.

"Oh, honey, didn't you realize what a danger signal that

was?" Lisa put an arm around Melanie's waist. "Bringing you here where you didn't know anyone, trying to control the people you met . . . Did he hit you?"

"N-n-no," Melanie said. "But he . . . I felt afraid of him, and I didn't know why." She choked on a sob. "I didn't know he was going to ruin your shop, Lisa. Or Katie's. I know you'll never forgive me. . . ."

"It is not your fault," Katie said firmly. "You are our friend."

"That's right," Donna said. "And thank goodness you found out what he was before you married him. Now . . ."

"Now you'll come home with me," Lisa said. "We'll have a good cry, and then tomorrow you can call your parents. It's going to be all right."

The enthusiasm was back in Lisa's voice. She had a new project, it seemed. Someone who needed her help. Katie didn't doubt that Lisa would take good care of Melanie, and that it would be good for her, too.

She watched the three of them walk away, Lisa and Donna on either side of Melanie. That was good. So why did she feel so bereft?

She turned back toward the shop, to find Chief Walker studying her face.

"She'll be all right, I guess," he said.

Katie nodded. "Lisa will take care of her." Katie forced herself to look again at the damage. "It is hard to believe."

"I know. I'm sorry. At least it's over now." He brushed his hands together, as if dusting off the problems Mike had caused.

It wasn't over for her. Or for Caleb. Katie's heart winced.

"Has . . . Has Caleb Brand been notified?" How she kept her voice even she didn't know.

"I sent someone to bring him." Chief Walker turned, looking down the street, and then nodded. "There they are now."

She couldn't face Caleb. But that was just being a coward. No matter what it cost her, she had to say how sorry she was.

The car pulled up, and the door opened. Caleb stepped out, the rotating lights turning his face different colors as he moved.

Staring at the shop, he walked toward them as if he were in a nightmare. Chief Walker took a step toward him, but Caleb didn't seem to register his presence.

Katie nerved herself to speak. "Caleb . . ."

He didn't turn toward her. He walked past, toward the shop, and didn't look at her at all.

Her throat thickened, and she struggled to gain control. She'd thought she'd have to settle for being Caleb's friend. Now, it seemed, she wouldn't even have that.

"Is it all right if we go home now?" She forced out the words, clasping Aaron's arm for support.

"Sure, sure." Chief Walker waved to one of his officers. "I'll have someone drive you. By morning, you should be able to get in to start cleaning up, so you can get back in business."

She gave him a meaningless smile and turned away. Back in business. To see Caleb every day and know what she'd done to him? She couldn't.

She would leave. She would admit that having her own shop wasn't to be, and she would go home.

CHAPTER NINETEEN

*K*atie had tried without much success to get some sleep in what was left of the night. She had wanted to cry, but somehow the tears didn't come.

Now, sitting at the breakfast table, she wrapped her hands around the mug of coffee Molly had poured for her and stared at it, trying to concentrate. Her mind didn't seem to work, either.

"It is time." Molly turned from the sink, drying her hands, a determined expression on her pert face. "We should get going to town. It might be best if Rhoda stays here to watch the baby while I go with you to start the cleanup."

Katie stared at her. "I don't think . . ."

"This is not a time for thinking," Molly said firmly. "This is a time to get to work. A bad thing has happened, and I'm certain-sure nothing will make you feel better than setting it right."

Finally tears stung Katie's eyes. "It can't be set right. All those quilts, all that work, are destroyed."

"Ja, and Melanie's hopes for her future are destroyed, too."

Molly, sweet, lively Molly, was implacable. "You are not the only one hurting, Katie Miller. You cannot sit around and feel sorry for yourself."

Stung, Katie pulled back. "I'm not. At least . . . Well, maybe I am. I have to face it. This dream of mine isn't coming true. You're right that other people have been hurt. Caleb . . ." She couldn't go on. "I should pack up and go home."

Molly sank into the chair opposite her and clasped her hand. "I have never known you to give up on anything you set your mind to. Is this about the shop? Or is it about Caleb?"

Katie pressed her lips together, blinking back tears. "How did you know?" she whispered.

"I've seen the way you look at him." Molly squeezed her hand. "And the way he looks back at you."

"No." Her voice shook. "I thought I could never love anyone else because of Eli. Coming here, starting my own business was supposed to take the place of that."

"And then you met Caleb." Molly's voice was soft.

"Ja. Somehow, even without my noticing it, I started to care for him. To love him."

"Well, then—"

Katie shook her head, silencing Molly. "He told me. He is where I was, stuck believing that he can't love anyone else because of what people believe about Mattie. Maybe worse, because he feels she took away his ability to love." She put her hands over her face. "I don't know how to fight that. And even if I could, I'm to blame for the damage to his shop. He'll never forget that."

"But it wasn't your fault. Who could know that Melanie's boyfriend was such a crazy person that he thought he could keep her by destroying her friendships?" Molly's small frame shuddered. "He might have gone after any of us." She glanced around the farmhouse kitchen, as if imagining what could have happened to her home.

"I started the group." Katie pressed her hands flat on the tabletop. "I invited Melanie. I was responsible."

"It is wrong to think that." Molly sounded as firm and solemn as Bishop Mose. "Mike is responsible for what he did. We must forgive him, but it's foolish and wrong to try and take the responsibility. And if Caleb thinks that, I will tell him so myself."

Katie managed a weak chuckle. "You are very decided all of a sudden, Cousin Molly."

Molly grinned. "I'm a mammi now. I have to be grown-up." She stood and held out her hand to Katie. "Will you komm?"

"Ja." Her energy seemed to have returned. "Denke, Molly."

They intended to leave right away, but nothing that involved a baby could be accomplished quickly. By the time Molly had settled little Jacob and given Rhoda detailed instructions on caring for him, Katie could have harnessed Daisy several times over. Finally they were off, but it was late morning by the time they reached town.

Katie averted her eyes as they turned into the lane next to the shop, wanting to put off seeing the damage for as long as possible. Too soon they were opening the back door, and she steeled herself as they walked in.

Maybe it wasn't so bad because the picture was already in her mind. Or maybe it was because people were already there, working.

Donna, high on a ladder cleaning the upper shelves, turned to wave at her with a sponge. "Katie, I'm glad you're here. We have about a million questions to ask you. Do you want the same things put back up here? Very few of them were damaged."

"For goodness' sake, let her catch her breath." Lisa, in jeans and with her hair covered by a bright silk scarf, put down the quilt she was holding and came to hug Katie. "How are you? Did you get any sleep?"

"I'm fine. But you—" It was hard to speak over the lump in her throat. She glanced around the busy store.

Myra and Rachel were there, along with Naomi and Emma and several other women from the Amish community, including Ruth Weaver, of all people. They'd even brought their spouses and a few teenage children. The Englisch merchants were there, too, along with Paula Schatz and the niece who lived with her. They moved back and forth through Katie's shop and Caleb's shop, everyone helping.

Katie started to say they shouldn't be doing all that work, but the words died in her throat. This was community. Her community. She couldn't deny that.

Myra held an armload of quilted table runners. "It's maybe not as bad as it first looked," she said. "Joseph and some of the other men are repairing the broken racks. And these table runners were hardly touched at all."

"The quilts . . ." Katie couldn't finish that question.

"The quilts took the worst of it," Naomi said, her voice brisk as if to deny emotion. "We've already sorted out those that can't be saved at all. But komm, look what Emma and I are thinking about some of these."

She led Katie to the display bed, which had taken the worst of the onslaught. Had Mike realized that the quilts were the most valuable items in the shop?

Probably he had, or else he'd just been lucky, from his point of view. He'd wanted to do the most damage possible.

"See this?" Emma disregarded the paint sprayed on part of a postage stamp quilt. "We can cut away the bad part, we're thinking, and rebind it to make a smaller coverlet. And some of them can be remade into place mats and table runners."

"They are not a total loss," Naomi added. "We can find something to save on almost all of them." Her smile was very sweet. "That is quilting, ja? We make something new out of what is left of the old."

The words seemed to resonate through Katie, but she wasn't sure she was ready to hear them. Still, even if she were closing the shop and going home, it would be wrong not to try with the quilts. Many of them were other people's work—people who deserved to have them made right.

"Ja," she said, trying to keep her voice steady. "We will save everything we can."

"Gut. And look at this." Naomi pulled a basket from under the bed. "Here are the patches for your new Lancaster Rose quilt. They were not touched at all. You can still make your new quilt."

Katie took one of the squares in her hand, tears welling in her eyes. "I can still make my new quilt." She swallowed the lump in her throat, wanting to turn the conversation away from herself. "How is Melanie doing?"

"Not so shocked," Lisa said. "But still upset. I wanted her to come and help, but she's blaming herself for everything."

Naomi clucked. "Poor child. At least she should be thanking God she didn't marry that man."

"I'm afraid she's not ready to see that yet," Lisa said. "Sometime, maybe."

"I just don't understand." Distress sounded in Myra's soft voice. "What would make the man act that way?"

Lisa and Donna exchanged glances.

"It happens," Lisa said. "Some men think loving gives them the right to control everything the loved one says and does. They don't want her to have any friends or any interests beyond them."

"That is not love," Myra said, with surprising firmness for one so gentle. "Loving is wanting the best for that other person, no matter what."

Lisa smiled. "Myra, I think you are very wise."

Myra flushed, shaking her head.

This closeness among the women was what she'd hoped for, Katie realized. Just not quite the way she'd visualized it.

She had thought they'd be bonding, Amish and Englisch women, over a quilting frame as they sewed. Instead, they were bonding over the wreckage of her shop. Even if she had to leave Pleasant Valley, she would have done something *gut* here.

Caleb tried to close his ears to the noise made by what seemed like half the community, all crowded into his shop and Katie's, all trying to help. He wanted to escape—to think about what had happened and try to process it all. But he couldn't. For someone who'd considered himself outside the community, he seemed to have almost too many friends, too many brothers and sisters.

He needed to talk to Katie—that much was clear in his mind. But what he had to say to her couldn't be said with an audience.

"We're taking this up to the shop." Aaron put his shoulder to the end of the blanket chest, while William grasped the other end. "The damage is all on the surface, so it won't take any time to refinish it. We'll be by tomorrow to help with that."

"I can't take you away from your own work," Caleb protested, but Aaron was already halfway up the stairs.

"No problem." His voice echoed down. "We can spare a few days to set things right."

Set things right. The words echoed in Caleb's mind. How did you set things right that had gone so far wrong?

A stir went through the workers as folks turned their heads toward the door. Chief Walker had come in. He beckoned to Caleb.

"Just wanted to fill you and Katie in on what's happening." He headed through the archway.

Caleb had no choice but to follow. He needed to see Katie, but not like this, under the eyes of the community, brought together by the law.

Chief Walker, looking a bit taken aback by the crowd that thronged Katie's shop, ushered the two of them into the back hallway. As if by unspoken agreement, the other women clustered toward the front of the store or into the back room.

Katie was pale, her eyes shadowed, probably by a combination of a sleepless night and the devastation that had hit her. She tried to smile, and pain gripped Caleb's chest at the sight.

"Well, now, I thought I should bring you folks up to date on the situation. Mike Franklin has been moved to the county jail, so you don't have to worry about him."

"Is he all right?" Katie's voice was soft.

For an instant Chief Walker looked surprised, but Caleb wasn't. That's the kind of woman Katie was, always concerned about others.

Chief Walker nodded. "A public defender . . . a lawyer . . . has been appointed to help him."

"And Melanie?" she persisted. "She is not in trouble with the law, is she?"

"No, no. Poor girl, she's had enough to cope with. We've taken a statement from her, but I don't think we'll have to bother her anymore. I understand her parents are coming to bring her home with them."

Katie took a deep breath. If anything, the strain on her face deepened. Was she thinking that her parents would want to do the same?

"Anyway, Mike has decided to plead guilty in exchange for a lighter sentence." Chief Walker shook his head. "Seems he got it into his head that you ladies were influencing Melanie against him, so he decided to get back at you, figuring we'd blame it on the usual teenage vandalism."

"What did he think he would gain by such a thing?" Caleb could only shake his head.

"Yeah, well, I know you folks will forgive him, but as for understanding what made his mind work that way . . ." Chief Walker shrugged. "It's beyond me." He glanced from Katie to Caleb. "Glad to see you're getting the help you need, but it's what I'd expect. Pleasant Valley's a good place to live."

He nodded and turned away, leaving Caleb alone with Katie for a moment, at least.

"The chief is right, you know," he said, trying to find his way toward what he really wanted to say. "This is a gut place to live. I hope . . . Well, I hope this doesn't change your mind about staying here."

Katie didn't respond. She just stood there, looking a little lost. Then she shook her head. "I don't know," she said, her words so soft he could barely hear them. "I just don't know."

Before he could say more, she'd walked off toward the women.

He stood looking after her, afraid of what his face must reveal at the thought of Katie going away. He'd told her he didn't have a heart left to love again. So what was it that seemed to be breaking so painfully in his chest?

"Caleb."

He blinked, hardly able to believe that Mattie Weaver's mother was seeking him out.

"Ruth . . . I didn't realize you were here helping." Helping Katie, of course. Neither she nor Ephraim had been in his shop since Mattie had left.

Ruth didn't respond to that. Instead, she nodded toward Katie, who was now surrounded by the other women. "You are not going to let her go away, are you?"

For a moment he could only stare at Ruth, not certain he'd heard her right. "I can't tell Katie what to do."

Ruth came closer, putting her hand on his arm and looking up at him. There were lines on her face . . . lines of sorrow and pain. She'd aged twenty years since her daughter had run away, he thought.

"You can tell her what you feel," Ruth said softly. "You must not let what happened with Mattie keep you from loving someone else."

He should not talk to Mattie's mother, of all people, about this. "I don't think . . ."

"Hush." She shook his arm, her fingers tight. "Listen to me, Caleb Brand. I know full well that you are not the father of Mattie's little boy."

"You know?" His feelings seemed to be tumbling around inside him. "How can you know?"

Ruth's thin lips tightened. "Ephraim is unforgiving. But I am not." Tears shone suddenly in her eyes. "We write now. She sends me pictures of her little Jamie . . . so handsome and smart he is. If only I could hold him in my arms—" She stopped, as if she could not say more.

"Mattie . . ." Caleb found he could say her name without bitterness. "Is she happy?"

"Ja, I think so. She is married to Jamie's father, and they live in Ohio, where he works."

"I'm glad for her." He *was* glad. Mattie had found whatever it was she'd been looking for.

"You need to be glad for you." Ruth shook his arm again. "Half the township knows that you are in love with Katie Miller. Don't let her go away. If it would help you for me to tell the church—"

"No, no." He might not be sure of anything else, but he knew that he could not subject Ruth to more pain. "I don't want that."

Ruth gave the slightest possible smile. "Then live your life, Caleb. Don't waste it." She spun and was gone as quickly as she'd appeared, leaving him standing there feeling oddly disoriented. His world had turned upside down in the past twenty-four hours, and he wasn't sure how to go about righting it.

· · ·

Somehow Katie managed to get through the day. Each time she wanted to give in to tears, someone would distract her, or ask her a question, or bully her into tackling the next task. Donna, of course, did much of the bullying, but Katie had to admit that might be what she needed. At least it kept her from thinking too much.

"It's really coming along." Lisa paused, holding the broom with which she'd been sweeping up scraps from the floor. "You'll see. It'll soon be back to the way it should be."

Katie gave her a searching look. "And what about your shop? Are we able to get in to help yet?" She held her breath, half expecting Lisa to say she was accepting her loss and closing.

"Another day or two at most," Lisa said, looking exasperated. "Honestly, sometimes I think the insurance is more trouble than it's worth. I have to wait for another adjuster, who's supposed to come tomorrow. Then I'll be able to clear up the mess and see what can be salvaged. But at least, eventually, I'll get a check so I can replace the ruined stock."

Katie's breath caught. "You're reopening, then?"

"I was ready to give up. I really was. And then I thought about what Mark would say. And Donna started pushing me on it." Lisa smiled. "You know how she can be. She just wouldn't let me give up."

"Ja. She's proved to be a gut friend." Despite her faults, Donna was just like all of them, Amish and Englisch. Not saints, just ordinary people trying to do their best.

"Fact is, we've decided that she's going into business with me." Lisa met Katie's surprised gaze and laughed. "Yes, I know. We'll fight all the time and drive each other crazy, but it'll be nice, even so. I like the idea of not going it alone."

"I'm glad." Katie was. The town wouldn't be the same without Lisa's energetic presence.

And would it be the same without Katie Miller's? Maybe. Or maybe she hadn't been here long enough to make a ripple in Pleasant Valley if she left.

The bell over the door jingled, and she was thankful for the interruption to those thoughts. Doubly thankful, when she saw who it was.

"Melanie." She went forward, holding out both hands toward the young woman, who hovered just inside the door as if unsure of her welcome. "I am so glad to see you."

Melanie clasped her hands, her anxious look dissolving into a smile. "I didn't know whether you'd want to see me or not, but I had to come and say I'm sorry. And to say good-bye."

She was leaving, then. Well, who could blame her?

"You have nothing to be sorry for," Katie said firmly. "Don't ever think that folks blame you for what Mike did."

Melanie's smile wobbled a little, but she kept it pinned to her face. "I know. But I blame myself. I should have been smart enough to see what was going on."

Lisa let the broom drop so she could put her arm around Melanie and give her something between a hug and a shake. "You're a smart person . . . smart enough to learn from your mistake. You're going to be all right."

Melanie nodded. "I think so. My folks have been great. They didn't say a word about Mike, just came to pick me up. They're waiting out in the car now."

"So you will go home with them," Katie said. That was natural enough, wasn't it? Melanie didn't have family or a business here. She could walk away and start over.

"Not for good," Melanie said. "Just until I can figure out what I want to do with myself. Anyway, I wanted to say thank you for all you did for me. All of you." A tear spilled over, and she wiped it away. "If not for you, I don't know what would have happened."

"It is our pleasure to have you for a friend," Katie said. She put her arms around Melanie for a last hug. "Don't forget about us, will you?"

"I won't. I'll write. Really I will." Stepping away, she glanced toward the street. "I have to go, but I'll stay in touch."

She went out, the bell jingling again.

Lisa shook her head. "She means that, but I suspect she's going to forget us as soon as she gets on with her life."

"Maybe that's for the best," Katie said. "We wouldn't want her to brood on the past, would we?"

"No, I guess not." Lisa picked up her broom. "I'd better finish this. I'm supposed to go to supper with Donna and her husband tonight."

Katie stood motionless for a moment as Lisa went back to work.

Endings. Beginnings. That was what made up life, wasn't it? She'd just like to know whether she was at an ending or a beginning.

CHAPTER TWENTY

The moment she and Molly reached the Miller farmhouse, Katie realized that something was different. She heard voices, familiar voices. She took one step into the kitchen, saw her father move toward her, and flung herself into his arms.

They closed around her, warm and strong and comforting, and she felt like a small child rushing to Daadi with a scraped knee and receiving the same unconditional love.

But she wasn't a child, and she shouldn't unload her troubles on him. She kissed his cheek, feeling the familiar softness of his beard, which was nearly all gray now. "Daadi, I am wonderful glad to see you."

"And I to see you." He kissed her forehead. "And here is your mamm, as well."

Mamm rose from the table, setting down her coffee cup. Glancing from Mamm's face to Rhoda's, Katie found it easy to see that they had been at odds already.

"Mamm, it is so gut of you to come." She hugged her, and Mamm pressed her cheek against Katie's.

Then she drew back and patted her cheek. "Of course we would come when our child is in trouble. Even if . . ." She broke off with a glance at Daadi. "We would have come straight to the shop, but we thought you'd be here."

Molly turned from greeting Katie's daad to give her mother a quick embrace. "Ach, I think half the church was at the shop today, helping to clean up. And a fine number of our Englisch friends, as well, ain't so, Katie?"

Molly sent an appealing glance toward her, and Katie suspected she was trying to think what she would make for supper in a hurry.

"Ja, lots of folks wanted to help." Sarah came in from the pantry carrying what looked like a chicken potpie. "You should see the pantry and the refrigerator, full with the food folks have been bringing."

Relief washed over Molly's face. "That is ser kind of them. Sarah, can you stay for supper?"

"Denke, but I must get back to Aunt Emma. She has a potpie cooking for us and has sent this one for you. It will just need to be heated up for your supper." She set it on the stove and went out the kitchen door.

A moment later Katie glimpsed her through the window, seeing Aaron meet her and walk her to her buggy, his head bent toward hers, his arm around her waist. A pang went through Katie . . . not envy of Sarah, surely, but maybe a sense of loss for herself. She would not have that closeness with a loved one, it seemed.

"Well, that solves the mystery of what we're having for supper." Molly hustled to the stove. "And here is dessert ready for us. Someone else has sent an apple crumb pie, as well. I wonder who it was."

Molly was chattering, Katie realized, because she sensed as well as Katie did that Rhoda looked on the verge of an explosion, while Mamm seemed to be controlling the lecture she wished to give both her daughters with a great effort.

"I'll get vegetables and applesauce to go with supper," Katie said, grasping Rhoda's wrist. "Komm, help me."

After one surprised tug, Rhoda went along quietly enough, following her around the corner and into the pantry. They'd no sooner entered the tiny room than the younger girl began to sputter like a teakettle about to whistle. "Katie, she . . ."

Katie put her hand over Rhoda's lips. "Hush, now. Do you want Mamm and Daadi to hear you?"

"I don't care," Rhoda said, but she lowered her voice to a whisper. "You don't know what she's been saying since she got here. Mamm said that you must give up the shop and come home, and me, too. And when Daadi said that was up to you, she said that I had to come anyway, and that you would if Daadi said so on account of him signing the lease, and then Daadi said to hush and he'd talk to you, and . . ." Rhoda finally seemed to run out of steam. Or breath, maybe, since she'd said all that on a breathless rush. Now she gripped Katie's hands. "You're not giving up, are you, Katie? Please say you're not."

Katie closed her eyes for a second. Whatever she said to Rhoda had to be the truth, if only she knew it. How strange that she had left home to get away from the situation with Eli, only to find herself in the same place again. Could she go on running the shop, being so close to Caleb, and knowing they could never be together?

"I don't know," she murmured finally. She cupped Rhoda's face in her palms before her little sister could erupt again. "But I will do my best for you. Can you trust me for that?"

Rhoda looked as if she would explode in a wave of pleading and anger, but somehow she managed to control it. She pressed her lips together firmly. Then she nodded.

"I trust you," she said softly. "Always."

"Gut." Katie gave her a quick hug. She scooped some jars from the shelves at random and put them in Rhoda's hands. "We'd best get in there before Mamm comes looking for us."

When they returned to the kitchen, it was obvious to Katie that Mamm and Daadi had probably had a whispered conversation of their own. Mamm's cheeks were flushed, and her lips formed a thin line.

Daadi stood and held out his hand to Katie. "Komm, Katie. Let's take a little walk."

They went out the back door and down the porch steps. Again she had to remind herself that she wasn't a little girl any longer.

Daadi had something white in one hand . . . a paper of some sort. The lease he'd signed with Bishop Mose, maybe? Her throat tightened.

"Aaron has a nice place here, for sure," Daad said. "I hear he and Sarah will move in with her aunt once they are married, while his brothers stay here with Molly and Jacob. It's gut to have them all close."

Katie stopped, looking up at him. "Does that mean that you

want Rhoda and me to come home and be close to you and Mamm?"

He smiled, shaking his head. "Always jumping to conclusions, my Katie. You did that when you were a little girl. I meant only that you have family here, too, if you decide to stay."

If. For a moment she couldn't breathe. "The cousins have been ser kind to us. But as for staying . . . is that up to me?"

He touched her cheek gently. "This thing that happened has been a bad blow, but it has not changed my mind about backing your business for a year. The decision is yours. If everything has been too hard, and you want to come home, that is gut. And if you want to stay, that is gut also. I . . . We will support you either way."

Her decision, and she didn't know what it should be. In a way, it would have been a relief to have Daadi make it for her, but she knew that she couldn't have been happy with that for long.

"What about Rhoda?"

Daad studied her face. "I never thought that was such a gut idea, but your mamm insisted it would be better for Rhoda, as well as Louise. And I knew you would be gut for her. But is she truly a help to you? Or is the responsibility too much?"

That question, at least, Katie had an answer for.

"It's a big responsibility, for sure. But I love having her here, and if I stay, I don't know how I'd get along without her."

"That is the answer, then." Daadi handed her the envelope in his hand. "And before I forget, I was asked to bring this to you."

No, not the lease, then, she realized. It was a folded piece of notepaper. She opened it and recognized the writing instantly. Jessica's handwriting. A knot formed in her throat.

Dear Katie,

I am so ashamed. How could I send your letter back that way? Now I will never know what it said. I hope it said that you forgive me, and that you are willing to be friends again.

I am so sorry to hear about your trouble. You are in our prayers.

With love,
Jessica

Katie stared at the letter for a long moment. A tear dropped on the paper, blurring the writing, and she blotted it away carefully. Teardrops, like streams in the desert.

Behold, I will do a new thing. The words came back, comforting, giving her strength, and she knew her decision was made. She would choose the new life, no matter what pain it might hold.

She lifted her head and smiled at her father. "If it is my decision, then Rhoda and I will stay," she said.

"Gut."

He nodded, and she realized that was the answer he'd hoped to hear.

Katie was late getting to the shop the next morning. Caleb had been listening for her, starting at every creak of the old building, glancing out the window so often that Becky stared at him.

"Is something wrong, Onkel Caleb?"

"No, nothing." That wasn't true. Everything was wrong, and he had to fix it and pray it wasn't too late.

"There's Katie's buggy," Becky called. "Gut, Rhoda is with her. I was hoping and hoping that she would come today." She skipped toward the back door.

Caleb caught her arm. "Will you do me a favor, Becky, and not ask why?"

Her eyes went round, but she nodded. "What?"

"I want to talk to Katie alone. Will you go and keep Rhoda busy? Maybe offer to help her in unharnessing Daisy so that Katie comes in by herself."

Becky looked as if she would burst with needing to ask why, but she nodded and darted toward the back door like a pebble from a slingshot.

Now, if only he knew what to say, once he finally had a chance to speak to Katie. He rubbed his palms on his pant legs. *I was wrong.* That was a good place to start.

It might be too late. She could have already decided to give up the shop and go home, and maybe nothing he said could make a difference.

He had to try. She deserved to hear the truth from him, at the least.

He heard the quick, light step he'd been listening for and went at once to meet her. "Caleb." She looked startled to see him. "You are at work early."

"Not so early as all that. I wanted to talk to you."

It seemed to him that a shield went up in her face at those words. "I must open the front door." She took a step toward the front of the shop.

He stopped her with his hand on her wrist. He could feel her pulse beating against his palm. Was it his imagination, or did it speed up suddenly when he looked at her?

"Wait," he said quietly. "Please wait, Katie."

She didn't answer, but she didn't move, either. She just looked at him, eyes questioning, guarded.

"I wanted to say . . ." He seemed to stumble over the words. Was this how William felt when he tried to communicate? *Just say it,* he ordered himself. "I was wrong."

There. It was out. That had to be the hardest part.

"Wrong?" The question seemed to deepen the blue of her eyes. "What were you wrong about?"

He gave a wry smile. "Quite a few things, I think. Like thinking that your shop wasn't a gut fit next to mine, for example."

"Ach, I knew you'd get over that quick enough." She managed a slight curve of the lips for that. "Don't give it a thought."

"And I was wrong about problems coming because of Pennsylvania Dutch Days, too. The problems were already here, ja?"

"I'm sorry," she said quickly. "Sorry that you suffered because of Mike's anger toward me. That was so unfair, so—"

"Hush." Caleb wanted to touch her lips to silence her blaming herself, but if he did, he suspected he'd never get the rest of this said, because he'd be kissing her. He contented himself with pressing her hand, holding it captive in both of his. "I want to tell you what I thought when I saw what he'd done that night."

Pain crossed her face. "You thought your work was ruined because of me, and you were right."

"No." He couldn't say it fast enough. "I didn't think that at all. Even before I knew who had done it and why, I didn't. I thought . . ." Holding her hand between his, he gave in to the impulse to lift it to his lips. "All I could see was that you had been hurt. That's all. I barely looked at my place, because I was so busy looking at yours. And that's when I knew I'd been wrong about the most important thing."

"What is that?" She whispered the words, the color coming up in her fine, smooth skin.

"When I told you that I had no love left to give anyone else because of Mattie. Because if I didn't, then how could I feel my heart break at the hurt to you?" He brushed her fingertips with his lips, seeming to feel that light touch through his body like a lightning strike. "I have known you only a month, Katie Miller, but I have never known anyone better than I know you. I love you. Don't go away."

Tears sparkled in her eyes, and her lips trembled. "I had already decided that I would not run away. I'm not going anywhere," she whispered.

He couldn't possibly resist. He put his arms around her, lowering his head to kiss her, holding her close, knowing in every fiber of his body that she was his and he was hers.

When he finally drew back a little, he still held her in the circle of his arms. She looked up at him, and he realized tears were slipping down her cheeks. The sight was like a blow to the heart.

"What is it? What's wrong?"

"Nothing." She smiled, not wiping the tears away. "I'm happy. God has given me a new life."

"God has given *us* a new life," he corrected gently. "Together."

EPILOGUE

*T*he Lancaster Rose quilt was stretched across the quilting frame, the colors of the flowers glowing against the white background. The quilters were gathered around the frame, their hands swooping like birds above the surface as they put in the final delicate stitching, their dear voices talking and sharing.

Katie looked at them all, her heart seeming to swell with love. Emma and Naomi, the most experienced quilters, sat across from each other, so that no one less quick would be embarrassed by trying to keep up. Then came Rachel, Myra, Lisa, and Donna. Cousin Molly sat across from Katie. The two girls, Rhoda and Becky, were at the foot of the frame, obviously nervous at being included in quilting something so important.

Katie's wedding quilt. She looked at it with a rushing sense of joy. Hers and Caleb's. It would adorn their bed in the house they'd bought across the street from their combined shops.

That had taken some negotiating, the decision to combine the shops. Some folks might expect her to give up the quilt shop when she married, but not Caleb. He understood how important it was to her.

She glanced at Rhoda, face intent as she minded her stitches. Rhoda didn't know it yet, but one day she would be equal partners with Katie in the shop. If she and Caleb were blessed with children, Rhoda would be there to help them manage. To say nothing of Naomi and Becky and all the other family and friends she'd found here in Pleasant Valley.

"Why so silent, Katie?" Naomi glanced at her prospective daughter-in-law with a twinkle in her eyes. "Dreaming of Caleb?"

The others laughed gently when Katie blushed, and Caleb's voice sounded from the doorway behind her.

"What is all this noise?" he asked with mock severity. "It sounds as if half the sisters of the church are here."

"We were saying that Katie is daydreaming of you, Onkel Caleb," Becky piped up with newfound confidence.

"She does not need to dream of me," Caleb said, and his loving gaze met Katie's. "I am here, and I will always be."